About the Author

Award-winning author Heather Peck has enjoyed a varied life. She has been both farmer and agricultural policy adviser, volunteer covid vaccinator and NHS Trust Chair. She bred sheep and alpacas, reared calves, broke ploughs, represented the UK in international negotiations, specialised in emergency response from Chernobyl to bird flu, managed controls over pesticides and GM crops, saw legislation through Parliament and got paid to eat Kit Kats while on secondment to Nestle Rowntree.

She lives in Norfolk with her partner Gary, two dogs, two cats, two hens and a female rabbit named Hero.

Also by Heather Peck

THE DCI GELDARD NORFOLK MYSTERIES
Secret Places
Glass Arrows *
Fires of Hate **
The Temenos Remains **
Dig Two Graves **
Beyond Closed Doors
Death on the Rhine (novella) **
Death on the Norwich Express (novella)
Milestones (thriller)

BOOKS FOR CHILDREN
Tails of Two Spaniels **
The Pixie and the Bear
The Animals of White Cows Farm

*shortlisted for the East Anglian Book Award prize for fiction
2021
**Firebird Book Award Winner

Beyond Closed Doors

DCI GREG GELDARD BOOK 6

Heather Peck

Ormesby Publishing

Published in 2024 by Ormesby Publishing

Ormesby St Margaret

Norfolk

www.ormesbypublishing.co.uk

Text copyright © Heather Peck 2024

Author photograph by John Thompson 2021

British Library Cataloguing in Publication Data

A CIP catalogue record for this book is available from the British Library.

Page design and typesetting by Ormesby Publishing

With thanks to Gary

for everything

Acknowledgments

Many thanks again to my beta readers Geoff Dodgson, Alison Tayler and Gary Westlake for their constructive criticism and extremely helpful comments. This book is all the better for your help.

Thanks also to Sharon Gray at CluedUpEditing for her meticulous and sensitive proof reading.

And to johnny_an for the cover design.

Contents

Key Characters

Police

Chief Constable Ralph Thornfield
Chief Superintendent Margaret Tayler
Main investigative team:
DCI Greg Geldard
DS Chris Mathews
DCs Bill Street, Jill Hayes, Jenny Warren, Steve Hall
& Phil Knight
DC Jeff Fellowes currently suspended without pay
Ned George senior crime scene investigator
PD Turbo springer spaniel
Police in Great Yarmouth:
Sergeant Briscoe
Constable Drake
Police in North Staffs:
PCs Darren Golding & Sue Hill
Sergeant Ryder

Legal services

Frank Parker Crown Prosecution Service
Harbottle, and Wallis Solicitors
Ruth Baker Appropriate Adult

Medical experts

Dr Paisley Police pathologist

Baddies

Constantin Gabrys – Lithuanian Mr Big, now in prison
Eva Gabrys – his wife
Helen Gabrys – his daughter
Peter Shinfield – (aka Peter or Patrick Ashfield/Ashton)
now a Protected Person
Tyson Strange – schoolboy

Other participants

Mr & Mrs Geldard senior – Greg's parents
Bobby – Greg's cat
Tally – Chris's foul-mouthed parrot
Kit Mirren – slaughterhouse worker
Anne, Karen and Jake Mirren – Kit's wife, daughter and son
Tim Simmons – friend of Anne Mirren's
Diana Grain – teacher friend of DC Jill Hayes.
Ella Pentney – secretary at Norfolk Police
Tom Harris – landlord of the Swan Inn

Glossary

ANPR Automatic Number Plate Recognition

APB All Points Bulletin

CCTV Closed Circuit Television

GP General Practitioner (local doctor)

IMSI International Mobile Subscriber Identity – a means of tracking unique SIM cards

'**on the huh**' Norfolk phrase meaning dodgy

IOPC Independent Office for Police Conduct

RIB Rigid Inflatable Boat

Tender a boat used to support another boat or ship

1

Introduction

Greg is attempting a romantic proposal of marriage by the River Bure, but it's not going to plan...

'I'm trying to ask you to marry me, woman,' said Greg, exasperated. 'I had a whole romantic speech rehearsed and now it's gone straight out of my head.'

'Say that again,' said Chris.

'I said,' said Greg, taking her by the elbows and turning her towards him, 'that I can't imagine any greater joy than working with you, other than being married to you.'

'Was that the romantic speech?' she asked critically, 'because if so, it wasn't bad, but it could do with a bit of work.'

'For God's sake, will you marry me?' demanded Greg. 'Yes or no?'

Chris opened her mouth, but her phone rang. 'Leave it,' said Greg as she glanced at the screen, but she held up her hand.

'Sorry,' she mouthed, listened, then put it on speaker phone.

'In short,' said the Chief Superintendent's voice, 'there's been a leak somewhere. The Protection Service got Peter

Shinfield away, but it was a close thing and they've taken casualties. They've had to change their plans for him. And we need a good hard look at how it got out. Tell Greg I need him here.'

Chris closed her phone and looked at Greg. 'You heard,' she said.

'I heard, but I haven't heard an answer yet.' He pulled her close. 'Will you, Chris?'

'Of course I will, you silly sod. Now get us over to Wymondham. It might be our last case together.'

2

After the event – 31 January 2020

Greg and Chris were the first to speak to the survivors. After the paramedics that is. They arrived at the Norfolk and Norwich Hospital at the same time as the back-up from the Protected Persons team. An ambulance left as they arrived, blue lights and siren both in evidence.

Head bowed to the wind, DCI Greg Geldard went to the car pulled up behind his, and leaned in through the window. The two armed police inside looked grim.

'I assume you're taking our witness, Peter Shinfield, off to another safe location,' said Greg. 'I don't need to know where. But I would like the chance for a few words before you leave.'

'Okay, if you make it quick,' said the man behind the steering wheel. His partner deployed to the hospital entrance and took up a watchful stance. The driver stayed in the car, which, in view of the weather, Greg couldn't help but feel was the better option.

Greg found the protected witness, Peter Shinfield, in a private room off the main A&E department, strapping on his forehead and still guarded by a dark figure wearing the logo 'Potters Property Services'. A nurse bending over Shinfield stood up as they went in.

'He's had a big shock,' he said. 'The doctor would like him to stay for a while, but I gather that's not on.'

Over by the window, the logoed figure from Protected Persons said, 'Don't worry. We'll look after him. It's better he comes with us.'

Greg looked up at the tall officer he'd met a few weeks earlier. 'Are you okay?' he asked.

'I'm fine,' he said, moving forwards into the light. Greg noted that he was paler than normal but appeared to be uninjured.

'And your partner?' asked Greg.

'He's taken a bullet to the abdomen. He's in theatre, I believe. It's not looking great. They said something about life-changing injuries.'

'Any other casualties?'

'One. The attacker. Tom got him, after he was shot. He saved Shinfield and me before he collapsed. It was a good shot. Straight to the chest and put him down just like that.' He snapped his fingers. 'As far as I know, the body's still at the scene.'

'Were there any others?'

'Not that I saw. If there were, they didn't break cover and got away. Your forensic team will no doubt be having a look around.'

'They're on the way there,' promised Greg. 'I just need a quick word with you and Shinfield before you set off again. I've been tasked with finding out how this happened.'

'Best someone does,' said the tall man. 'The shooter was waiting when we came out of the house this evening. Which means, not only did he know where we were, but also that we were planning a late start.'

'Not necessarily,' argued Chris. 'He could've been there all day, just waiting for his chance.'

'I don't think so. We ran a check when we got back from the court. All clear. And we checked all the way back to the main road. There were no vehicles that we couldn't account for. This evening, there was a car a couple of hundred yards from the cottage, parked on the verge. It's the perp's car, I'm sure of it.'

Chris made a note and picked up her phone to make sure the team in Bacton were preserving the probable crime scene.

'There're a couple of armed officers waiting for you outside,' Greg said. 'I assume as escorts to wherever it is you're going. I'll be quick with my questions, so you can get on. You first.'

Greg and the Protected Persons officer moved back to the window, and Greg switched his recorder on.

'Who exactly knew where you were and what time you were heading out this evening?' he asked in an undertone.

'Your chief superintendent, our office head and ourselves,' he replied. 'As far as I'm concerned, no one else. You'll have to ask around at your end to find out where the info went.'

Greg nodded. 'Who knows where you're going now?' he asked.

'Our HQ. Even I don't know until we're on the way. My instructions are, to leave here at 19.45, head for the A47, westbound, and wait for further instructions.'

Greg turned to Peter Shinfield, who was still sitting on the edge of the bed. 'Did you tell anyone when you were leaving? Anyone at all?'

'No.' Shinfield shook his head to reinforce his negative, then winced and put a hand up to his forehead.

'You're sure about that? No sad goodbyes to family or girlfriends? No hints at all that this was your last night in Norfolk?'

'No. Definitely not. In the first place, I'd had it drilled into me by these chaps that it would breach our agreement. In the second, I'm much more afraid of Constantin Gabrys and his employees than you are. I'm not taking any risks, believe me.' The slick wetness on his face and his extreme pallor bore out the truth of his statement.

'Okay. Thank you. I had to ask.' As Greg turned away, one of the two armed men from outside came into the room.

'Ready?' he asked.

'Ready,' chorused Shinfield and his minder.

'I'm done here for now,' confirmed Greg, then turned back to Shinfield. 'Good luck, Peter,' he said.

***

When Greg and Chris reached the holiday cottage on the edge of Bacton, a sheeted body still lay in the drive. The rather short-handed local police team were doing their best to keep sightseers at bay, assisted by Constable Weather. The rain and the east wind powering in from the Urals were undoubtedly making their task easier.

While Detective Sergeant Chris Mathews shot off to advise and support the uniformed team, as she deemed appropriate, Greg went for a quick word with his scenes-of-crime manager, Ned. Then, with a wave, he called Chris over and they went into the small bungalow.

The living space was mainly taken up by a large sitting room, with a dining area at one end and a kitchen alcove. Through the rain streaming down the windows, he could see a patio with a hot tub in the foreground and the tumbling North Sea behind. The sound of crashing waves formed a background to the sounds of a diesel engine as the mortuary van arrived. Ned had followed them into the cottage.

'Whose is the body outside?' asked Greg.

'Not identified yet. We'll be checking fingerprints and DNA with our records. But...' and Ned shrugged.

'Any signs of bugging, or of communications between Shinfield and the outside world?'

'Not yet.' Ned regarded Greg sympathetically. 'If you're hoping for evidence that the leak came from here, I'm going to disappoint you.'

3

One month later

The Chief Constable, Ralph Thornfield, or 'the Almighty', as he was colloquially known, was not a happy man. From the vantage point of his office window, the tall man in immaculate uniform watched his chief superintendent cross the car park in the pouring rain. Margaret Tayler's normally fluffy brown hair was draped limply over her face, and she stumbled over a rough area of asphalt, clutching an increasingly soggy cardboard box to her chest. As she reached her car, she seemed to sense the gaze from the second-floor office window and turned. Margaret and the Almighty exchanged glance for glance, then she put the box in her car, got in and drove away.

He turned back into the room to focus on the man sitting quietly by the desk.

'In view of the latest developments, I hope to God you've finished with that disaster at Norwich railway station.'

'If you mean the investigation of the death on the Norwich train[1] and the consequences, then yes.'

'I should damn well think so. I can't have you being sidetracked. If you can't keep your mind on the job, perhaps I should give the job to someone else.'

Greg opened his mouth, the words *Be my guest* on his lips, then thought the better of them and amended his reply to, 'I kept the Chief Superintendent fully informed of my priorities at all times.'

'Yes, and look where that's got us,' snapped Thornfield, more than a little unfairly, and threw himself into his chair. Greg remained silent, considering that the maxim, *Surplus words turn septic*, had rarely felt more apposite.

'Sum up where we're at,' commanded Thornfield.

'The two protected witnesses from the trial of Constantin Gabrys are safely in their new locations with their new identities. Both identities and locations are known only to the Protection Service.

'We've ruled out any leaks from the Bacton safe house that might have led to Peter Shinfield being targeted as he left. The only other places where that location was known were the Protection Service, and here at Norfolk police. The Protection Service has engaged investigators from Essex Police to check how they handled the information. So far, nothing.

'In Norfolk, both DS Mathews and I knew the location, because we had interviewed Shinfield there. Chief Superintendent Margaret Tayler knew, because the Protection

---

1. See Death on the Norwich Express

Service had told her. The forensic team have checked the phones and IT of all three of us and can find no leaks via those routes. They have also crawled over my car, and it's neither bugged nor tracked. We were about to start wider investigations when DS Mathews's fellow train traveller dropped dead right in front of her, and we were, as you put it, sidetracked for a few days while we identified his murderer and dealt with the aftermath. Then, as you know, came the accusations that the Chief Super and her son were involved.' He paused and Thornfield jumped in.

'What next?' he demanded.

'The allegations about the Chief Super obviously created another level of complexity. The source is dubious, but we can't ignore it. On the other hand, I don't want what is very likely no more than malice to distract us from other lines of enquiry. So, my plan is to check out the specific accusation that Margaret Tayler's son has been benefitting financially from links with organised crime, while DS Mathews chases down any possible routes for a leak from Margaret's office to the Gabrys empire, what's left of it.'

'Tell me about the dubious source,' demanded Thornfield.

'I assume you're aware of the background.'

'Assume I'm not. Give me the short version of why this officer, Constable Fellowes I believe, is dubious.'

'Okay.' Greg paused for a moment to order his thoughts. 'First, he was found to be circulating inappropriate images of a female colleague to a closed WhatsApp group. The images were of DI Sarah Laurence at the moment she was rescued from kidnap and false imprisonment. Another officer, also being disciplined, had taken the photos, but it was Fellowes who uploaded them to the WhatsApp group he shared with some of his old friends from the Met. He also added the offensive captions. He has been suspended pending dismissal ever since.

'Second, despite my advice to him on his first day about behaviour that was unacceptable here in Norfolk, there have been repeated complaints about his misogynistic attitudes to female staff, and indeed the public, and also about inappropriate language. He described Sergeant Mathews, for example, as a "short-arsed slut".

'Third, his responses to the complaints against him have included a series of complaints about other people, specifically Sergeant Mathews and now Chief Superintendent Tayler. It won't have escaped your notice that both are women in authority, something he seems to have a problem with. The two complaints against Sergeant Mathews have already been investigated and dismissed by HR. The associated complaint, that it was inappropriate for Sergeant Mathews and me to be working together in the circumstances, is partly dealt with by the fact I'm not her line manager and haven't been for a long time. And while it's not actually forbidden for colleagues to have social relationships, to keep things clear she is looking for a transfer. That leaves the latest complaint against Margaret Tayler. Of course, I will look into it as part of my search for the mole, but I think you can see why I regard Fellowes as a dubious source.'

Thornfield swung his chair to look out of the window for a long moment, then swung it back.

'I don't want to believe it's Margaret either,' he said. 'But if the investigation is to be thorough, we need to approach it dispassionately. If you can't do that, if you're unable to think the unthinkable, then I'd better put it into the hands of someone else.'

Greg took a moment to consider the challenge and decided to answer frankly. 'If you want someone else to do it, you'll get no objections from me,' he said. 'In fact, I'm surprised that an internal investigation has been regarded as acceptable. But equally, if you want me to carry on, I will. And I'll give it my best shot, even if I uncover something uncomfortable in the process.'

Leaning on his desk, Thornfield gave Greg a very straight look. 'That's more or less what I expected you to say. Thank you. And in answer to your question, the reason we're happy for you to take this on is because there's evidence to prove that links to the Gabrys empire pre-dated your arrival in Norfolk. That puts you in the clear. I'll get what information we have sent over to you.' He stood up. Greg took that as a signal the meeting was over and left the room.

He had scarcely reached his office, when the Almighty's secretary arrived with a sealed box.

'He says you must have these, and you're to sign to say the box arrived safely and with the seal unbroken.' She flourished a bit of paper at him, which Greg signed, then she whisked herself away. Feeling a little silly, Greg locked the door behind her, and cut through the signed tape on the box. Inside were three cardboard files, stuffed with papers linked together by a treasury tag. He settled down to read.

A couple of hours later, he emerged from the paperwork with a budding headache, to find the pounding wasn't only in his temples but also coming from his office door. Pushing the last file back into the box, he went to let Chris in.

'Hi,' he said, as she shook rain from her coat and hung it on the back of the visitor's chair. 'Anything yet on the dead assassin at Bacton?'

'He's been ID'd as a migrant worker from Romania,' she said. 'His fingerprints were on file after a case of assault at the Immigration Removal Centre at Yarl's Wood. He apparently absconded a few weeks ago. Is that the box of secret papers on the mole?' she asked, nodding at Greg's desk then throwing herself into the chair.

Greg was torn between exasperation and amusement. 'I know you always know everything, but really,' he said. 'How did you know that? The Almighty is carrying on as though this is the biggest secret since Lord Lucan.'

'He shouldn't ask his secretary to cart it down the corridor then,' she replied. 'She's tight-lipped enough, but the assistant under her is not, and everyone in that office knew what she was delivering. Is there anything I need to know?'

'Probably several things,' said Greg. 'The first being the suspicion that organised crime, and drugs dealers in particular, have been tipped off before raids for at least three years.'

'Jim and I could have told you that,' agreed Chris, nodding. 'He's been frustrated as hell that plans seemed to be known in the wrong quarters even as he put them together. Tell me something I don't know.'

'The most interesting info I've found so far relates to an old investigation into an inspector working in Great Yarmouth. He retired before I came to Norfolk, but you might remember him – Inspector Smart.'

'Sure do,' replied Chris. 'He was a clear demonstration of the fallacy of nominative determinism. You know, the theory that names determine jobs, like someone named Ditchfield ending up as a land drainage contractor.'

'I take it he wasn't known for his intellect.'

'Correct. How he passed his exams, Lord knows, and, in general, when things went wrong on his watch, it was usually cock-up rather than conspiracy. So how did he get fingered as a criminal mastermind?'

'It seems he had a lifestyle that couldn't have been funded from a police salary. Someone considered him worth a closer look and, as far as I can see, that someone was Margaret. The investigation got as far as saying that his explanations of betting wins and bequests were shaky, but if the money was dirty someone had done a good job of laundering it and the banking investigations ran into the ground too. The final note says he retired to Spain. It's probably worth taking another look to see how he's living now.'

'Anything more recent?'

'There are some well-documented instances of raids that failed, and the investigator at the time appears to have done a good job of identifying who knew what, when, and therefore could have been in a position to brief Gabrys. The problem is, there's not one common thread linking all the cases. Sometimes it was officers A and B in the know, other times it would be C or D. Or any combination you can think of, but never one person linking all the occasions word got out to Gabrys or his fellows.'

'Could there have been several people involved?'

'Possible of course, but that doesn't fit the other evidence. Apart from Smart, there's no one who seems to have been benefitting financially.'

'Who was the investigating officer?' asked Chris.

'Margaret Tayler.'

4

On the brink – 12 March 2020

Chris was watching the news on the TV when Greg got home. He started to speak as he entered the room, but she held her hand up for silence. He sat on the sofa beside her, Bobby purring on his lap, and watched with her. At the end of the coronavirus briefing, Chris reached for the remote and silenced the talking heads.

'You got that?' she asked. 'Risk raised from moderate to high. It looks like we're in for an unusual year. Any guidance from the top of the office yet?'

'Not that I've seen,' replied Greg. 'I'm just glad I didn't get stuck with standing in for Margaret. I don't like paperwork at the best of times.'

'Who is deputising?'

'Someone dropped in from uniform; I don't know them. Hopefully it's only for a short time. At least, I think that's what the Almighty's hoping, whatever he says about keeping our minds open. As for the virus, the only thing I've heard is complaints that the Home Office is being slow to brief police forces. So, no change there. Let's get some supper.'

'Yes, sorry. I meant to get something out of the freezer, but I got sidetracked by the news. I'll bung something in the microwave.'

Greg was already surveying the contents of the fridge. 'I think we need to do some shopping,' he pronounced, assessing the possibilities of a wedge of cheddar, some rather withered carrots, half a pint of milk and a couple of bottles of beer. 'Oh good, we have got some butter and some salad that needs eating before it walks away on its own. How about jacket potatoes with tuna and salad?'

'Fine for me,' said Chris. 'Then I want to talk to you about a new job. I'm thinking of applying for this.' She waved some printed sheets of paper at him.

Greg took a moment to put two potatoes in the microwave then rejoined her on the sofa.

'What is it?' he asked.

'DI in Suffolk, in the domestic abuse unit. It's based in Lowestoft, so the travelling is do-able, and the switch of police authorities would completely do away with any more accusations that our relationship is improper.'

'And it would mean promotion, which would be absolutely brilliant and well overdue. I think you should go for it, Chris. Anything I can do to help, of course I will, even though I'm not sure how I'll manage without the best sergeant ever!'

'I have to get it first,' she said practically. 'But I do think it would be good for both of us in the long run. Even if that mutt Fellowes hadn't raised the issue, there's no way I could be a DI under you, and I *am* still ambitious.'

'As you should be.' The microwave pinged and Greg got up to get the potatoes out. 'I'll put these in the oven for a bit to crisp up. Can you make the salad, and while you're doing that, I'll open a bottle to celebrate the next stage in your career.'

Half an hour later, they were both back on the sofa, meal eaten and glasses in hand.

'Champagne goes remarkably well with tuna,' reflected Chris.

'Better not drink any more though,' said Greg, picking the bottle up. 'Oh, it's nearly empty anyway. Might as well finish it, then off to bed. We have an early start in the morning. I've arranged for us to see Margaret first thing.'

'Before we go up...' Chris found herself addressing the back of his head as he went to drop the empty bottle in the recycling bin.

'Sorry, what was that?' he said as he reappeared in the doorway. 'I missed what you said.'

'I was going to ask,' she replied, 'who will you replace me with?'

'Now, there's a question. I think it's probably best we advertise the role openly in Norfolk, but the front runners, to my mind, are Bill and Jill.'

'Jill, every time.' The response was instant and firm.

'Why so?' he asked.

'Because while Bill has a lot of good qualities, I think he'd make a better sergeant in uniform than in CID. Jill, on the other hand, is a great detective. Think how much you rely on her already.'

'You're not worried she'll fall for my irresistible charms?' Greg lay back on the sofa, and tried to look like a lounge lizard.

'No, I'm not,' said Chris and hit him with a cushion. 'That's for being big-headed. But seriously, not only am I pretty confident of your loyalty, but she bats for the other side.'

'Does she really? I never noticed.'

'Why should you? It's not something a woman makes very obvious in the police even today. But take it from me, she does. She has a long-term partner who's a teacher.'

'When will you put your application in?'

'Tomorrow, assuming I have time after we see Margaret.'

5

13 March 2020

The Taylers lived in a large house set back from the A149 near Rollesby. It was surrounded by a high, curving brick wall with large wooden eagles on the gate posts. Greg had rung ahead, so wasn't surprised to find the tall wooden gates open, ready for his car to turn in to the sweeping drive. They closed behind him as he pulled up near the front door.

The house was modern, although the mixed brick and flint facade reflected an older style. The multi-paned windows were reflecting the early morning sun as he rapped on the sage-green door. Behind him, Chris was winding up a phone call to Suffolk police as the door opened and Margaret beckoned them in.

She took them through to a small, book-lined study and sat them down on a sofa facing the window overlooking the drive. As she took a seat in a leather armchair to the side, Greg noticed that she was her usual self: neat suit, pale jumper and scarf at her neck, her hair moderately tidy, for her.

'Well, this has the potential to be embarrassing,' she began. 'So let me say straight away that I understand the need to investigate the allegation made, even if it makes my blood boil. I am surprised it's you though! I was expecting the whole issue to have been handed over to the IOPC by now.'

'So did I,' replied Greg. 'When you asked me to investigate the leak, I assumed I'd be replaced pretty swiftly by a formal team from outside. To be blunt, I'm still expecting that to happen. According to the Almighty, this is in the nature of a preliminary inquiry. It's already been referred to the IOPC and they are likely to take over in the near future.'

'That's my understanding too,' said Margaret.

'But even though this is a preliminary inquiry,' Greg went on, 'I thought you might have wanted a Federation rep present, or a solicitor.'

Margaret leaned forwards to the low table in front of her. 'Coffee?' she asked, waving a cafetière, then poured without waiting for an answer. 'I didn't feel the need for either,' she said. 'I know what I'm doing, and I know what I haven't done.'

'There are two areas I wanted to ask about,' said Greg. 'First, the allegation your son has been involved in drugs locally, and second, the investigation you carried out prior to my arrival here, into information being leaked to Gabrys and the like.'

'I expected you'd want to talk to Anthony,' she replied. 'He's waiting in the kitchen, and, on my advice, he's got his bank statements ready for you to see. Incidentally, he does have our solicitor with him, as he's much more naive than me.' She flashed a smile. 'But to give you the short version: he was stupid enough, like a lot of young men, to experiment with drugs while he was at university in York. He was caught in possession of a small quantity of cannabis and some steroids. He was cautioned by North Yorkshire Police. He has never been in trouble in Norfolk, for drugs or anything else, not even a parking ticket.'

'Where do you think the accusation came from?' asked Chris.

'We all know who it came from,' said Margaret. 'Fellowes. As to why that specific allegation, my guess is that he went looking for dirt on all those of us who had tackled his bad behaviour. In your case,' – she nodded impartially to Greg and Chris – 'all he could dig up was your relationship with each other and Greg's marital breakup. In my case, I'd guess he found the information about Anthony in my file, as I reported it to senior management at the time. The interesting question is, how did he get at the file?'

Greg scribbled a note to himself and decided not to mention that they'd already done a background search on Anthony Tayler and his bank accounts. It would be interesting to see if the information they had already tallied with anything he said today.

'Thank you,' he said. 'We'll have a word with your son in a moment. Before we do, what did you conclude from the investigation you carried out earlier?'

'You've seen the files, I take it?' Margaret took a sip of her coffee. 'Then you know that, apart from Inspector Smart, I couldn't pin anything on any single officer. Smart was stupid and started flashing the cash. In my own mind, I'm certain he was corrupt. But someone much smarter than him was laundering the money, and I couldn't pin it on him. He retired to Spain, as I assume you know. When you flushed out Standish and his money-laundering activities for Gabrys,

I thought it might be worth taking another look for any link with Smart, but I was overtaken by events.' She shrugged.

'And even if we can tie Smart to Gabrys in the past, that doesn't explain what happened at the safe house.'

'No, it doesn't.'

'Exactly who *did* know when Shinfield was due to be moved from the safe house in Bacton? And who knew its location?'

'To answer your second question first, the Protected Persons Service, you, Chris and I all knew about the cottage. Me, because I was told; you two, because you'd been there.

'As to when, the service personnel again, and me. I can't imagine they invited a lethal attack on themselves, and I told no one.'

'Did you commit anything to paper?'

'No. Nor to my computer, before you ask.'

'Why were you told?' asked Chris suddenly. 'On the face of it, you didn't need to know. At least, telling you could have been postponed until after the event.'

'True,' said Margaret. 'I needed to be able to stand down the extra patrols once Shinfield had gone, but I didn't need to know in advance. My contact at Protected Persons said they were telling me as a courtesy and telling me early because they were about to go on leave.'

There was a long silence before Greg said, 'So if they'd stuck to normal procedure, you wouldn't have known in advance and none of this would be necessary.'

'Precisely,' said Margaret and drank up the last few drops of her coffee. 'Shall I take you through to Anthony?'

The kitchen was warm from a wide, red Aga against one wall, and redolent with the smell of more coffee. Already sitting at the scrubbed-oak kitchen table were a nervous young man with fuzzy brown hair very like Margaret's and an older man in a baggy pinstriped suit with very little hair at all.

'Harbottle,' said the latter, standing and holding out his hand. The younger man stood too, half held out his hand, then seemed to think the better of it and sat down again.

'I'll leave you to it,' said Margaret, and left, closing the door behind her. Greg and Chris pulled out two of the kitchen chairs tucked under the table and sat down opposite.

'This is just a preliminary conversation,' said Greg, 'but I think we'll do it under caution, if you don't mind. That will keep everything tidy just in case we need to follow up on anything.' Harbottle nodded, obviously not surprised, Chris got her recorder out and Greg administered the caution.

Once everyone had identified themselves for the tape, Greg got stuck into the questioning and rapidly discovered that there seemed little new to learn. The bank statements Margaret had mentioned were duly provided and scrutinised. He exchanged a look with Chris as they both noted the close match between the paperwork now provided and the information they already had.

'Can we take these copies away with us?' he asked. Anthony Tayler nodded and shuffled them together to hand them over.

'Is Mum in the clear now?' he asked. 'None of my mistakes were anything to do with her. They didn't even happen in Norfolk, and I've kept my nose clean ever since.'

'I can't say anything about that,' said Greg. 'But thank you for your cooperation today. At present I can't see any reason why we'd need to talk to you again. But if we do want to get hold of you, where will you be?'

'Here,' he said. 'For the next month or so anyway. Then I plan to go travelling on my gap year.'

'Let me know before you plan to leave the country,' said Greg. 'And thank you again.'

As he and Chris went back into the hall, Margaret rejoined them from her office.

'I imagine I'll hear from the Almighty,' she said. 'Hopefully I can get back to work soon.'

6

Great Yarmouth – that same day

Karen was excited when she rushed home from the local junior school.

'Mum, Mum, I came top,' she shouted even before she was through the kitchen door. 'I came top.' She ground to a halt and fell silent, as she picked up on the atmosphere in the room. Her mum was sitting at the kitchen table, her face red on one side. Her younger brother, Jake, was hovering by the door into the hall and, from the look of the stains on his face, had been crying. Her father was leaning on the sink, the usual can of lager in his hand.

'Well look who's here, old brainbox herself.' His words were slightly slurred as usual. 'P'raps it's because she's so bright, so clever, that her mother thinks she can move up in the world 'erself. Thinks she can get a job, no less. And a smart job at that. In an office.'

'I just thought it would help out,' her mum said quietly. 'A bit extra money...'

'Meaning my job's not good enough, eh?' her father shouted. 'I'm not smart enough to earn enough for the likes of you p'raps.'

Karen knew that speaking was a mistake. Saying anything was a mistake when he was in this mood. She stopped where she was, by the door, and hoped her mum would keep quiet. It was a forlorn hope, she knew.

'I just thought,' her mum began again, and her father lashed out with his fist, knocking her mum off the kitchen chair onto the floor. Jake cried out and ran up the stairs. Karen ran to her mum and sat on the floor with her as the angry man shouted at them both.

'Ever think that if you smart folk did a bit less thinkin' and a bit less spendin' on crap like phones and computers, my hard work would be good enough for us all. But no, you 'as to go lookin' for trouble, don't you. You 'as to think you're better 'n me, better 'n anyone. Oh, you make me sick. I'm goin' out.' As he slammed his hand on the table, both Karen and her mum flinched. Then as his stamping steps went through the kitchen and off down the yard, they both relaxed and sat up.

'Sorry, Karen,' said her mum.

'You shouldn't say anything,' said Karen. 'It always makes things worse.'

'I know. I didn't intend to say anything about the job, but he opened the letter. I thought I could do the work while he was at the abattoir and be home before he got back. But...' She shrugged. 'Maybe next time,' she said.

She got up and inspected the damage in the old spotted mirror. There were the clear red marks of fingers on one cheek, and she winced as she eased the shoulder he had struck with his fist. 'That's going to show for a bit. He's slipping,' she said. 'He doesn't usually leave a mark. Come on, Karen, fetch Jake down and we'll have some tea. I've got sausages.'

Karen went into the hall, then came back, and hesitated by the kitchen door. 'Mum, why did you marry him?' she asked. 'Was he nicer once?'

Her mother turned, surprised. 'You're growing up, aren't you, Karen?' she said. 'You've never asked me that before.'

'So was he?' Karen persisted.

Her mum shook the packet of sausages into the frying pan and sighed. 'Yes, I suppose he was. Before—' and she stopped herself.

'Before what?'

'Let's just say, before life got complicated and he had to take a job in a hurry. And the only one he could find was in that place. It's not all his fault,' she added. 'Don't be too hard on him.'

7

Evening of 13 March

The afternoon had proved to be paperwork heavy, so much so Greg and Chris were still at it into the evening. While Greg had found his desk half buried in what he mentally filed as MC – miscellaneous crap – Chris had divided her time between bank statements, registry details for HR files and attempting to fill in her application for the DI job in Suffolk.

When Jim Henning made the mistake of passing too close to her desk, he found himself hijacked into helping rephrase her blunt first drafts into something approximating diplomacy.

'You can't say that,' he pointed out.

'It's the truth,' she muttered rebelliously but only half seriously.

'Yes, but you don't need me to tell you that a reply to *Why do you want this job?* that reads *Because a misogynistic mutt from the Met objects to me sleeping with the boss* is not well designed to achieve what you want. It's not even wholly true, is it? I know you've enjoyed working with Greg, but don't pretend you don't want this promotion.'

'Yes, but my first attempt was just too creepy for words. I tried my first thoughts just to see how they read.'

'What was the creepy version?'

Chris scrabbled in her waste basket, then read out, '*Because the job deals with issues I care about and sets challenges that play to my strengths of determination, empathy, energy and local knowledge. I am also highly organised and a good manager of people.*'

'What's wrong with that?' demanded Jim.

'It sounds as though it was written by a robot for a start.'

'But it also has the benefit of being true. If I were you, I'd start from that. Let's look at the rest of the form. Okay. The problem with the way you've answered these questions, is that you keep saying "we" rather than "I".'

'But these things were all team achievements,' objected Chris.

'Yes, I know that,' replied Jim. 'But they want to know what *you* did, not what the team did. So say something like, *I led a team of x officers to...* then list the achievement, and what your contribution was. If your contribution was organising the team, re-energising it when the going got hard, and prioritising tasks when it threatened to be overwhelmed, then say that. Give examples.'

'Oh God. I hate filling these forms in. It makes you wonder if it's worth it.'

'You know it is, really,' said Jim. 'You'll be brilliant in that job, and it is important. What's all this other stuff?' he asked, picking up another wodge of paper from her desk.

'That? Oh, that's the bank stuff from Anthony Tayler. I've been comparing what he gave us this morning with what we already knew. It seems to match up okay.'

Jim had run his eye down the top sheet, then started flicking through the rest of the pile.

'Where's the statement from his building society?' he asked.

'What building society? I don't think I've seen a building society account,' replied Chris, looking up from her forms.

'That's my point. There seem to be regular payments into a building society savings account, but I haven't seen that account. It's probably nothing, but we should see it, for completeness.'

'So we should.'

When Chris took the issue to Greg, he was still wrestling with Home Office paperwork, but looked up when she came in.

'I'll ring Margaret,' he said. 'Hopefully it's just an oversight. By the way, just to make you feel even better, Mother has announced they're going to pay us a visit next Tuesday.'

'Oh,' exclaimed Chris, hesitating over the word that would have followed, and rejecting several attractive possibilities. 'How nice,' she said, in the end. 'Is this because you told them we're engaged?'

'That's right,' said Greg with a grin. 'They're coming so Mother can give us the benefit of her planning expertise.'

'How about we introduce her to my mother and leave them to fight it out between them?' suggested Chris.

'That's a bit hard on your dad and mine,' objected Greg. 'What've they done to deserve that? I can't imagine anyone being brave enough to referee that battle.'

'When are we going to break it to them that we've got our own plans?' asked Chris.

'When we have. I know we keep saying we know what we'd like, but we haven't actually booked anything, have we?'

'Oh God, more forms,' said Chris.

'Rubbish. A few minutes online, that's all it'll take. Let's do it tonight, then we can present them with a fait accompli next week.'

'Okay. If I've got my job application forms done by then.'

'You go away and finish your first draft, and I'll ring Margaret,' recommended Greg.

As it happened, it was Anthony rather than Margaret who answered the phone. He seemed surprised to be asked for his savings account details but promised to email the statements over as soon as he'd found them. When nothing had appeared by 7pm, Greg rang again. This time he got Margaret.

'Silly boy,' she said in a brisk tone. 'I'll let you have them straight away.'

Minutes later the emails were on Greg's desk. And moments after that, he was back on the phone to Margaret.

'May be nothing,' he said, keeping his tone non-committal, 'but there are regular cash payments going out of the account and, notwithstanding the payments in from his bank account, there's not much of a balance left. What are the payments for?'

'I'd love to tell you,' replied Margaret, 'but Tony went out soon after you rang this afternoon, and I haven't seen him since. I'd like to know why that is too.'

Her voice was brittle, and reading between the lines, Greg was left with a conviction that Margaret had reached the same conclusion as he.

'I'll be going home soon,' he said. 'You can get me on my mobile if there's anything to report.'

'Okay Greg. Speak later.'

In the car on the way to Acle and home, Chris asked for an update.

'Looks like it could be regular payments for something expensive, which could be drugs or could be something entirely innocent. But, if the latter, why make himself scarce this afternoon? Or if not that, then it could be payments to a blackmailer.'

'Or both,' said Chris.

'Or both.'

8

Great Yarmouth – 14 March 2020

Karen woke on Saturday, aware that, for some reason, there was something to look forward to. For a few minutes her fuzzy morning brain struggled to access the memory, then she was forced violently into full consciousness by the arrival, right on her tummy, of her brother in mid-leap.

'Wake up, Karen. Wake up,' he shouted happily. 'We're going out today, remember? Dad's working and Mum promised us a trip to the shops and to the beach. Even a picnic, she said.'

Karen gasped breath back into her body and pushed at her brother. 'Get off me, you great lump,' she said. 'Yes, I remember. Go and get your breakfast, and I'll be down in a minute.' Pulling on jeans and jumper and looking at the amount of wrist now showing from the end of her sleeves, she wondered if the shopping might include some clothes. She'd grown out of nearly everything she had, and while that meant Jake could have her old jumpers, it left her with hardly anything.

It was the first question she asked her mother when she joined them in the kitchen.

'Yes, I'd noticed,' her mother said. 'And you need new trainers too, both of you. Uncle Tim is going to give us a lift to a supermarket at Gapton Hall, and we'll see what we can find.'

'But what about the beach?' asked Jake, who was a lot more interested in fun than clothes.

'We'll go to the beach after,' said his mother. 'But that doesn't mean slot machines, so get your head around that.'

A mulish expression came over Jake's face and he pushed his dish of cornflakes away. 'I don't want to come then,' he muttered.

'Don't spoil the whole day before we've even started,' his sister said. 'Come on, we'll be getting a ride in a car too.'

'Well, a van anyway,' said her mum. 'Uncle Tim's swopped his car for a van, so we'll be going in that.'

It was a white Bedford van that pulled up outside. Tim wound the driver's window down and enjoined them to *Hurry up now* as they rushed round to the other side. Then all three squashed onto the bench seat. Jake had cheered up and, in order to keep him in a good mood, the other two gave way to his demand to sit next to Tim, who was looking across at their mum sitting by the window, and frowning.

'I can see the marks, you know, Anne,' he said.

'Shush,' said their mum. 'Not now, Tim. Not in front of the children.'

'Not what in front of us?' demanded Karen.

'Not telling you what we've got planned,' said her mum, frowning at Tim and shaking her head slightly. He took the hint and drove off.

***

If Karen was disappointed to find that the 'supermarket' was yet another charity shop, she soon cheered up as she explored the wide choice of clothes and shoes available. By the time they got back in the van, each clutching a paper bag containing a Greggs Cornish pasty and a can of Coke – a treat from Uncle Tim – there were several bags in the back of the van, containing three jumpers, a nearly new quilted jacket only a bit too big for Karen, a pair of jeans each and a pair of trainers for Jake. Unfortunately, there were no trainers in Karen's size. She'd lusted after a pair of high heels, but her mother had said a firm no.

'What time do you need to be home?' Tim asked in an undertone. Karen looked up from her pasty as her mother replied.

'No later than three. We need to be back before Kit.'

'When are you going to get out?' asked Tim, still in a low voice. Karen buried her face in her greasy Greggs bag but carried on listening.

'When I think it's safe,' her mum said, then added, 'Don't ask me now, Tim. Not in front...' and she nodded to Jake. Tim fell silent, screwed up the remains of his paper bag and tossed it over his shoulder into the back of the van.

'Okay,' he said loudly. 'To the beach and the slot machines!'

'Yeeaah,' shouted Jake, ignoring his mother's frown and shake of the head.

9

Same day – where is Anthony?

When Margaret rang Greg on Saturday morning, her voice sounded strained.

'He didn't come home last night,' she said without preamble.

'Anthony?'

'Yes. Greg, I'm sure he can't have had anything to do with the leak. He had no access to any information, either this time or on any previous occasion. But I am worried now. Worried that he might have got mixed up in drugs again after all. Otherwise, why has he disappeared?'

Phone held to one ear, Greg poured himself a coffee from the cafetière in his other hand, and sat down at the kitchen table opposite Chris, engaged in completing her application forms.

'Is this unusual for him?' he asked Margaret. 'Are we perhaps overreacting? Maybe he just stayed out with a mate. He is over twenty after all. I remember what it felt like. Just!'

'It's not unusual for him to stay out, but it is unusual for him not to let me know he wouldn't be back. He's normally very considerate like that. And I've rung the obvious suspects. I'm worried, Greg.'

'I'll have a word with Jim,' he promised. 'I don't suppose you have his phone on your *Find My* app?'

'No. Not any more. He's too old for that sort of parental scrutiny.' There was a pause. 'On the other hand, *you* could probably find him via his phone, if he's using it.'

'I'll have a word with Jim,' promised Greg again.

'You'll let me know, if you find him?'

'Of course. I'll keep you posted,' said Greg.

Chris looked up from her laptop. 'I've just hit send,' she said. 'Now it's in the lap of the gods and I can think about something else. I take it that was Margaret.'

'Yes. Anthony didn't come home last night and she's worried.' Greg was dialling Jim as he spoke. It took only moments to put him in the picture.

'Are you happy we have enough to justify tracking his phone?' asked Jim.

'I think so. Can you get an IMSI catcher organised, so we can track the phone and any messages?'

'I'll get it sorted straight away,' Jim promised.

'Let me know when you find anything.'

'Okay. But aren't you supposed to be on leave today?'

'I was, but I don't want to leave you exposed. As I say, let me know when you have anything.' Greg looked at Chris. 'I imagine you got that?'

'Yes. With luck, we can fit in a quick bit of shopping before we need to join Jim. Come on. We need to stock up if we don't want to starve. I've got a list.'

In the car and heading for the supermarket in Acle, Chris said, 'Are you thinking that Anthony looks like being the mole?'

'Not really,' said Greg. 'But he might be a link in the chain. Even if he is, it doesn't explain how the intelligence got out of Wymondham.'

'Margaret could be lying, when she says she told no one.'

'Yes, she could. But I find that hard to believe, unless some extraordinary pressure was being put on her.'

'Because of Anthony?'

'That seems the most likely possibility. Which is another good reason to find him.'

'Something else that occurs to me,' said Chris. 'Margaret knew where the safe house was, where Peter Shinfield was being kept, I mean.'

'Yes, as did we.'

'She'd known that for a while, like us. She also knew, like us, that he would be giving evidence at the trial. But no attempt was made on him until the evening *after* the trial, when he was due to leave Bacton.'

'Yes,' said Greg. 'It was clearly a revenge attack, not an attempt to keep him quiet, and that's very like Gabrys, as we know.'

'More than that, it suggests that it was the message about him being moved that triggered the precise timing of the attack. So, we need to focus on that particular message at that particular time. I want to go back into Margaret's office and see if we missed anything.'

'Okay. That's good thinking. After we've done the shopping, we'll go to Wymondham. You to Margaret's office, and me to catch up with Jim.'

'Agreed.'

***

It was late afternoon by the time Jim had any news. As Greg reflected, he'd missed out on his day off, but at least he'd had the opportunity to get rid of the remaining paperwork. He'd just filed the last of it – a request for comment on a wellness initiative – in his wastepaper basket when Jim came in.

'Some progress but not much,' he replied to Greg's elevated eyebrow. 'We tracked the phone onto a train to London. It seems he took the late express into Liverpool St and paid for his ticket with a credit card. It was a return ticket. After that we lost him for a while, possibly onto the Underground. Last spotted today in the vicinity of Victoria Station. After that, nothing. He may have turned the phone off or run out of battery. The issue is that from there he has access to rail and bus networks as well as London airports. He could be anywhere.'

'Are you keeping an eye on credit-card usage? That might be our best indication of his next move. Assuming he doesn't wise up, and switch to cash.'

'We'll keep on it,' said Jim. 'Keep the low profile for the present? No media appeals?'

'Yes. No point alerting him to the fact we're looking for him. I'll let Margaret know he's in London and see if he's made contact with her.'

One floor up, Chris was chatting with the only secretary on duty at the weekend.

'How're you getting on with Margaret's stand-in?' she asked.

'He's okay. Bit indecisive,' said Shelley, tapping away at her laptop. 'He says one thing, then half an hour later, he says something completely different. S'pose it's all part of the learning curve. Either that, or he's a shopping trolley,' she added.

'A shopping trolley?'

'You know,' – she looked up from her screen with a grin on her wide, cheerful face – 'wobbly wheel, keeps changing direction.' They both laughed.

Chris made herself comfortable on the edge of the desk. 'Who do *you* think leaked?' she asked.

Shelley looked at her for a long moment. 'Is this just between you and me?' she asked.

'Is it interesting enough?' replied Chris.

'Depends what you've heard already.' Shelley glanced over to the office door. Chris took the hint, got up and closed the door, then returned to her perch on the desk.

'Go on then,' she invited.

'Truth is,' said Shelley, 'it could have been any of us.'

'How do you make that out?' asked Chris. 'Margaret says she didn't tell anyone.'

Shelley laughed. 'Come on, Chris, you know how this place works. Everyone talks in front of someone. If it's not the driver, it's the secretary.'

'But—' began Chris, but Shelley interrupted again.

'I'm not saying Margaret was indiscreet in front of any of us, not on purpose at least, but I don't think she's any idea how much her voice carries through that door, even when it's closed. Whoever is in here, hears pretty much everything she says in there,' – she nodded at the inner office – 'unless we've got headphones on. It doesn't matter normally, at least it shouldn't matter, because we're all discreet. It goes with the job. But if someone wanted to leak, they would have got the information very easily.'

'You're talking as though that's a large pool of folk,' said Chris.

'It may be more than you think. Three of us work in rotation because we job share. Then there are visitors like the Almighty's PAs, and so on.'

'Could you make me a list?' Shelley frowned and leaned an elbow on her desk.,

If you're worried about getting someone into trouble, think of it this way,' said Chris. 'Anyone who's innocent can only benefit from us finding out who our mole is. And even the guilty person might be better off with us knowing, than being coerced to work for Constantin Gabrys.'

'Okay.' Shelley nodded and started scribbling on a bit of paper. 'But please don't say where this came from. I have to work with these folk.'

'Okay.' Chris nodded. 'It came from HR if anyone asks.' She took the piece of paper with six names on it and went straight to Greg.

When she arrived in his office, Jim was just leaving. 'You might want to stay for this,' she said as she closed the door behind her. It took just a moment to fill the two men in on what Shelley had said. Greg looked sceptical.

'You believe they really do overhear enough to be effective moles?' he asked.

'Shelley was very convincing. So yes, I do think it's possible. They hear a lot just by accident, and anyone deliberately eavesdropping would gather a lot more.'

'Okay. Let's take this list, Shelley included, and run the usual checks: bank statements, lifestyle changes, contacts, etc. I doubt we'll get very far tomorrow, but we can pick this up on Monday.'

'We can narrow it down a bit,' she pointed out. 'First we need to know who was in the office around the time Margaret got the key message from the Protection Service.'

'Of course. Thanks, Chris. You happy, Jim?'

'I'm happy,' he confirmed.

10

Monday 16 March 2020

Monday morning began with a lengthy email from Greg's mother. From the look of it, she'd been working on it for days. Chris read it in an ominous silence.

'Well?' said Greg.

'Well what? None of this is acceptable, you know that. She's selected a venue, suggested dates, recommended a guest list and even gone so far as to pick my wedding dress for me! This would be bad if she was the bride's mother let alone the groom's. Even *my* mother hasn't gone this far!'

'She hasn't actually picked a dress, as such,' said Greg, trying to look on the bright side. 'She just recommended a dressmaker.'

'And suggested a style to ... hmm, what did she say now? ..., *to make the most of my good points*. She makes it sound as though they're few and far between.'

There was a pregnant pause, then Chris sat down on the sofa and laughed until she cried. After a moment, Greg joined her with a reluctant grin on his face.

'I'm sorry, Chris,' he said. 'I should've known a wedding would bring out all her worst tendencies. I'll reply, setting her straight.'

'No, don't do that,' she said, wiping her eyes. 'As long as she's not committing any money to these pipe dreams, let it go until we see her tomorrow. Then we can set her straight.'

'You realise there'll be a row.'

'No there won't,' said Chris with determination. 'It takes two to row, and we're not going to. So long as we stick together and stay calm, there won't be a row. We just explain clearly and quietly that we are going to get married on a beach in Mexico, that the only guests will be your parents and mine, and that we'll organise a celebration for friends and colleagues after we get home.'

'And that the guest list and venue for that will be down to us,' added Greg.

'Exactly.'

They looked at each other and laughed again. 'She's still going to kick off, isn't she,' said Chris.

'Yes,' said Greg. 'And so will yours. Come on, let's forget about it for now, and get to work.'

At Wymondham they separated, Greg to catch up with Jim, and Chris on a mission to the HR department.

'I just need to know,' she said to the HR assistant minding the shop, 'who, of the clerical team on the top floor, was at work on this date in the late afternoon and early evening.'

'Shouldn't be too difficult to check,' said the young man with a crew cut, tapping busily on his computer. 'Give me a few minutes and I'll have something for you. Grab a coffee while you're waiting.' He nodded to the kettle and mugs in the corner.

'Thanks,' said Chris, surprised. She wasn't usually welcomed so warmly in HR. He looked up with a grin at the note of surprise.

'I've been wanting to meet the sergeant who called a certain Constable Fellowes a "dingbat waste of space",' he admitted.

'Oh, I see,' she said. 'You've met him, I take it.'

'For my sins.'

'Then you'll understand.'

'No comment,' he said with another grin, and turned back to his screen. 'I will say, however, that the account of the altercation definitely enlivened our day, and the epithet currently ranks Number One in our informal "most innovative insult" competition.' Chris snorted slightly into her coffee, thinking that HR had more of a sense of humour than she'd expected.

'What's standing at Number Two?' she asked.

"I smell something burning. Are you trying to think again?"

'But that was...'

'Yes. You're currently occupying both the Number One and Number Two slots. Congratulations, Sergeant Mathews. It's a record. Would you like to go for the hat trick? Don't answer that,' he said hurriedly. 'That's the lot. I'll print this list off.'

'Done already?' she said.

'Yup.' He picked up the sheet of paper that emerged from the printer and handed it over. 'The top two names are Chief Superintendent Tayler's secretaries on duty that day. As you probably know, three of them job share. The next two names are the PA and her assistant from the Almighty's office and the last is the messenger who was delivering post that day. I've included him for completeness just because he works on that floor, but it's likely he did his last round before midday.'

'Thank you.' She turned back at the door. 'Let me know if I get knocked off the top spot, won't you? And thanks for the coffee.'

Back in the main office she spotted Greg and Jim, heads together in the far corner. She decided to leave them in peace for a moment and went over to the desk with the two big screens where Jill was, as usual, hard at work.

'Jill,' she said quietly, 'I have a confidential job for you. Come into Greg's office for a minute and I'll explain.' Greg looked up and nodded as they left the room, then turned back to Jim.

In the small office, Chris handed over the list of names to Jill.

'It's been suggested that one of these may have been eavesdropping on Margaret Tayler on the afternoon she was told about the plans to move Shinfield from the safe house. Can you run some background checks, please? You know, the usual bank statements, unusual lifestyle changes, anything you can find out through paperwork and discreet enquiries.'

'Sure,' said Jill. After a hesitation she added, 'Can I ask you something, Chris?'

'Of course.'

'Rumour has it you're applying for a job in Suffolk.'

'That's right. And you'd like my job?'

Jill flushed. 'I'd like the opportunity, if you really are on the move.'

'And I'd like you to have it too,' replied Chris. 'If I get the promotion, and I mean if, I think the job will be advertised. I'd be happy to give you a hand with your application, although,' she added, 'I wouldn't claim to be an expert on forms!'

Jim and Greg were poring over yet more phone tracking reports when they were interrupted by a civilian assistant at the desk beside them.

'I think he's on the move,' he said. 'The phone's in use again and it's now somewhere near the Keele services on the M6.'

'Who's he ringing? Is it a number we know?' asked Greg.

'Looks like, yes, it's his mother, the Chief Super,' was the reply.

Even as he spoke, Greg's phone rang. Glancing at the screen he said, 'It's Margaret,' and moved a few feet away to take the call.

Watching, Jim saw his back stiffen. The call was soon over, and he came back to Jim.

'We have a problem,' he said quietly, and moved away again to the side of the room. 'Margaret rang to say she's been speaking to Anthony, and she's very afraid he's going to do something silly. She says he is indeed at Keele Services and asks if we can get someone to him quickly.'

'We need to contact Staffordshire Police. Find out if they have a team anywhere near. Either that or we try the North Staffs mental-health lot.'

'Staffs police,' they said in unison.

'Especially as we want a quick response. Make it clear it involves one of our own,' said Greg as Jim picked up a phone.

'They've a traffic team near Stoke, southbound on the motorway,' reported Jim after a moment. 'They've been alerted, and I've given them a description. Have we a photo?'

Greg put down his phone. 'I've just asked Margaret,' he said. 'She's emailing one over right now. I'll forward it to Staffs Police HQ at Stafford.'

'They said they'll get a rapid-response team on to it, but Traffic are closer.'

'Okay. We'll have to leave it to them for the moment.'

'Any idea how he got there?' asked Jim.

'Margaret says on a National Express coach.'

'I'll have a word with National Express, see if they know whether the coach has left Keele Services yet.'

'While you're doing that, I'll contact security at Keele,' said Greg. 'They must have someone. See if they can help.'

11

Keele motorway services – later the same day

A drama was already unfolding by the time local traffic cops, PCs Golding and Hill, stepped out of their car. A figure was visible on the roof of the restaurant block and as they watched he used the 'Welcome Break' sign to help him scramble up to the next level, the top of the motorway bridge.

'Bugger,' said Darren Golding succinctly as he strode towards the entrance. Sue Hill secured their car and followed in a hurry.

'Okay, how'd he get up there?' Darren demanded of the small, but growing crowd near the entrance. A man in liveried track suit, apparently a security guard, stepped forwards.

'Waste bin to top of the phone boxes, then up onto the cafe roof,' he said pointing. 'He was already up there by the time I was told we had an incident underway.'

A plump lady clutching a KFC box pushed to the front. 'He came off that coach,' she said. 'The National Express. I was sitting behind him on the way from London.'

'Did he say anything?' asked Sue Hill.

'Not to me. I didn't notice him really, until he ran over from the coach and started climbing. I seem to remember he spent a lot of the journey on his mobile phone, but that's not unusual, is it? He was still on the bus when I got off. I saw him running over when I came out with my supper.' She indicated the box of fried chicken. 'Going cold now,' she said dismally.

Darren had moved over to the bin and surveyed the options. 'Suppose I'd better get after him,' he said to Sue. 'Radio it in and ask for back-up.' Sue looked at her senior colleague.

'Shouldn't you wait for the back-up?' she asked. Never one to follow rules, Darren shook his balding head and settled his belt firmly round his still slim middle.

'No. It might be too late. If he jumps off that bridge into traffic, he's a goner.'

'Don't take risks,' said Sue, and Darren grinned.

'Not learned yet the whole job is about risks?' he said. 'You just have to be careful which ones you pick. And I'm careful. Make that call.

'You,' he said to the security guard. 'Make sure no would-be heroes follow me up here.'

He scrambled inelegantly onto the rubbish bin, and then swung himself with impressive ease to the top of the telephone box. It shook a little under his weight, but he wasn't hanging about, and made his way swiftly along the line of kiosks to the first building. His quarry was lingering on the roof of the bridge but started to move as he saw the uniformed policeman coming towards him. He slipped as he did, and for a moment Darren thought his problem would be solved by the young man falling back onto the cafe roof. Unfortunately, it wasn't to be as easy as that. He regained his footing and, on all fours, headed back towards the centre of the bridge.

Darren stopped by the Welcome Break sign and made no attempt to go any further. 'Hang on,' he shouted. 'There's no hurry. I'm not coming any closer.'

The young man stopped in his mad scramble, paused, then turned to sit on the curving metal. He was still facing away from Darren and towards the motorway with the speeding cars and lorries, but Darren took the hesitation as a good sign.

'So,' he said, trying to lean nonchalantly on the edge of the bridge looming beside him. 'What's the story? Why are we here on a chilly March Monday afternoon? Please don't tell me you don't like Mondays!'

The young man just shook his head, and Darren wished he'd done that course on talking down potential suicides. He was pretty sure cracking jokes didn't figure in the curriculum, but he was making it up as he went along.

'We could go inside and talk about it in the warm,' he suggested. 'Me, I could murder a burger. How about you?' Another shake of the head but, on the other hand, to Darren's relief, he hadn't moved any further onto the bridge, and Darren took that as a good sign. *Whoops, spoke to soon*, he thought to himself, as the boy – he seemed little more than a boy – suddenly got up and moved several steps further onto the bridge. Darren turned to see what had precipitated the move, and was furious to see the security guard moving slowly and clumsily towards him.

'I told you to stop anyone from following me,' he shouted. 'That didn't give you carte blanche to play the fool. Pillock,' he muttered as he turned back to the lad now wobbling in the wind as he balanced precariously on the curving roof. 'Sorry,' he shouted. 'He's gone now. It's just me. You were saying?'

'I wasn't,' the lad answered. 'I hadn't said anything.' Darren took some comfort that he had now.

'How old are you?' he asked abruptly.

'Twenty,' the lad replied.

'My God, I wish I was twenty again,' said Darren. By this time, he was saying the first thing that came into his head. Anything to keep a conversation going. He hoped that Sue had got some help arriving soon. This was a bit beyond him. He was much happier chasing speeding motorists and flagging down lorries driven by texting maniacs.

'You wouldn't if you were me,' was his answer. 'Being twenty is shit. You get into a mess, and you've no power to get out of it. Then you drag other people down with you, and suddenly it's all too late.'

'The one thing about being twenty, is that it's definitely not too late. Forty now. At forty it's too late for all sorts of stuff. Too late for me to win a race, play football for England or take a gap year to travel the world. But at twenty, no matter what your mistakes, you still have loads of time. Unless, of course, you've killed someone,' he added, taking a risk. 'That would be a bit of a bummer. Have you killed anyone?'

'No,' said the lad.

'I'm Darren,' said Darren, belatedly remembering he was probably supposed to have introduced himself. 'Are you Tony?'

'Yes, I'm Ant ... I'm Tony,' said the lad after a slight pause.

'And the people you think you're dragging down with you. Would that be your mum by any chance?'

'Yes,' he said. 'How did you know?'

'Just a guess, because your mum is why I'm here. She's worried about you.'

A pause, while Darren looked over his shoulder. He could see Sue was now keeping people back, and as he watched he saw a second car, this one unmarked, pull up beside theirs. He turned back to Tony.

'Come on, Tony,' he said. 'Give me and your mum a break. We're both in the last chance saloon, but you've got years, like I said. Come inside, have something to eat with me, and tell me what the problem is. I might have some suggestions.'

Another long pause, while cold winds blew around both of them, and Darren had time to realise how cold he was getting. Then Tony made a move, slipped on the metal roof, but recovered himself and came towards him. When he reached the edge, Darren held out his hand to help him down.

'Good man,' he said. 'The burgers are on me.'

They both retraced their steps, via phone kiosks and bin, to ground level, to be met by a spattering of applause. Darren noticed a few mobile phones held up in the air and understood, with resignation, that they were likely to be figuring on social media before the day was out. Sue came over with a blanket from the car, which she wrapped round the shivering Tony, and sat him in their car. Darren leaned on the door frame.

'Beef or chicken?' he asked. 'The burger: beef or chicken?'

'Beef, please,' said Tony.

'Coffee with sugar or without?'

'With,' said Tony. Darren nodded at Sue.

'I'll get you something too,' he said. 'Just make sure our friend doesn't leg it away before I get back,' he added quietly.

On his way to the cafe, he was intercepted by the colleagues from the unmarked car.

'Well done,' said Detective Sergeant Ryder, casually dressed in jeans and loose jacket. 'You can hand him over to us now.'

'With respect,' said Darren, 'I promised him a burger, and I think he'll talk to me. Let me give him his tea and have a chat. Then I can take him to the station.'

Ryder thought quickly. He knew Darren of old, both his strengths and weaknesses.

'Okay,' he said. 'We'll meet you at the station, and I'll let the Norfolk lot know he's safe, thanks to you. But don't waste too much time. See you in an hour? And I'll want a full report.'

'Gotcha,' said Darren, and returned to his burger quest.

***

The news, both that Anthony Tayler had been apprehended, and was safe, was greeted in Norfolk HQ with relief. Greg passed on the glad tidings to Margaret by phone, and had some difficulty deterring her from leaping into a car and heading north.

'You'll probably pass him on the way here,' he argued. 'It would be a pointless trip. Leave it with me and I'll let you know as soon he arrives, I promise.'

'He's definitely unharmed?'

'Definitely.'

'Any idea yet why he ran and what he's been up to?' she asked.

'Not yet, but I haven't had a full report. I will get back to you as soon as I can.'

Chris came into the room as he put the phone down. 'Something you need to watch on the BBC,' she said. A moment's clicking through websites, and both were watching the Prime Minister standing at a podium flanked by the Chief Medical Officer and the government's Chief Scientist.

At the end, they looked at each other. 'Work from home if you can, and no unnecessary travel,' said Greg, breaking the silence. His phone buzzed as he spoke. 'That'll be a call to a meeting to discuss the implications,' he predicted.

'You'd have thought we'd have had a bit more notice,' complained Chris.

'Well, working from home isn't going to happen for us, is it?' he replied. 'Apart from a few civilian office staff, we'll be carrying on as normal on the grounds that it's necessary. On the other hand, I think our wedding's off for the foreseeable future. We won't be going to Mexico any time soon.'

'Oh God, yes,' said Chris, then broke into a smile as another thought struck her. 'On the plus side, your parents won't be coming tomorrow.'

12

Great Yarmouth – evening of 16 March

When the news finished, there was a long silence. Karen looked at her mum, and then at her father. Jake, already in his pyjamas, was more interested in his toy car and pushed it around the threadbare hearthrug while providing engine sound effects.

'That's that then,' said her father. 'We all stay home. No job for you, my lady, like it or not.'

'Surely *your* work is necessary,' said her mum nervously. 'People still have to eat. People will still need meat.'

He leaned back in his chair and popped another can of lager open. 'You'd think so, wouldn't you. But I've been told I'm not needed at the moment,' he said, taking a long swig, and wiping his mouth with the back of his hand. 'I've already been told to stay home till I'm called for. They told me on Saturday.'

'You never said anything,' her mum said with a blank expression.

'None of your business,' he replied. 'I've told you now, haven't I?'

'Are they closing the whole place down?' asked her mum.

Karen wished she'd say nothing. Keep quiet. Didn't she know that asking questions just made things worse? Her father slammed his hand on the arm of the chair, making them all jump and lager spill out of the can.

'Mind your own business,' he shouted. 'I've told you all you need to know. I'll be home until they tell me to go in. And you'll be home too if you know what's good for you.'

'But what will we live on, if there's no money coming in?' Her mum seemed to be made reckless by panic and earned the reaction Karen had been expecting. The thrown can sprayed lager all over the room and caught her mum on her forehead. A small splash of blood bloomed and grew.

'Now look what you made me do,' her father snarled, and got up to fetch another can from the fridge.

Karen went to the bathroom and fetched some toilet roll, then went to her mum, and offered it in silence. Her mum didn't look at her. She just took the tissue and held it to her forehead, then said, 'Go to bed, Karen. Both of you.' Jake was already halfway up the stairs. Karen followed him.

'What do we do if he's home all the time?' Jake asked.

'I don't know,' Karen whispered back. 'But we can go to school. They haven't said anything about not going to school. We should just get ready as usual in the morning, and slip out quietly before he's up.'

'What do we do if he's up early?' asked Jake.

'I don't know.' Her voice was rising with irritation and she stopped short, taking a nervous look over the banisters. 'I don't know,' she said more quietly. 'How should I know? Go to bed, Jake, and we'll go to school as usual. I hope.'

13

Tuesday 17 March 2020

At breakfast, with yet more gloomy news of deaths, sickness and runs on toilet paper at the supermarkets, Chris was in a thoughtful mood. Greg was arguing with his mother on the phone. By the time he put it down, he was a little pink in the face and running late.

'Coffee?' asked Chris, waving the cafetière.

'No time. I'll get one at the office. I'm expecting Anthony Tayler in the next half hour, so we need to get a move on. You ready?'

'No problem,' said Chris, shrugging into her purple duffel coat.

In the car and heading down the A47, she said, 'I assume they're not coming. That you won the debate.'

'Just, and only with my father's backing. Between him putting his foot down and refusing to drive her, and me pointing out that the subject of our wedding was now on the back burner for the foreseeable future, we eventually got an agreement.

'Chris, it occurs to me there's other things we need to talk about.'

'Yes, I've been thinking too. You first.'

'If these rules go the way we're expecting, then I think we need to simplify our living arrangements. At the moment, you're dividing your time between staying at mine and your place. How do you feel about moving in with me full-time right now? Then we're a proper household and—'

'You don't have to convince me,' she interrupted. 'I think it makes sense too. Your place is much bigger than mine, and mine is only rented, so all in all, it makes much more sense this way. It's what we'll be doing when we're married, isn't it?'

'I'm glad you see it that way,' he said, indicating left and pulling into the exit lane for the A11. 'As far as I'm concerned, the only reason I haven't suggested it before is because of the you-working-with-me issue, and your application for the Suffolk job will solve that one.'

'If I get it,' she interrupted, her fingers crossed against bad luck.

'Of course you'll get it. But we need to decide about furniture and such.'

Chris grinned. 'I imagine "and such" refers to my parrot.'

Greg risked a sideways glance. 'Yes. Your parrot. Tally. I assume she'll be coming with you.'

'Yes, please,' said Chris. 'My mother's made it clear that looking after her when I'm staying at yours was okay as a temporary arrangement, but that's all. She doesn't want to take her on permanently. For that matter, I'd miss her too. And she does like you. Tally that is, not my mother. I mean,' she added, spotting a potential for misunderstanding, 'of course my mother likes you as well, but...'

'Yes okay,' said Greg.

'Is that, yes okay, Tally can live with us too?'

'Yes, of course she can. Bobby got on with her okay when she stayed before. I suppose she can get used to her again. Is she still swearing as much?'

'My mother, or Tally?' asked Chris, deliberately misunderstanding.

'Tally of course. She considerably broadened my vocabulary last time.' After a pause, he added, 'Something else occurs to me. When I explain to my mother that a foul-mouthed parrot with a razor-sharp beak has taken up permanent residence, I think her enthusiasm for visiting will diminish sharply.'

'Now that's what I call a win-win,' replied Chris. 'I'll fetch her round tonight. If you come with me, we can decide what, of my furniture, we want to keep as well.'

***

It felt strange in the office, without all the civilian office staff bustling around. On their way through reception, they were told a list of the functions now being carried out by homeworking had been emailed to all staff, and a second list of the senior staff who were in the office that day was handed to them.

'We're to assume anyone not on this list is working from home,' said Greg. 'I see the Almighty's at home today.'

'Probably so he doesn't have to make his own coffee,' said Chris. 'The secretaries are all working from home too.'

Greg looked at his watch. 'Anthony Tayler should be here any moment. Jim and I will have a chat with him. Let me know if you and Jill turn anything up.'

'Will do,' said Chris as they parted company.

Jim was ready and waiting in Greg's office. 'The Tayler lad arrived from Staffordshire about ten minutes ago. I've had them put him in an interview room, with a constable keeping an eye on him.'

'What about our Staffordshire colleagues? I'd like to thank them.'

'They've gone straight back. Busy at their end, apparently, and they were under instructions to keep their distance, to avoid virus transfer.'

Greg raised an eyebrow. 'I suppose we need to get used to this,' he said. 'Come on, let's have that chat with Anthony. Has he a solicitor?'

'Yes. One organised by Margaret. And Margaret's on her way as well, I believe.'

'That's going to be tricky,' remarked Greg. 'We'd better park her somewhere neutral. As she's suspended pending conclusion of the investigation, she hadn't better go into her office and we can't leave her in the main waiting room.'

'Ask her to wait in her car,' suggested Jim. 'We can use the virus as an excuse. I believe that's where most visitors are being asked to wait now.'

'Good idea. Tell the front desk that, and that I'll come out to speak to her as soon as I can.'

Anthony was accompanied by the solicitor Greg had met at the Tayler's house a few days before.

'Mr Harbottle, isn't it,' said Greg, holding out his hand, then remembering and removing it. 'Sorry, forgot. We're not supposed to shake hands now, are we.'

Harbottle and Anthony were sitting, some feet apart, on the far side of the table. Greg and Jim sat down their side, and Jim started the tape.

After the introductions and the caution were recorded, Greg explained. 'I'm conducting this interview under caution because we have reason to believe you may have been procuring illicit substances. But to be frank, I am aware that there may be another explanation for the expenditure that has reduced your savings account to almost zero. This is your chance to set the record straight.'

There was a pause, during which Anthony looked at the floor, and Mr Harbottle looked at Anthony.

'I'm told by Staffordshire Police, that when they picked you up at the Keele services, you said you were worried about "dragging your mother down with you". What did you mean by that?' asked Greg.

Anthony sighed, then said, 'I suppose I'm going to have to tell someone.'

'That's right,' said Greg when there didn't seem to be any more forthcoming. Mr Harbottle shifted in his seat but stayed quiet.

'It started a couple of years ago,' said Anthony.

'What started?' asked Jim.

'I expect you know I got caught with a spliff or two in York,' he said. 'When I came home that summer, I promised

I wouldn't do that again. And I didn't. But then I got offered stuff at a rave near Great Yarmouth.'

Mr Harbottle started to say something, but Anthony held up his hand. 'It's okay. I'm not about to incriminate myself,' he said. 'I said I got offered stuff, but I didn't take it. I handed it back. Then, next thing I know, I'm getting photos sent to me that someone must have taken that evening. They made it look as though I was getting stuff off a dealer. Then I'm getting threats, that if I don't pay up, the photos are going to my mother.

'I said go ahead, she won't believe you. I'm not completely stupid,' he added.

'Then I got more photos and some videos. Some were the same as those I'd seen at first. Others were videos from the rave. I probably was a bit tipsy,' he admitted, 'but those videos made me look as though I was high as a kite. And the threats changed. Now they were saying they'd put the pictures on Facebook and name both me and my mother. So I paid up. Fifty pounds didn't seem so much. Not at the start.'

'How much are they demanding now?' asked Jim.

'It got up to two hundred per month. Then I ran out of money.'

'What did they ask for next?' asked Greg.

'Information. But I told them I hadn't any. That Mum never talks shop at home and doesn't bring paperwork home either. That wasn't quite true, but it was true that I never saw any, and that I had no information I could share, even if I wanted to. I thought about just making stuff up, but decided that might be even more dangerous. I tried to sell my bike to raise some cash, but no one seemed very interested in it, and

I didn't know what else to do. That's why I decided to go on a gap year to get away from them all. And give it time for the dust to settle if they did go public.'

'How were you going to fund your gap year?' asked Jim.

'My grandfather offered to buy me some rail tickets to get me started, but said it was up to me to work my way after that. He's quite keen on me standing on my own two feet.'

'How did the blackmailer contact you?' asked Greg.

'Always by mobile phone. Either a phone call or a text message. The photos and videos were attached to text messages.'

'Did you ever meet anyone?'

'No. Not to my knowledge.'

'How did you pay the cash over? You did pay them cash, I take it?'

'Yes. I had to put it in an envelope and post it to an address they gave me. But when I checked it, it was just a shop that acted as a sort of postbox.

'I tried watching it, but I didn't see anyone I recognised in the short time I was there. Without a car, it was a bit difficult to hang about watching, without attracting attention. People started to look at me funny, so I decided to leave.'

'And the address of the shop?'

Anthony provided it and Jim made a note. When he'd wound up the interview with the usual warning about not leaving the area without letting him know, Greg said, 'Your mother's waiting for you in the car park. I'll take you to her.'

Walking down the corridor, with Harbottle a few paces behind, Greg said to Anthony,

'I realise you've had a bad time. You were in a bad place, and you didn't know how to get out of it. Can I give you a little advice?'

Anthony nodded, walking along looking straight ahead.

'Don't hide stuff from your mum. She's in your corner, and she knows better than most how to deal with the bad guys. And she's tough. The only thing that would really get to her, would be if something happened to you.' Greg paused at the door to the car park. 'If you need to talk to me anytime, this number will find me,' he said, and handed over a card. 'Come on. I think you've had a long day already.'

Handing him over to Margaret, he said, 'We're not making any charges. Anthony has just been helping us with our enquiries. I'll leave him to explain what's been going on.' And he waved as he turned to walk away.

'Greg,' Margaret called after him, her voice softer than normal. 'Thank you.'

'No problem.'

14

A gossip of secretaries

Jill was looking frazzled when Chris leaned over to ask, 'Got anywhere?'

'Nothing clear,' she said. 'And if I have to listen to any more backstairs gossip about who kissed, hugged or bonked whom in which cupboard, staircase, car or office – delete as appropriate – I might go mad! According to the dictionary, the collective noun for secretaries is a pool, but I think a gossip might be more appropriate. No wonder nothing stays secret round here.'

Chris sat on the edge of the desk and swung a foot reflectively. 'I always found them a good source of intelligence. In fact, I cultivated them as such. I suppose I assumed they kept their information exchange within the family. Which may have been stupid of me. In fact,' she went on, 'if I think about it, I never heard anything truly sensitive, just operational stuff a bit ahead of time, so perhaps they were exercising some discretion and we're being a bit harsh now.'

'That's my frustration,' replied Jill. 'I'm not hearing anything other than personal gossip. One of the secretaries is being singled out for being more indiscreet than most, but that's all so far and I'm still waiting on some of the other data.'

'I hate to say this, given how much time you've spent checking ANPR data recently,' said Chris, 'but is it worth looking at car movements around a few key dates?'

'The data only goes back so far,' warned Jill. 'But I could look to see, for example, where their cars went on the day Margaret was told about the safe-house changeover.'

'Worth a try,' said Chris. 'I'll catch up with you later. In the meantime, I'm going to try a little experiment.'

The upper floor was eerily silent, with so many staff working from home. Chris nodded to the one PA she saw passing down the corridor, then went into Margaret's office. There was a sign on the desk giving contact details for the on-duty secretary, and she knocked on the inner door, which was slightly ajar. The acting Chief Superintendent, a temporarily promoted chief inspector from Norwich, looked up in surprise. He was a heavyweight man who probably looked better in uniform than he would in civvies, reflected Chris. And he looked harassed, as well he might in the circumstances. When he took over Margaret's desk, he presumably hadn't anticipated a pandemic on top of everything else.

'Can I help?' he asked.

Chris explained briefly what she wanted to do. A variety of expressions passed over his face as she spoke, starting with irritation and working their way through surprise to interest.

'What do you want *me* to do?' he asked.

'Nothing really, sir,' she replied. 'If I can just set up my equipment then go into the outer office for a few minutes, that will be all.'

'Okay. Go for it. I'll go and fetch myself a coffee while you're doing that.' And picking up his mug, he left the room. Chris put her small recorder on the desk, fiddled with it for a moment, then set it to play, and left the room closing the door behind her.

She was still standing in the secretary's room, listening, when the acting CS returned with his coffee.

'I can hear that!' he exclaimed. They both listened to Chris's voice from inside Margaret's office, then the sound cut off.

'That was the last version of the recording,' Chris explained. 'The loudest. I recorded the speech at four volume levels. At the first, the quietest, I could hear a voice but not make out any words. With all the others, the words became successively clearer.'

'Proving what?'

'Not much if I'm honest, sir,' admitted Chris. 'But it does suggest that the eavesdropping theory is practical. You *can* hear a voice through that door, even when it's closed.'

Back in the main office, Jill was buried in ANPR recordings, but surfaced briefly to wave Chris over.

'Got some banking data,' she said. 'There's a couple of odd entries I'd like you to look at. I've mailed them over to you.'

'Okay, I'll check that out next,' replied Chris.

'How did your experiment go?' Jill remembered to ask. Chris gave a thumbs up, as she went over to a spare desk and logged on. It didn't take her long to spot the anomalies Jill had referred to, and she took it straight to Greg.

'I hear you've been with the acting Chief Superintendent,' he remarked.

'Not deliberately,' she replied. 'It was his office I wanted. Unfortunately, he happened to be in it. He was quite reasonable though, and I found out what I wanted.'

'Which was?'

'That the eavesdropping theory has legs. I made several recordings of me reading a speech, and I could clearly hear words through the closed door, even at quite low volume. That wasn't why I came in though. Jill's turned something up.' She put a wodge of papers on his desk and pointed to an item listed on the top.

'This is it. A surprisingly large sum of money was paid into this account the day after the attack in Bacton. The account it came from has been linked to that accountant we arrested. The one who was money laundering for Constantin Gabrys and his drug-running schemes. There was a second payment yesterday.'

'You mean Standish? The accountant?'

'That's right.'

'But he's still in gaol, isn't he? Surely all the bank accounts were shut down after we got him and Gabrys?'

'You'd think so, wouldn't you? But it seems one, at least, is still functioning. It'll be interesting to find out if there's more than one. We only got on to this because Jill is so thorough. As soon as she spotted the odd payment, she ran a wide-ranging check to see if the originating bank account was known to us. And voila!'

Greg got up, stuck his head out of the door and hollered, 'Jim,' in stentorian tones.

Once Jim had joined them, Greg brought him up to date. 'So, I'd like you to check out the Standish end with Jill. Chris and I will interview Kath Irwin.'

'Margaret's secretary?'

'One of the three, yes,' said Chris,

The interview with Kath Irwin was short and sweet. She claimed to have no idea that the payments had been made into her account, let alone any idea where they had come from. Then she clammed up and refused to say anything else without a solicitor present. A quick telephone call between Greg and the head of HR, and she was suspended and sent home. Then Greg rang the Working-From-Home Almighty.

'It's looking less and less likely that Margaret had any involvement in a leak,' he said. 'To me at least. When are the IOPC coming to conduct the formal investigation?'

'It should have been this week,' was the reply from the Almighty. 'But it may not happen just yet. The designated lead investigator has got Covid, and all his team are currently in isolation. Their HQ updated me this morning. Let me have your report, Greg, and then I can take soundings. It may be we can have Margaret back off suspension if your evidence justifies it. I'll speak to the IOPC about it. It's not what would normally happen, but these aren't normal times.'

15

The end of everything

For the next couple of days, Karen kept her head down and worked hard at school. At home, the atmosphere continued to be ... well, weird was the only word that came to mind. Mum was on edge and kept having long telephone conversations every time her father was outside the house, which wasn't very often. Her father was even more bad-tempered than usual. He snapped when her mum asked if she could go shopping, and shouted at her when she wanted to take Karen and Jake on the beach.

'It's not permitted, you fool!' he shouted, so loud that Karen could hear from the next room. 'Which bit of "stay at home" isn't clear to you?'

'Surely,' Karen heard her mum say, 'surely that doesn't mean you can't go for a walk? Or let children play on the beach?'

'Of course it means that!' her father shouted. 'Are you really stupid? The virus doesn't care about walks or beaches. They said stay home and stay home you will.'

'You just don't want me to go out.' Her mum was almost shouting now. 'It's just any excuse to keep me in.'

'It's an ill wind, as they say,' he replied, and laughed in her face. The door banged as she left the kitchen and walked straight into Karen.

'Karen,' she said. 'You shouldn't be listening. It's rude! Go to bed!'

Karen wanted to say that she hadn't been listening, she just couldn't help hearing when they shouted so loud. And to point out that it wasn't bedtime yet. But neither comment seemed a good idea.

The stresses of home seemed to spill over into school. At least, she assumed that was why Miss Grain asked her what was wrong.

'Nothing,' said Karen.

'You just seemed a little worried,' said Miss Grain. 'Is it because of Covid? You don't need to worry too much. It doesn't seem to hurt children.'

'I'm not worried,' said Karen again.

'Because, if anything is wrong at home, you can always tell me, you know.'

'Nothing's wrong,' said Karen. 'Can I go now?'

Notwithstanding Miss Grain and her intrusive questions, school was still Karen's favourite place. Her safe space, filled with friends and books.

It was the end of Karen's world when she was told that school would soon be closing and all lessons would be online.

16

Gorleston, near the golf course

It took Jim mere minutes to establish that the accountancy firm of Standish & Partners had folded when its owner – and one and only partner – was confined at Her Majesty's pleasure. It took rather longer to find out where Mrs Standish was now living. Eventually he pulled up outside a small, neat house with a tidy front garden not far from the golf course in Gorleston. The rain had stopped at last when he and Jill got out of the car.

'Seems odd to see so many cars in drives at this time of day,' Jill remarked.

'So there are, I hadn't really noticed,' said Jim. 'The owners are all working from home, I suppose.' He rang the doorbell and waited, Jill behind him on the gravel path.

When Mrs Standish opened the door, they hardly recognised her. It seemed she'd had a makeover since parting from her money-laundering ex-husband. The dark hair was now cut in a glossy, short bob and she seemed to have lost a couple of stone in weight.

'Come in,' she said. 'You remember my son, Nathan, I'm sure. He's in the kitchen.'

'Of course we remember Nathan,' said Jim. 'I especially remember how brave he was, coming forward to give evidence.[1]

We'll help now if we can,' replied Mrs Standish. 'But I doubt we know anything useful.'

A pot of coffee was already in evidence on the kitchen table, and Nathan was engrossed in his laptop.

'Just finishing something,' he muttered without looking up. 'Be with you in a moment.'

Jill noted that the mother's transformation had not extended to the son. He still looked scruffy and he was still engrossed in IT.

'You said something about a bank account,' his mother said, pouring coffee.

'Yes. It appears that an account associated with Standish and Partners has been active recently. As the business was closed down, that surprised us. We were wondering if you knew anything about this particular account.'

'What's the sort code and account number?' asked Nathan.

'It's a Santander account,' replied Jim, not sure he was ready to hand over any more details.

'It's not one of ours then,' said Nathan, and his mother agreed.

'Our accounts are at Lloyds,' she said. 'And a right old hassle we had opening them. I have one account, and Nathan has

---

1. see Dig Two Graves

another. That's our lot, these days. As far as I know, all the business accounts were closed after the court case, when the business was wound up.'

'Who had access to them, when they were open?'

'Apart from my ex, I've no idea,' she replied. 'I assume office staff may have had some access, and, for all I know, those Lithuanians he was working for may have had access too. You'd know more about that than I do.'

'Do you have any paperwork from the old business?' asked Jim, clutching at straws.

'No,' said Mrs Standish.

'Yes,' said Nathan. She looked at him, startled.

'Not paperwork as such,' he said, managing to convey from his expression the view that anything on paper probably belonged in the sixteenth century. 'I do still have some files on my laptop that I copied from my father's, but I assumed you'd have copies of all that stuff from when you arrested him.'

'Not necessarily,' said Jim. 'A lot of files disappeared off the server at the time of the arrest. Can you let Jill here have copies of what you've got?'

While Nathan and Jill got their heads together over paired laptops, Jim moved away a little with his mug of coffee and stared into the back garden. Mrs Standish joined him.

'I'm glad to see you looking so settled,' he said. 'It must be difficult getting your life back on track after the sort of experience you two had.'

'Easier in some ways than carrying on with the old life,' said Mrs Standish. 'Yes, there are some who assume that if one member of a marriage is dirty then so is the whole family, but thankfully not everyone thinks that way. The school was great with Nathan, and my boss has been supportive, so we've got by, and I was thinking we were coming out the other end.' She turned to look at Jim. 'It isn't all going to start up again, is it?'

'Not for you,' he said, his fingers metaphorically crossed behind his back.

Back in the car, he looked at Jill. 'Anything look useful?' he asked.

'Possibly,' she said cautiously. 'I need to give it a close look.'

***

Over at Police HQ, time was passing more quickly than was convenient. Piling into the passenger seat of Greg's car, Chris checked her watch as she fastened her seat belt.

'We're running late,' she remarked, rather unnecessarily.

'I know,' said Greg, 'but I had a whole succession of phone calls just as I was trying to leave. In fact, it was still ringing as I left. Even as he spoke, there came a 'ting' from the phone in his pocket. 'Obviously a text message,' he said. 'It'll just have to wait. Now, what do we need to do at yours?'

'Most importantly, pick up Tally and her equipment, and the rest of my clothes and stuff. Then make our minds up what we want to move to your house, and what we want to sell or put into store. I can organise a man with a van to deal with that in the next few days. Then I can let the landlord know I've moved out. And that's it!'

'Sounds simple, doesn't it,' replied Greg with a smile sideways. 'I cleared out more wardrobe space for you this morning, but I think at least some of your furniture we need to bring over should be chests of drawers. For your extensive collection, that is. Oh, and by the way, it's *our* house now, not mine.'

Chris reached over to pat his knee. 'For that, I'll ignore the dig about my clothes,' she said.

In truth, as Greg discovered when they arrived at Chris's tiny cottage, there was a lot less than he had feared. Two big suitcases and a rainbow pile of clothes on hangers constituted the clothes element. Tally gave Chris the big hello, with cheek rubs and ear nibbles, then extended the same courtesy to Greg who was, not for the first time in his life, wrestling with Tally's supposedly demountable perch.

'Bugger,' announced Tally conversationally.

'Took the words out of my mouth,' said Greg.

Chris came over to critique his efforts. 'I don't know why you make such a meal of this,' she remarked, leaning over to twist one nut, and remove a pin. The perch collapsed to half its height, almost removing Greg's index finger as it did so.

'Careful,' he exclaimed, rocking back on his heels. Tally, flapping her wings to keep her balance on his shoulder, opened her beak to add a, no doubt salty, expression of her own, then took note of Chris's wagging finger and limited herself to 'Rats'.

'Look, you put the stuff in the pile over there in the car, then come back and see what I'm suggesting we keep,' said Chris.

By the time Greg reappeared in the living room, Chris had tied coloured labels to most of the furniture and was putting crockery in boxes. She stood up as he came in, rubbing the small of her back.

'When I moved in here, I swore I'd never move again,' she said. 'Now I remember why. Look, I've put green labels on the stuff I'd like to keep, and red labels on stuff to sell or give away. The orange labels are for stuff to put into store, either in your little barn or in a container. What do you think?'

Greg took a quick glance round the room, then went upstairs. Chris could hear his footsteps moving in the two tiny bedrooms and the bathroom. Then he reappeared in the living room.

'Looks fine to me,' he said. 'It makes sense to keep your bedroom furniture. It can go into the guest room at the house. And there's plenty of room for that wardrobe and chest to go into our room.'

'Your furniture is pretty sparse,' she agreed.

'I never got round to adding to the minimum I needed,' he said. 'Too busy. That leaves the sofas and kitchen table.'

'I'm happy to give the kitchen table away, if you're okay with swopping my sofas for yours. I think mine are newer and more comfortable.'

'Sounds good to me,' said Greg. 'Are we done here? We still need to unload the car at home and settle Tally in before we can go to bed.'

'Sure. And I vote we pick up a takeaway on the way home. We can call at the chippy in Acle.'

Chris locked the cottage behind her and got into the passenger seat with Tally on her arm. 'There's no room for her in the back,' she said in answer to Greg's raised eyebrow.

'Just keep her out of my way,' he said. 'And pray we don't get stopped on the way home.' His phone tinged again as he reached for the gear lever.

'I'd better have a glance at that before we set off,' he said, and pulled the phone from his pocket. 'Well, well. The first was from the Almighty. He's reinstating Margaret and says there's a longer explanation in my emails. The second was Margaret. She wants to see me in the morning.'

17

Reflections

By the time Chris came downstairs, still tired from their late night, Greg was up and about, as evidenced by the half-full cafetière on the kitchen table and the plate littered with toast crumbs on top of the dishwasher. Pouring herself a coffee she went looking, eventually spotting him on the riverbank. He was standing near a bed of reeds, mug in hand, watching the water swirl around their stems.

'Penny for them,' she said, disturbing his reflections.

'Not sure they're worth a penny,' he replied. 'I was just thinking about policing in a pandemic. You know,' he said, turning towards her, 'I'd been comforting myself with the thought that even if we were short-handed from sickness and hampered by new procedures, it would be compensated by the sort of drop in crime that we get when the weather is bad. But that's probably wishful thinking. The angry men won't stop being angry. The violent won't suddenly become meek and kind. It's just that instead of it happening on the streets, it'll happen in homes, where we can't see it and can't stop it.'

'That's a depressing thought,' said Chris. 'But probably correct.'

'Which makes your new job all the more important.'

'If I get it,' she said again.

'How are Bobby and Tally getting on this morning?' asked Greg, changing the subject with a clash of mental gears.

'In the middle of an inter-species Mexican stand-off,' replied Chris. 'Staring at each other across the conservatory.'

'That's okay then. Come on, we'd better get off. Margaret will be expecting me.'

They turned back towards the cottage, leaving the wind to rustle in the reeds behind them. 'You haven't told me what the explanation was, you know, about Margaret,' said Chris. 'Are you allowed to share it?'

'I think most of it will be common knowledge soon, if not already,' replied Greg. 'The Almighty has pronounced himself satisfied of Margaret's innocence, and by agreement with the IOPC – who have no spare investigators anyway, courtesy of Covid infections and quarantines – has called off the independent investigation. His view is that, with the balance of probability being that the culprit is a member of the civilian staff, we can complete the investigation in-house. That's not to say he won't call the IOPC in again if we fail,' he added.

'No pressure then,' commented Chris.

***

Entering Margaret's office, and seeing her familiar figure behind her desk, Greg felt as though she'd never been away. With personal photos and curios replaced, her big coffee pot in evidence and with her familiar, slightly wind-blown look also unchanged, she was clearly deep in the task of picking up the reins.

'Greg. Good. I need a quick briefing on what you've got on hand. Bring me up to date.'

Greg sat down. He had anticipated the request and he'd already thought how to present his summary.

'On the leak enquiry,' he started, 'we have two leads we're following up: some odd bank transfers into the account of Kath Irwin from an account linked to Standish and thereby to Gabrys, and some background files obtained via Nathan Standish.

'Regarding your son, Anthony, as you know he's in the clear, but we suspect he was targeted because of who he is. We're checking out the shop acting as a poste restante and a couple of other leads.

'That's about it at present, apart from the final stages of the Norwich Express case.'

'What about the Yarmouth stabbing?' asked Margaret.

'What stabbing?' questioned Greg. 'I haven't had one referred to me.'

'Oh, for Lord's sake,' Margaret stopped herself. 'I was afraid of that when I heard who was covering for me,' she said. 'He's notorious for his belief that uniform should handle more and CID less. In that case, I've got bad news for you, Greg. There was a case of a stabbing outside the Town Hall in Great Yarmouth nearly a week ago, witnessed by several staff from the Town Hall. It was in the local papers. I'm surprised you didn't see it. To the best of my knowledge, which isn't as good as it should be because of a lack of detail in my paperwork, the perpetrator is still on the loose. Here's the file I do have.' She proffered a thin bundle of papers. 'I need you to take this on as well.'

'Okay,' said Greg. 'Resources?'

'What you have. And just keep your fingers crossed none of them go down with Covid, or we're stuffed.'

Greg was pleased to run into Jim, stuffing his face with a chunky bacon butty, on the way back to his office.

'Where'd you get that?' he demanded. 'I thought the canteen was closed.'

'It is,' said Jim, clearing his mouth briefly. 'But an enterprising cafe owner has started a van run providing refreshments, and it calls here twice a day. The bacon rolls are brill.'

'So I see,' said Greg. 'Well it's good you're fuelled up, because I have a new job for you. A stabbing in Yarmouth.'

'The one that was in the *Mercury*?' asked Jim. 'I wondered why it hadn't come our way.'

'I didn't see it in the paper, but yes, that's the one. It's ours now. Apparently, it was left with uniform, but the perp is still at large and now it's our problem. Can I leave that with you and Bill? Chris, Jill and I will follow up on the Standish stuff.' Greg held out the file.

'Okay. I'll report later. Pity we didn't get it while it was fresh.'

'No comment,' said Greg.

Chris was waiting in his office when he got back. 'Jill wants a word, and I've got an interview.'

'You have. When?'

'Tomorrow, with apologies for the short notice, but they're keen to get on while they have the senior staff available to form a panel.'

'How many are they interviewing?'

'I don't know for sure, but rumour has it it's three. Me and two from Suffolk.'

'Congratulations, Chris.' Greg looked round swiftly to make sure the door was closed, then dropped a quick kiss on her hair. 'I'm very pleased for you. Make sure you get home early today, to prepare.'

'I'll try,' she said. 'Don't forget to talk to Jill.'

Greg followed her out of the door, and walked briskly down the corridor to find Jill, feeling suddenly cheerful. He'd miss working with Chris, but it was truly great that she should get her chance.

Jill was, as usual, at her desk with her attention on multiple screens. She took a second to refocus her eyes when she realised Greg was speaking to her.

'Sorry, didn't hear what you asked,' she said, rubbing her face with her hands.

'How long have you been looking at those videos?' asked Greg. 'You should take a break regularly, you know.'

'I know,' she said. 'But I get fascinated and then I lose track of time.'

'You wanted to speak to me,' Greg reminded her.

'Yes. A couple of things. On the bank accounts, the Santander account, as we know, has been accessed quite recently, so definitely by someone other than either Standish or Gabrys. The payments were set up through a banking app and all the passwords etc were used correctly, but the IP address was different from that used before Standish was arrested. The current IP address is in Great Yarmouth, but obviously I can't find out any more detail unless we get the internet service provider to hand over the precise geographical location. That's why I wanted a word. Are you happy to go for that?'

Greg thought quickly. 'Nothing more precise than Great Yarmouth?' he asked.

'No. Could be anywhere in that general area.'

'Okay. Do the paperwork and I'll sign it off. What was the other thing you wanted to tell me?'

'I've been checking ANPR in the vicinity of the newsagent's that Tony Tayler mentioned to us. The nearest camera is on the A1243 running down to Haven Bridge. Of the car number plates I fed into the system, the camera has captured quite a few belonging to people here, as you'd expect, including mine and yours. But only one of the numbers belonging to Margaret's secretaries. And it wasn't Kath Irwin's.'

'Whose was it?'

'Ella Pentney's.'

'Well, well. But it could be completely unrelated,' said Greg. 'Mustn't get too excited yet.'

'Quite. But what I'd like to do, right now before the evidence disappears, is get over to that shop and see if they, or any of their neighbours, have CCTV. If we can identify anyone actually visiting the shop, we'll be getting somewhere.'

'But will the shop even be open? Most are closed at the moment, remember.'

'Damn. Hadn't thought of that. I keep forgetting everything has changed. I suppose if it sells food, it might be worth us taking a look?'

'Okay. Let's do it. Come on.'

With Greg and Jill on their way to Yarmouth, Jim and Bill were already there and sitting in the police station with two uniformed constables and their sergeant a safe distance apart.

'Sorry if this puts you out,' Jim said easily, but the decision was taken above my pay grade. So, where've you got to, and who are we looking for?'

The two constables looked at their boss, who stepped in to the breach.

'We're pleased, to be honest,' he said. 'We've got enough on at the moment with all the new stuff coming through about isolating and lockdowns. But you asked who we're looking for. That's the problem, we don't know. The witnesses all report seeing two, not very tall, assailants wearing loose hoodies and jeans. They were talking to a youngish man, then stepped forwards and both stabbed him, each in turn. The unlucky victim is still in hospital and hasn't regained consciousness yet, so we have no evidence from him. One knife was recovered. It was a kitchen knife and there was no DNA on it that matches anything we've got on our database. The two in hoodies ran down a side alley towards the town centre and disappeared off camera. None of the witnesses followed them, being occupied in rushing to the help of the victim. We have a bit of video from the Town Hall CCTV, but it doesn't show us any more than the witnesses have described.'

'Were the assailants kids too?' asked Jim.

'Could have been,' said the constable with a brush cut and beard.

The other, clean-shaven but with hair as long as is permitted, chipped in. 'I think they were. And I think they took their hoodies off when they got out of range of a camera and mingled with the crowds. They'd be impossible to identify after that.'

Reflecting that his two colleagues looked like reversed images of each other, Bill asked them if they found any discarded hoodies?

'No,' they admitted. 'Not yet anyway.'

Not very likely now, thought Bill, and made a note.

Back in the car outside, Jim and Bill looked at each other.

'Wish we'd been brought in sooner,' said Jim.

'My thoughts exactly,' agreed Bill. 'I wonder if they asked any questions at the Sally Army place? It's only just round the corner, and if anyone picked up discarded clothing, it might be one of their clients.'

'True. But if they went round in uniform, everyone would clam up, as you know.'

'We could try?' said Bill. 'Even now, there could be blood spatter, even if it's been washed.'

'Let's try,' said Jim. He looked Bill up and down, then himself. 'Don't take this the wrong way, but I think you'll fit in better.' Bill grinned.

'It's a good job I've known you for a while,' he said, 'otherwise I'd think you just told me I looked like a tramp!' He got out of the car, hitched up his jeans under his old Barbour jacket, and went off round the corner. Jim smiled too and wriggled down in the driving seat to check the messages on his phone.

18

On Cobholm Island

The newsagent's was tucked away in the network of streets that criss-cross the drier end of the old island of Cobholm. On a map, the yellow network of roads to the east is mirrored by the blue pattern of dykes on the marsh land to the west. Everywhere is close to water, and the sounds of seagulls filled the wide Norfolk skies as Greg pulled up across the road from the shop. They watched for a few minutes. It didn't seem very busy, not at that time of the day, but at least it was open. As they waited, an elderly gentleman left the shop, closing the door behind him, and striding off with a newspaper and a loaf under his arm.

'Now's as good a time as any,' said Greg. 'Come on.'

A bell tinged sharply as they went through the door, and a sharp-featured old lady looked up from where she was leaning on the counter.

'Good afternoon,' said Greg. She watched them in silence for a moment as they looked round the shop, noting the presence of a CCTV camera by the door, and another on the wall behind the counter.

As they approached the counter the old lady asked, 'What can I do for you?'

Greg produced his warrant card. I'm Detective Chief Inspector Geldard and this is Detective Constable Hayes. We're investigating a crime, and we have reason to believe someone of interest to us has been using your shop to collect post. We'd like to see your records, and your CCTV footage, please?'

'Have you a warrant?' the old lady asked, then laughed. 'Don't worry,' she said. 'I've nothing to hide. You can see my records and the CCTV, but I warn you, I've no idea how far back it goes. My grandson deals with all that.'

She pushed a large accounts book across the counter towards them. 'I'm old school,' she said. 'I keep it all in there. The CCTV,' – she nodded to the camera behind her – 'like I said, my grandson set that up. I haven't had it all that long. If you don't know how to work the thing, you'll need him. I haven't a clue.'

'May I?' said Jill, and came behind the counter to examine the camera. 'It feeds to a tablet or a phone,' she said. 'Is it on your phone?'

'This?' asked the lady. 'By the way, I'm Maud Weeks. Pleased to meet you. I think.' She proffered an old iPhone to Jill.

'What's the password?' enquired Jill.

'Maud12,' replied the lady. 'Maud without an 'e'. Dan said I'd never remember anything more complicated, and he's right.'

Jill input the password, guessing correctly that Maud used a capital letter, and found the security app. She scrolled through a few images.

'We could do with copies of this, Boss. I can download images from both cameras via this phone, if Mrs Weeks is willing.'

'Help yourself,' said the lady. 'Is it going to take long, because if so, I could make us all a cup of tea.'

'Not long,' said Jill. 'I'll just fetch my iPad from the car.'

Greg chatted to Mrs Weeks while Jill performed her alchemy with the phone and her iPad. 'Do you have many customers wanting you to take their post in?' he asked.

'Not so many for post. These days it's mostly Amazon parcels for people who aren't around during the day. Or at least it was, before they all started working from home. That's partly why I got the camera, in case there was any dispute over deliveries.'

Greg was looking through the accounts book. 'Do you remember this one?' he asked, pushing the book over so she could see where he was pointing.

'Oh yes, she's a regular, or used to be,' she said. 'For post and parcels. Elisabeth Pentney. Like the lakes.'

Greg looked at Jill, who nodded. 'I think she's on the CCTV too,' she said.

'Mrs Weeks,' said Greg, 'I'm afraid we're going to have to take this book away with us. I'll give you a receipt for it, and it should be possible to let you have it back in due course.'

'But what am I going to use now?' she demanded.

'You could start a new book,' suggested Jill, indicating some ring-bound notebooks on a shelf. Grumbling, Mrs Weeks took one down and flipped its pages.

'I suppose,' she said grudgingly. 'But I'll want my big book back. Asap.'

Greg handed over a receipt and put the book under his arm. 'Of course,' he said. 'But that may not be very soon.'

Declining a repeated offer of tea from the hospitable shopkeeper, they returned to the car.

'That was easy,' remarked Greg in surprise. 'You'd think Ella Pentney would have taken more care. Been more secretive.'

'Did the dates match the times Tony Tayler sent money to his blackmailer?' asked Jill.

'At least one of them did. We can go through in detail, back at the office.'

Only a couple of miles away on the other side of the Yare, Bill was getting on like a house on fire with an ex-fisherman named Ernie, and a retired docker named Nick. Sitting in relative, though chilly, comfort on a bench outside the Salvation Army HQ, they'd been chatting for some time. Although difficult to distract from long-practised, and longwinded, tales of the Yarmouth riverbank, he eventually managed to establish that a mate of theirs, rejoicing in the name of Miggsy, had been the lucky finder of a couple of hoodies.

'Bu' ee knew they were on the huh,' said Nick. 'Blud on 'em, there were.'

'Where are they now?' asked Bill.

'Miggsy's probly wearin' one on 'em,' said Nick. 'T'other might be in ere.' He nodded over his shoulder. 'In store like.'

'And where would I find Miggsy?'

'In t'market most like. After chips.'

'Thank you,' said Bill. 'Have a drink on me.' He dropped some cash on the table before them.

Indoors, a middle-aged man with a bald head and a paunch was sorting through a pile of second-hand trainers. He looked up as Bill approached.

'Wish to goodness people would tie the laces together,' he grumbled. 'It's a devil of a job finding pairs when they don't. Do you reckon these match?' He held up a grubby pair of once white trainers with yellow soles.

'Look like it to me,' said Bill, and explained what he was looking for.

'Your best chance is Miggsy then,' said the trainer sorter. 'The other is probably already out there on someone's back, and I wouldn't know whose.'

The marketplace was busy with the sounds of people selling everything from bananas to pyjamas. The several chip stalls were doing a roaring trade, and at least seven massive herring gulls were lurking on rooftops and bench backs, ready to snatch at a moment's notice.

Jim's enquiries at the first chip vendor elicited the information that Miggsy had already collected some fries and would probably be found near the Feathers, hoping for a drink to wash them down. He waved Bill over, and the two of them turned down the back street towards the Feathers. Sure enough, a man in a hoodie was leaning on one of the outside tables, eating chips. Jim nodded to Bill and went further down the street. Bill went up to Miggsy, who took one look at a man he clearly identified as a copper, notwithstanding the worn leather jacket, spun round and headed off, straight into Jim.

Jim took him by the arm. 'Calm down, Miggsy,' he said. 'You're not in any trouble. We just want to ask you about your hoodie.'

Miggsy wasn't reassured and embarked on a long string of explanations and excuses.

'It's okay,' said Bill. 'I've just been talking to a couple of your mates, Bill and Nick. We just want to ask a couple of questions.'

The three of them went to sit on a market bench; an unusual trio, eyed with curiosity by passers-by.

'Is this the hoodie you found near the Town Hall a week or two ago?' asked Jim.

'Not the Town Hall,' said Miggsy. 'Nearer the market.'

'But it's one of two you found in the street?' asked Jim, noting without comment the educated voice in evidence now its owner had calmed down.

'Two what?' asked Miggsy, confused.

'It's one of the two hoodies you found?'

'Yes,' said Miggsy, enlightened.

'How would you feel about coming to the station with us and swopping it for a nice thick fleece?' asked Bill.

'Can I have the fleece as well?' asked Miggsy.

'Not as well,' said Bill. 'But we might throw in the price of a couple of pints. After we swop the hoodie for the fleece.'

At the police station a couple of streets away, Miggsy reluctantly agreed to come in, and waited with Bill in a hurriedly borrowed interview room, while Jim went looking for an appropriate fleece.

'Do you mind me asking, but you don't have much of a local accent,' said Bill. 'Are you from round here?'

Miggsy looked up, then down again at his hands. 'You mean, I speak better than you expected,' he said. 'We're not all idiots you know. All sorts land up on the streets. All it takes is a bit of bad luck.'

'Yet you kept a hoodie with blood on it, rather than hand it in to the police,' remarked Bill.

'I was probably drunk at the time,' replied Miggsy. 'And, as you see, it's a dark fleece. The blood wasn't obvious. And it was warm. Don't expect an apology for keeping something warm I found in a bin.' Bill fell silent.

When Jim returned, it was with a fleece, scarf and bobble hat. Once the clothing exchange had been effected, he nodded at Bill as he put the hoodie in an evidence bag.

'Are you willing to sign a statement saying where you found it?' Jim asked. 'I got a summary of what you've told us typed up while I was out.' He proffered the single sheet to Miggsy. 'It just says...' he went on.

'I can read,' said Miggsy, and took the sheet of paper. He read it in silence, then put it down on the desk and held out his hand for a pen. 'Where do I sign?' he asked.

The formalities completed, Bill put his hand in his pocket for his wallet. 'I promised you the price of a pint' he said.

Miggsy shook his head. 'Don't give me cash,' he said. 'I'll only bet it. If you want to do me a favour, buy me a sandwich or a pie.'

Jim nodded to Bill. 'See you back at the car,' he said, as Bill and Miggsy headed off in the direction of the marketplace again.

Bill was silent when he got back into the car. 'Cost us the price of a couple of pasties, a sausage roll and two ham butties from Greggs,' he said at last. 'That was an educated man, you know.'

'So I guessed,' replied Jim, starting the car. 'Drink or gambling?'

'First one and then both,' replied Bill. 'Makes you think!'

'Let's get this hoodie to Forensics, and take it from there,' replied Jim.

19

19 March 2020

The morning of Chris's interview dawned bright and still. When Greg saw her come down the stairs, he was impressed.

'Perfect,' he said.

Chris did a twirl in front of the mirror at the bottom of the stairs. 'I'm pretty pleased with it myself,' she said. 'I couldn't go all boring, that wouldn't have been me. But equally, I didn't want to scare them off. I thought this was a good compromise.' She twisted to scan her back view in the mirror. A perfectly fitting navy trouser suit with scarlet shirt and matching handbag met her self-congratulatory gaze.

'Perfect, as I said. Got everything?'

'Yes, thanks.'

'Good luck then. And don't forget, they'll be really lucky to have you.'

'Thanks.' She kissed him then checked her lipstick in the mirror. 'I'll be off then. Bye.' And she was gone.

Greg checked Tally had food in her bowl, double-checked the fruit bowl was put away in the larder after her depredations of the day before – when she'd sampled two bananas and an apple – petted Bobby and locked up before setting off for his meeting with Jill and the CCTV footage from Cobholm.

As luck would have it, the first person he walked into, on arrival in Wymondham, was Ned, his chief crime-scene manager.

'Got some results on the stabbing hoodie,' was Ned's opening gambit. 'There's definitely DNA from the victim, so it's the right hoodie. There's another set of DNA too, but we don't have a match for it yet. We're still trying for a familial match, but...' And he shrugged. 'I'll keep you posted,' he said, and dashed off.

'I've heard,' was Jim's comment. 'So far, it's the only lead we have. According to the surgeon at the James Paget, there were two knives involved. One was probably a serrated-edged kitchen knife and it's disappeared. The other was what appears to have been a commando knife, or a lookalike version, and we haven't found that either, despite an intensive search. The only other news is that it's looking bleak for the victim. He hasn't come round from his coma. Given the blood loss, the hospital thinks there's irretrievable brain damage and he's not likely to survive, in which case this will become a murder investigation. Get anywhere with the newsagent's at Cobholm?'

'Enough to suggest that we've been looking at the wrong secretary; probably thanks to a nice piece of misdirection. I'm just waiting on Jill's review of the CCTV, and then we'll be re-interviewing a certain Ms Pentney.'

'Ella?' Jim stopped himself and looked round to make sure he hadn't been overheard. 'Well, well. That's very interesting. She certainly has a bit of a reputation as a wild one. Somehow, that sits better with me than the suggestion it was Kath Irwin. That always looked unlikely.'

Jill was raring to go by the time Greg got to her desk. She tapped her notebook. 'I've got chapter and verse in here,' she said. 'The main thing is, you can be confident the CCTV sightings of EP that we have match with both the dates in Maud Weeks's record book and the dates of withdrawals from Tony Tayler's savings account. I've set up a program to review the videos using facial recognition software, but that can run on its own, so I'm ready to re-interview Ms Pentney, if you are.'

Greg grinned, recognising her enthusiasm from his earlier days on the verge of an important promotion opportunity.

'Let's go,' he said.

'I'll go and escort her down, shall I?' asked Jill.

'Yes, please. And we'll do this one under caution.' Sparing a moment to wonder how Chris was getting on in Lowestoft, Greg picked up his notes and headed for an interview room.

Somewhat to Jill's relief, Margaret was not in evidence when she reached the upper floor. Ella Pentney was, however, exactly where the rota said she should be: on duty in Margaret's outer office.

'Hi Ella,' said Jill. 'Can you come with me for a moment. We need a word.'

'Can it wait a bit?' asked the harassed-looking secretary. 'I'm a bit pushed at the minute.'

'Sorry, no,' replied Jill. 'DCI Geldard wants a chat with you, and he's waiting.'

'Oh dear, and we can't have that, can we?' said Ella sarcastically. 'Just a second then.'

Jill waited with increasing impatience for the secretary to stop messing about and make tracks for the door. After a lot of shuffling papers and gathering personal property, she eventually did.

'What's this all about?' asked Ella.

'Just following up on the statement you made earlier,' replied Jill. 'In here, please.'

Entering the room, Ella Pentney was still protesting loudly about the interruption to her day and how much work she had to do. She fell silent abruptly when she saw Greg's expression, and paled when he administered the caution.

Jill took a deep breath. 'Ella,' she began, 'we have clear evidence, both from a witness and from CCTV, that you were the woman who collected the payments which Anthony Tayler made to his blackmailer via the newsagent's in Cobholm.'

'No comment,' interrupted Ella. 'And I want a solicitor.'

'Of course,' replied Greg. 'Do you want one of your own, or a duty solicitor?'

She hesitated, then said, 'A duty solicitor. I'm saying nothing until I've spoken to one of them.'

'No problem. We'll have one with you shortly,' answered Greg.

Outside the interview room he said to Jill, 'Don't worry. I anticipated this and I've got one on standby. We'll reconvene in an hour.' He strode off down the corridor, whistling. Jill went back to her desk, feeling more than a little frustrated.

She sat down at her desktop, checked messages, looked at her watch, sighed and decided to see if the facial recognition program had turned up anything interesting. What she saw catapulted her out of her chair and along the corridor to Greg's office. She burst in so precipitately she caught him leaning back in his chair having a rather personal scratch. His hands shot to his desktop as his chair fell forwards, and he hoped she hadn't noticed.

'Boss,' she said. 'I've got something. You know I ran the CCTV images through my new program?'

'Yes,' he said, slightly pink in the face and picking up his coffee mug to hide it. 'What've you found?'

'This.' She slapped a fuzzy photo on his desk. 'Do you recognise her? You've met her.'

Greg studied the photo. 'It's not terribly clear, but she does look familiar. Hang on, is it? It's not Helen Gabrys?'

'It is.'

'Well, blow me down with a toffee trombone! Of all that crime-riddled family, I thought she was clean. The father was a megalomaniac and totally ruthless with it. I've never been more relieved to put a man behind bars. And the brother Mica – he was another nutter. But I thought she was the sane one.'

'Could be a coincidence,' said Jill. 'But worth investigating?'

'Absolutely.' Greg was thinking quickly. 'Get Steve to give you a hand. We need to know whether she's visited her father in prison and when, whether she's still living at Horses Mill House, and, if not, then where, her employment, if any, her car registration and recent movements, friends, colleagues and contacts, you know the routine.'

'On it, Boss,' replied Jill and went to the door. 'And Ella Pentney?'

'We'll see her as soon as you've got Steve started.'

This time it was Jim who delayed the start of the interview. 'I've got something you should know before you speak to Ella Pentney,' he said. They were in the corridor just outside the interview room. Jim looked left and right to make sure there was no one else in the vicinity.

'You know we got some old Standish and Partner files from Nathan Standish...'

'Sorry,' interrupted Jill. 'I never got chance to finish going through them.'

It's okay,' said Jim. 'When Greg poached you for the visit to Cobholm, I put Bill on to them. He turned up something just now. Ella Pentney used to work part-time for Standish and Partners, in the finance team. It looks likely she had online access to the bank account that paid money into Kath Irwin's account. And she wasn't the only one. Someone else has been using the account but we haven't yet managed to trace where the money went.'

This time, with the duty solicitor present, Ella started off cocky and recalcitrant. It didn't last long, as Jill laid out the evidence.

'So,' she said, 'if I can summarise, you were in the office on the day Chief Superintendent Tayler got the heads-up about the movements from the safe house in Bacton. You are on CCTV and have been identified as the woman who collected the money that Anthony Tayler was paying to his blackmailer. You worked for Standish and Partners at the same time as working here, and had access to the bank account that recently paid money into Kath Irwin's account. If we show your photo to Anthony Tayler,' she said with sudden inspiration, 'is he also going to identify you as the woman who tried to sell him drugs at a rave in Great Yarmouth in 2018?'

It was a lucky stroke. Ella, who'd had her mouth open to say *No comment* again, closed it on a gulp. Jill looked at Greg, who nodded, and took over.

'Ella,' he said. 'You're in big trouble. You're looking at years in gaol for aiding and abetting all sorts of serious crimes, let alone charges relating to supply of drugs, blackmail and the unauthorised disclosure of information. Your only chance now is to cooperate.'

'Like that worked well for Shinfield,' she said bitterly.

'He's well and living his new life, unlike the police officer who was shot – mainly because of you,' pointed out Greg.

Ella fell silent again, and Jill took the opportunity to place a photo on the table between them. It was of Helen Gabrys, taken at her graduation in York. Then she placed a second photo on top of it, this one from the CCTV footage filmed at the Cobholm newsagent's.

'Do you know this woman?' she asked.

Ella looked at the photos and was about to shake her head, when Jill placed a third photo on the pile.

'But, of course, we know you do,' she said, 'because this is a photo of you in the shop at the same time. Look at the time signatures on the screen shots.'

Ella didn't bother to look but burst into noisy tears. 'Okay, I'll tell you what I know,' they managed to make out.

Outside in the corridor again, Greg and Jill high-fived just as Jim came galloping round the corner.

'Just heard that Nathan Standish has been targeted for a knife attack outside his school,' he gasped. 'Can't be a coincidence. I'm off to the James Paget.'

'I'll come with you, Jim,' said Greg. 'Jill, tell Pentney we're keeping her in custody tonight. We've got until tomorrow to charge her.' And he chased off after Jim.

20

Evening of 19 March – at the James Paget Hospital

The two detectives found, on arrival, that the hospital was at one and the same time, madly busy and oddly quiet. Patients there were in plenty, and a lot of staff and volunteers doing their level best to keep possible Covid victims and other patients apart. But once inside, the lack of any friends and relatives accompanying arrivals made for a strange atmosphere.

It took some argument and waving of warrant cards, but eventually they succeeded in reaching Nathan Standish's bedside. He was pale and plentifully wrapped in bandages, but conscious. A doctor intercepted their progress.

'He's going to be okay, but he'll probably need an operation to tidy up the damage done to his abdomen,' she warned. 'And although he seems calm, we're keeping a careful watch on him for shock. So please, while I understand why you're keen to talk to him, keep it short. His mother's with him. We make an exception for children,' she added as Greg looked surprised.

'Will do,' said Greg, and they approached the bed with caution.

Mrs Standish was sitting by the bed, clutching his hand. Greg found it reassuring that the lad was quick to remove his hand from his mother's grasp when he saw the two men approaching.

'I thought you'd be along,' he whispered, shifting in the bed and wincing.

'Can't this wait?' asked his mother.

'No, it can't,' said all three males present, the two older ones adding, 'sorry.'

'I'll wait outside, but only for five minutes,' she said threateningly.

Nathan got straight to the point. 'I recognised one of them,' he said. 'He was from our school. The form above mine. The thick end,' he added, apparently feeling that he had some excuse for a less than politically correct expression. 'I think the other could have been from school too, but his balaclava was better at hiding his face.'

'Do you have a name?' asked Jim.

'No. But if you tell the Head, Miss Wilkes, it was the boy she caught scratching a rude word onto her car last term, she'll know who it is.'

'Did they say anything?' asked Greg. 'Were you threatened, for example?'

'No. They just cornered me after school in the alley nearby. I don't think they expected anyone else to be around, but there'd been a chess tournament and a whole bunch of players came out just after me. I guess that's why they ran.'

'Did they drop the knife?'

'Knives,' said Nathan with a grimace. 'I think they dropped one. A kitchen knife, I think. But there were definitely two. The other was humongous! An army knife maybe. Not a pretty sight, believe me.'

Jim started to say something, and then shut up again.

'Any idea why you were picked on?'

'None. Unless it's because of the files I gave you. It didn't feel random,' he added. 'They were waiting for me, I'm sure. They let a boy ahead of me go by safely and chose to gang up on me. I didn't do anything to provoke an attack, honest. I'm not stupid. One of them looked at his phone I'm sure, just before they stepped up to me. I remember because I thought, at the time, he was about to send a text. But now, I wonder if he was checking a picture of me.'

'Is there anything else we need to know before we leave you in peace?' asked Greg.

'I don't think so. Tell Mum she can go home, will you?'

'I doubt she'll want to go just yet,' said Greg. 'But we'll pass the message on.'

Back in the car park, Jim removed the surgical mask he was wearing, and leaned on his car.

'Something a bit odd,' he said. 'The description of the two knives sounds very like the types the pathologist says were used in the attack by the Town Hall.'

'You never got to speak to the victim in that case, did you?'

'No. He died here in the JP without regaining consciousness. But the suspicion was that he was a new drug dealer on the block and the incumbents weren't amused at the competition. We have some DNA from that attack, so we can run a check, if Nathan's evidence gives us a name.'

A couple of phone calls to HQ established both a phone number and an address for the East Norfolk Academy's headteacher. A further phone call caught her on the way to bed, judging by her initial reaction. She became instantly cooperative when Greg explained the reason for the call.

'Oh my God, is Nathan going to be all right?' was her first exclamation. Her second was horror that fellow pupils might have been involved. 'I know the boy he means,' she said. 'Tyson Strange. Always a very difficult child. Anger issues, you know, and very poor impulse control. But, as you might guess from the choice of name, his family exemplars were not, shall I say, pacifist. I don't know his address, but it will be in the school records. If you give me a minute, I can log on remotely and look it up for you.'

'That would be really helpful,' said Greg.

'I need to put the phone down. Bear with me.'

There were sounds of keys being tapped and some heavy sighing, then the single word: 'Eureka!' Now back on the phone, 'Got it,' she said. 'Are you ready? ... 49, Hampshire Street, Great Yarmouth.'

'Thank you,' said Greg.

'Not a problem,' came the reply. 'Log it as one of the unintended benefits of Covid. I wouldn't normally be able to access the school database from home. I can't help hoping Nathan was mistaken,' she added. 'Tyson is not the brightest spark in the box, but he never really had a chance.'

Greg rang off, with further thanks, and looked at Jim, purveyor of local knowledge.

'I know where that is,' he responded. 'It's not far from the seafront. Uniform tends to spend a lot of time around there. If it's not antisocial behaviour, it's shoplifting.'

'We'll go straight there,' decided Greg. 'But warn uniform. We may need back-up.' Jim got into his car and reached for his radio while Greg turned his BMW, and the two of them headed back into Great Yarmouth.

By the time they turned into Hampshire Street, a marked car with two occupants was already parked at the corner. Greg pulled up alongside and wound his window down.

'Evening, sir,' said a sergeant he recognised.

'Haven't we met,' asked Greg.

'Yes, sir. The Clean Boats Inc operation last year.'

'Knew I recognised you,' said Greg. 'But sorry, I don't recall your name.'

'Sergeant Briscoe, sir,' said the sturdy sergeant with grizzled hair and beard.

'You know why we're here?'

'Yes, sir, the stabbing earlier today. To apprehend a suspect. And if you'll forgive me, sirs, for mentioning it, but you two should be wearing stab vests.'

'Quite right,' said Greg. 'We'll put them on before we go in. What I'd like you to do is to deploy at the back of this address, in case our lad legs it out the back door. Thank you.'

With some difficulty they found spaces for both their cars then, appropriately kitted out, Greg and Jim rang the doorbell at No 49. It was a two-up two-down mid-terrace house with a front door opening straight off the street and, as they noted a few moments later, directly into the living room.

'Mrs Strange?' Greg asked the woman who answered the door in pyjamas and dressing gown.

'Yes? And?' she said. 'It's a bit late to be knocking folk up!'

'We'd like a word with your son Tyson,' said Greg, noting at least two faces peering over the stairs that led out of the sitting room to the floor above.

One of the faces disappeared abruptly as his mother shouted, 'Tyson, what you been up to this time?'

'May I?' said Greg as he pushed past Mrs Strange and headed for the stairs, Jim just behind him.

'Oy, I 'aven't said you could come in. Don't wake Doug, for God's sake. He's on earlies and 'e gets right crabby if 'e don't get 'is sleep.'

Reflecting that if he'd managed to sleep through her shout, he was unlikely to be wakened by anything short of a bomb going off, Greg brushed past a younger boy on the stairs, assuming he was too young to be Tyson. He got to the top just in time to see what he guessed was his quarry heading into the bathroom, and hammered on the door as it slammed in his face. Jim, guessing the next move, went through the living room to the back of the house, and saw a shape fall past the kitchen window, pick itself up and head for the back gate. It was with relief Jim saw the fleeing figure neatly trapped by Sergeant Briscoe waiting in the alley.

On the landing, Greg turned to find himself facing a tousled, and unpleasantly aromatic, angry man recently roused from sleep.

'Police,' he said briefly, holding up his warrant card, and headed back down the uncarpeted stairs. The man behind him rubbed his face and head, yawned and, to Greg's amazement, turned to go back to bed. He could only conclude that evening police raids were nothing new in this household.

Jim was in the garden, watching with approval as Sergeant Briscoe handcuffed the now unresisting shape on the ground. Once Tyson was picked up and dusted down, the sergeant bent down to something lying in the shadows, and picked up a long shape in his gloved hand.

'You'll be wanting this, I think,' he said. 'Looks like an army survival knife. Might be what you're looking for.'

Jim took it from him with care, and placed it in an evidence bag. 'Excellent. Find anything else on him?'

'Just this.' Sergeant Briscoe held out a piece of paper. Taking it from him, Jim illuminated it with his phone: *WHAT HAPPENS TO A GRASS.*

'Well, well,' he said. 'Tyson Strange, you're under arrest for the attempted murder of Nathan Standish. You do not have to say anything, but it may harm your defence if you do not mention when questioned something which you later rely on in court. Anything you do say may be given in evidence. Do you understand?'

'Yer wha?' said Tyson, shaking his head.

'Better bring his mother in too,' said Greg. 'He's probably under eighteen. Sergeant, I'd like a thorough search conducted of this house and garden.' He turned to find Mrs Strange just behind him.

'Mrs Strange, we have just arrested your son for attempted murder and we're now going to search this house, because we have reason to believe he may have concealed evidence material to the case. In these circumstances we don't need a warrant for the search.

'Jim, get Ned's team here asap. Sergeant Briscoe, can you and your chap keep an eye on things until the forensic services arrive. And thank you for your help this evening.

'Jim, when you're ready we'll take this lad to Wymondham.'

Organising the transport of their arrestee took longer than Greg would have liked. It was after midnight before he and Jim could go home for a few hours' sleep before starting their interviews in the morning.

When he did get home, Chris was already in bed.

'How'd your interview go?' he asked when he realised she was awake.

'Good, I think. I'll tell you all about it in the morning,' she replied. 'You're asleep on your feet!'

21

Friday 20 March 2020

At least two Norfolk homes were in a kerfuffle that morning. In Thorpe St Andrew, Jill was rushing round in preparation for a long day's interviewing, with both Ella Pentney and Tyson Strange lined up in the cells. Her long-term partner, Diana, was simultaneously dashing about in preparation for her last day of in-school teaching for the foreseeable future. There were frequent collisions in the narrow spaces of their small cottage, accompanied by 'sorry' and 'damn', depending on whether or not the impact resulted in someone dropping something. In the end, Jill sat down on their battered but comfortable sofa with a sigh.

'Look, I'll just sit here until you've left,' she said. 'It'll be quicker in the long run.'

'Sorry,' said Diana again. 'There's just so much to think about if I'm not going to see any of these children in person for weeks or even months. And how the devil I'm going to run lessons from here with our dicky wi-fi, goodness knows? Now, where did I put my list of lesson materials that I need to bring home with me?'

'Is this it?' asked Jill, holding up a sheet of A4 with what looked like a list of addresses on one side, and a list beginning 'map of the world' on the other.

'That's it.' Diana seized it with relief, and headed for the door, came back to kiss Jill, then headed for the door again. 'Okay, I'm out of your hair. See you for supper?'

'I don't know when I'll be back,' said Jill, getting up from the sofa now it seemed safe to do so. 'I'll let you know. It might be a long day.'

'Okay. Byeee.' Diana was already out the door.

Jill tidied a couple of mugs and glasses into the dishwasher, hung Diana's forgotten coat on the hook near the back door, and picked up her laptop to set off for Wymondham.

Near the Bure, the chaos was largely psittacine, with a bit of feline aggression thrown in. Bobby had taken a dislike to Tally using her litter tray and had expressed her irritation with a sharp-tipped paw. Tally had retaliated with a peck to the cat's bum and a full-blown whirlwind of yowling, spitting and screeching had ensued. By the time a pyjamaed Chris had rushed to the rescue, the ball of fur and feathers had resolved into its two component parts. Bobby was sitting on the sofa engaged in licking her assaulted rear end, while Tally had retreated to her perch and was resettling her feathers.

Examining both parties, Chris could find little damage other than wounded pride, and concluded the affray had largely been for show. By the time Greg came down, fully dressed for the day, she had made coffee and there was bread in the toaster.

'What was all that about?' he asked. 'It sounded like war had broken out in a zoo.'

'A disagreement over something,' said Chris. 'Probably the litter tray since there's no food about for them to quarrel over. I said we should put two trays down in this space. I'll try to pick another up on my way home. We need cat litter too.'

'Now tell me about your job interview.'

Chris handed Greg a mug of coffee and sat down with the other. 'I think it went well,' she said. 'I'd anticipated all the questions and, at the end, when I asked them what planning had been done to deal with domestic incidents during a lockdown, they seemed interested and we had a good discussion. I don't think I blew it, so basically it'll come down to how good the other candidates are. As you know, one of them is in-house, so they may have an advantage.'

'When do you hear?' asked Greg.

'They said in a couple of days. I took that to mean Monday, which gives them the weekend to think about it and clear it with senior management.'

'Do you know when they'd want you to start, if you get it?' he asked.

'Sooner rather than later. I asked about that too, and they said they'd look to negotiate an early start with my management if I accepted the job.'

'Sounds promising,' said Greg. 'I'm going to miss working with you, but having you as a contact in Suffolk would be really great, never mind the pay rise.' He tried to keep his face straight but failed miserably.

'I always knew you were only after my money,' replied Chris.

They both left the house, each with a piece of toast in one hand and car keys in the other.

'I'd like you to pop over to the James Paget, to see if Nathan has remembered anything else from his assault,' said Greg. 'The way things are going, we may not be allowed in at all soon! I'll interview Ella Pentney first, but hopefully you'll join me in Wymondham before I get round to Tyson Strange.'

'Busy day,' said Chris, and kissed him goodbye before she got into her car. 'Will do. See you later.'

At Wymondham, Jill had put half an hour to good use, bringing herself up to date on Helen Gabrys. When Greg called her into his office, she already had a printed list of key points in her hand.

'I've brought Steve with me,' she said, somewhat unnecessarily, given that the six-footer was not exactly unobtrusive in an office environment, 'since he's done all this digging. Steve, you tell him.'

Steve cleared his throat. 'Helen Gabrys, graduated with a 2:1 in law from York last summer. Applied for a couple of jobs in Norwich but no evidence she got any and, as far as I can see, she's not in employment. It's assumed she lived with her mother at Horses Mill House after graduating, but the family sold the house in January. I haven't been able to trace a house purchase and I don't know where they're living now, but it can't be too far away because Helen has been a regular visitor to see her father in prison, and post addressed to her from the prison has been going to a newsagent's in Stalham.

'I've also found evidence of car sales. It seems that all Gabrys senior's cars and boats were sold at the same time as the house – all bar one, that is. The remaining car is a small BMW hatchback and I'm assuming it's the car Helen Gabrys is using, so I've asked for an ANPR check on that number.

'Oh, and I've spoken to her tutor in York, and he's given me some names and phone numbers of people he thought she was friendly with, but I haven't got very far with that yet.'

'Well done, Steve, in a very short space of time. She certainly seems to have a fondness for newsagents as postal addresses. Okay. The main priority now is to find out where she, and presumably her mother, are living. Stalham seems like a good place to start, but we need to narrow it down. Can I leave that with you, Steve, while we interview Pentney and Tyson? The clock's ticking on those two.'

Ella's coiffure had suffered from a night in the cells, but someone had obviously supplied a change of clothes, as she was now in jeans and jumper. Her expression was predominantly sulky as Greg ran through the preliminaries, and her solicitor jumped in swiftly with a reminder that they needed either to charge her or release her within a matter of hours.

'I'm well aware of that, thank you,' replied Greg. 'If your client is minded to cooperate with our questions, I think we can wrap this up fairly swiftly.

'To summarise where we got to yesterday, Ms Pentney, you admitted offering Anthony Tayler drugs at a rave in Great Yarmouth two years ago, drugs which had been supplied to you by Mica Gabrys. You also admitted to passing information acquired through your work here in Wymondham to various people connected with the Gabrys family, including, most recently, Helen Gabrys. You admitted to assisting Helen Gabrys to blackmail Anthony Tayler, and to using a bank account previously connected to Standish and Partners and through them the Gabrys business interests, to frame Kath Irwin for leaking information. In passing, I note that you failed to declare your employment with said Standish and Partners when you were also employed here. I rather imagine our HR team will have something to say about that.

'The one thing I don't yet understand, is why you let yourself be used in this way. Was it pure greed? Resentment for some reason? Come on, Ella, enlighten me.'

There was a long silence, then Ella looked up with anger written plain on her face. 'So easy for you lot, isn't it,' she spat. 'So comfortable on your high ground. Never anything to worry about. No money worries, no temptations, no having to deal with threats or violence.'

If memories of certain incidents in the recent past flashed though Greg's mind, he didn't let them show on his face. Jill was less impassive, remembering both Greg's rescue of a suspect from the River Bure, which nearly resulted in his drowning, and the revenge attack on his home and Chris only a few months ago by Gabrys senior himself. She opened her mouth and Greg trod on her nearest foot to silence her.

'So what was it?' he asked. 'Money or fear?'

'Both,' she said. 'You try dealing with Mica Gabrys on the rampage. Oh wait, Sarah did that for you, didn't she, when she stabbed him.'

'So with him gone, why were you still handing over information to the family?' asked Greg.

'Because they threatened to shop me to you if I didn't, and they paid handsomely when I did. Happy now?' she sneered. Looking at her, Jill found it hard to recognise the woman she'd worked alongside for several years.

Greg leaned back in his chair. 'DC Hayes here will let you have a statement to sign,' he said. 'In the meantime, Elisabeth

Pentney, I'm charging you with the unauthorised disclosure of information and aiding and abetting blackmail. Other charges may follow. You will be remanded in custody to appear before the magistrates in the morning.'

'Hang on,' said Ella. 'What about my immunity from prosecution and a new identity?'

'What about it?' asked Greg. 'You haven't been offered any such thing.' And he left Ms Pentney with mouth open as he and Jill left the room.

***

Over at the James Paget Hospital, Chris found Nathan on the general paediatric ward, and pretty disgusted about it. He had a bed in a corner and was wholly engaged with his EarPods and laptop when Chris entered the room.

'Look at it,' he said, gesturing at the cartoons on the walls with one hand, while removing his EarPods with the other. 'What am I doing in here? I'm not a child.'

'By law you are,' replied Chris, sitting down at his bedside. 'Anyone under eighteen is defined as a child in law. I think the NHS regards you as transitional. How are you, Nathan, apart from cross, that is?'

He smiled unwillingly, but Chris noted that his colour was poor and suspected he was putting a brave face on things.

'Thinking about how lucky I've been,' he said. 'Lucky to be alive, that is. It's quite scary being attacked by a nutter with a knife the size of a machete,' he added.

'That's an understatement,' agreed Chris. 'We've got the boy you identified in custody. He's being interviewed this morning, so hopefully we'll soon have the other one too.'

'Was I targeted because of the info I gave you?' he asked.

'We don't know yet, but it seems likely,' agreed Chris. 'Do you remember anything else about the attack now you've had chance to think about it some more?'

'I've been trying not to think about it,' he admitted. 'It gives me the horrors. I don't think I'll shake this off as easily as I thought.'

'We can get you some counselling,' replied Chris, then, when she saw the disbelief on his face, added, 'It does help, honestly. You ask Greg about it. He's had counselling in the past.'

'The Chief Inspector has?' asked Nathan in amazement.

'When he's got a minute, I'll ask him to pop in and talk to you about it,' Chris promised. 'Honest, it's not just for wimps, you know. Heroes need it too.'

Nathan laughed, then stopped hurriedly, clutching his stomach. 'That hurts. Don't make me laugh,' he pleaded.

Chris started to gather up her things. 'I need to go,' she said. 'Do you need anything?'

'No,' said Nathan. 'Mum's got that covered and hopefully I'll be out of here soon. They need my bed. But before you go, there is one thing.'

'You remembered something?' asked Chris, half in and half out of her chair.

'Just about the other attacker. Thinking about it, I don't think it was another pupil after all. He was wearing dark clothes, like I said, and he wasn't much bigger than the other one, the boy. But somehow, I think he was older. But I can't quite work out what's given me that impression.'

'Did you see his face at all?' asked Chris.

Nathan thought hard, his eyes closed as he tried to examine his mind's eye. Chris waited patiently.

'I saw a bit of his face,' he said. 'Not his eyes, but his chin... Got it!' he exclaimed suddenly. 'His chin was dark. He had stubble. He wasn't a child. He was a man.'

***

'So,' – Chris wound up her telephone conversation with Greg – 'we're looking for a man with a boyish figure. Oh, and I've committed you to having a chat with the lad, about counselling. I think we owe him.'

Greg sighed, looking at his heaped in-tray and mentally reviewing the long to-do list in his head. 'I suppose you're right,' he admitted. 'I'll make time when I can. Are you far off the office now, Chris?'

'About ten minutes,' she said.

'In that case I'll hold off my next chat with Tyson Strange until you get here. A new face might be helpful.'

The first interview with Tyson had not gone well. Given the boy's age, and what Greg suspected about his cognitive abilities – or lack of – Greg had asked his mother to sit in as an appropriate adult. Unfortunately, Mrs Strange had failed to grasp her role, and constantly interrupted to answer questions on behalf of her son.

'Mrs Strange,' Greg had said for the umpteenth time, 'you are here to support your son, not to answer for him. I need to hear Tyson's answers to my questions, not yours.'

'Ee's just a lad,' she answered, as she had many times before.

This time Greg interrupted before she could repeat, yet again, her now well-established speech about being a mother. 'Mrs Strange, I am advising you again, for your benefit and for the record, that while you are not expected to act simply as an observer, the reason you are here is to advise Tyson, to observe whether the interview is being conducted properly and fairly, and to facilitate communication with Tyson. If you can't do that, if you continue to obstruct me in asking him the entirely proper questions I have been putting to him, then I will have you removed and replaced with another appropriate adult.'

The maternal tirade began again, and Greg reached the end of his tether. 'Interview suspended,' he said. 'DC Hayes, please remove Mrs Strange to the waiting room. I'm going to see Chief Superintendent Tayler about replacing her with another appropriate adult.' The duty solicitor rose to object, but Greg was gone.

By the time Chris arrived, permission to replace Mrs Strange had been granted, and an appropriate adult had been sourced from Norwich.

'We're just waiting for her to arrive and introduce herself to Tyson, then we'll get going again,' explained Greg. 'Let's have a quick sarnie and a catch-up with Jill, while we have the chance.'

Sandwiches from the mobile shop in the car park were proving popular. Greg had to stand in a queue to collect a couple of tuna and cucumber baguettes for himself and Jill, plus a corned beef and tomato for Chris. They sat down in a corner of the ops room, but observing the now regulation two metres apart, and tucked in. The phone rang just as they all took their first mouthfuls.

Jill swallowed hastily, then said, 'It's Steve,' and put him on speaker phone.

'I'm in Stalham,' the echoey voice announced. 'I've just had a chat in the newsagent's that Helen Gabrys is using for her post. She's been using the place for some months, and this time I don't think it's just to cover her tracks as a blackmailer. Luckily, the proprietor is nosy. He doesn't just store the post, he reads what's written on the envelopes and, judging from his chat with me, he asks a lot of questions. One way or another, he's certain that Helen is living on a boat. He says several letters have been from TechMarine, who service boats, and some from a boatyard here in Stalham.'

'Which one?' asked Chris.

'Rivers Edge Marina,' replied Steve. 'I'm going there now.'

'Keep it low-key,' requested Greg. 'Establish whether she has a boat moored there and identify it, then get out.'

'Got it, Boss,' said Steve, and rang off.

Barely had Jill got stuck into her butty again, when there was another phone call.

'My turn this time,' said Chris, reaching for the phone. 'The appropriate adult is here, and they've shown her through to meet Tyson,' she reported. 'We can get going.'

'Okay, this time let's try it with Chris and me,' said Greg. 'Jill, you observe, as I might want you to step in. Come on, let's see if we can get some sense out of him now.'

The appropriate adult was a white-haired lady with a no-nonsense expression and a clear, low voice. She introduced herself as Ruth Baker and added, 'I've explained to Tyson why I'm here.'

'Still don't see why I need anyone,' he muttered. 'I tole you I din't need Mum, and I don't need 'er.' He tilted a thumb towards Mrs Baker.

'It's the law,' said Greg briskly. 'You're underage, so you must have an appropriate adult. Now, let's see if we can make some progress. For Mrs Baker's benefit, I'll now show you again the CCTV footage of you in the road behind the East Coast Academy school, just before 4pm yesterday. Do you agree that's you?'

Tyson looked at the footage in silence.

'Do you understand the question, Tyson?' asked Mrs Baker.

'Course I do,' he said. 'I'm not stupid.'

'You don't have to answer the questions,' his solicitor reminded him.

'I know that too,' said Tyson, clearly irritated. Then he pointed at the screen, now showing an enhanced image of the face turned towards the camera. 'But it's obvious that's me, innit?'

'What can you tell me about the attack on Nathan Standish that occurred immediately after?' asked Greg.

'No comment,' said Tyson.

'The CCTV footage places you there at the time of the attack,' said Greg. 'You've just agreed that. So, what did you see?'

Silence from Tyson, who was using the moment to attempt to dig a hole in the table in front of him with his fingernail.

'You know that Nathan Standish has identified you as the person who stabbed him with this knife.' Greg showed Tyson, his solicitor and Mrs Baker, a photo of a paratrooper's knife in an evidence bag. 'And that your fingerprints are on the knife. Is this your knife, Tyson?'

Tyson muttered something.

Chris said, 'Sorry, Tyson, I couldn't hear that. What did you say?'

'I said yes,' said Tyson. 'It's mine. I collect military stuff.'

'So, are you admitting to stabbing Nathan?'

Silence again.

'Tyson,' said Chris, with a nod from Greg, 'let's just go over it all again. You've admitted being there at the time Nathan was stabbed, and we have you on CCTV confirming the time and date. Nathan has given evidence that you stabbed him. You've agreed he was stabbed with your knife, and we have your fingerprints on it. And then, there's this!' She produced from the file in front of them, a further evidence bag, this one containing just a piece of paper. On it were printed in bold capitals, the words '*WHAT HAPPENS TO A GRASS*'. 'This was found in the pocket of your fleece when you were taken into custody,' she added. 'Were you supposed to leave this on Nathan's body? As a warning?'

There was a pause. Mrs Baker looked at the solicitor then, as he remained silent, she cleared her throat.

'I wonder if you might rephrase that question?' she suggested.

Chris looked down, then looked up again at Tyson. 'Fair enough,' she said. 'Tyson, where did you get this piece of paper?'

'From Miss Gabrys,' he said.

'What did she tell you to do with it?'

'Leave it with Nathan. After...' Tyson hesitated.

'After what?' asked Chris.

'After I did what she asked,' said Tyson.

'What did she ask you to do?' asked Chris patiently.

'To cut Nathan. Then leave the paper with him. I forgot,' he added. 'I'll be in trouble now.'

'Can you describe Miss Gabrys?' asked Chris, then at a glance from Mrs Baker amended her question to 'What does Miss Gabrys look like?'

Tyson looked confused. 'She has fair hair,' he offered. 'And she's not fat.'

Greg shuffled through the file, then came up with a photo of Helen Gabrys from the previous year. 'Do you recognise this lady?' he asked.

Tyson scrutinised the photo. 'It looks like Miss Gabrys,' he said uncertainly, 'but she's got shorter hair. And it's curly.'

'What did you get out of doing stuff for her?' asked Greg. 'Did she pay you?'

'I'm her man,' boasted Tyson. 'Her *number one* man, she says.'

'But why?' persisted Greg. 'How does she pay you?'

'Cash only,' said Tyson, proud of his financial acumen. 'Always cash.'

'And the other boy with you? Did she pay him too?'

The expression of confusion came back to Tyson's face. 'Don't know,' he said. 'E just said 'e'd been told to be there. In case I blew it, like.'

'Who was he?' asked Chris.

'Don't know,' replied Tyson. 'Niver seen 'im afore. Called 'imself Red.'

'Where did he go after you stabbed Nathan?'

'Off. Down the street. Aven't seen 'im since. But 'e weren't a boy. 'E were older.'

Greg leaned back and exchanged glances with Chris. 'Interview suspended,' he said, and the two of them left the room. A few seconds later he popped his head back in. 'Would you like me to see if we can rustle up some teas and coffees?' he asked.

In the next room, Chris and Jill were comparing notes.

'He admits being there, that the knife is his and that Helen Gabrys asked him to cut Nathan then leave a warning,' summarised Jill.

'There's details we don't have yet,' said Greg, overhearing as he came into the room. 'Like how did they meet? Who set the whole relationship up? How much and how does he get paid, etc? And the million-dollar question, who is Red?'

Sounds like Tyson's relationship with the Gabrys family is fairly longstanding,' said Chris. 'I bet it all goes back to Mica. We know he was close to the county lines operation that involved the Academy.'

'Very likely, but I think we can leave that to another day. We have enough now to charge Tyson with the attack on Nathan. That'll keep him under wraps and get the press off the Chief Super's back while we follow up Steve's work in Stalham and find Helen Gabrys,' responded Greg.

'And Red?' asked Jill 'What about him? He was a witness at the least and may have been directly involved.'

'See if there's been any mention of a "Red" anywhere in our records. Try Jim. He might be able to help.'

22

Everything changes

Karen was devastated. The news crashed around her ears like winter breakers on a beach. School was always her favourite place. Now, with the angry atmosphere at home, it was even more of a refuge, a place where she could distract herself with new facts and hide in the multi-coloured worlds of books. To hear that it was to be taken away was the end of everything.

She spent Thursday in a daze, collecting books, writing down login details, making sure she had her list of assignments from the teachers, knowing all the while that with only one phone and an old laptop between herself, Jake and her parents, she would struggle to keep up. Friday was a day of goodbyes, of promises to keep in touch, to send messages, to join WhatsApp groups, to ask for permission, which she knew would not be granted, to keep up on Twitter and Facebook. At the end of the day there were tears and hugs, even though the latter too had apparently been forbidden in this cold new world.

Then she went home on Friday afternoon to a world without lessons, friends or respite from tension – just screens and bad temper.

23

Saturday 21 March 2020

Even in normal times, Saturdays were always difficult, because you never knew what might happen. Some Saturdays their father would go to work, and they could go out with their mum and sometimes Tim. Those were good days. Other Saturdays, if he wasn't working, it all depended on what he was doing. If he was going to the football, or to play pool, and the matches had gone well, then everything would be quiet at home. But if he'd lost, or won but celebrated too well, then they had to watch out.

These weren't normal times, and this Saturday started badly because their father was still at home and decided he was going to play football with Jake in the yard. Jake didn't want to play football. He wanted to finish the drawing he'd begun the day before. But his father was having none of it and forced him outside.

After a while, Karen heard shouts and sobbing. She hesitated about fetching her mum, and in the end went cautiously to the back door and opened it a careful crack. Jake was standing against the back wall, within a white rectangular

131

shape drawn in chalk. She realised it was meant to be a football goal. Jake was bent double, his arms wrapped round his head, and, as she watched, her father took a powerful kick at the football, which shot towards the goal and ricocheted off Jake's back into the corner of the yard.

'Come on, boy! Defend your goal,' her father shouted. 'Stand up and kick it back!' He took another kick at the ball, which this time narrowly missed Jake's head. 'Are you a boy or a girl? Oh, I give up,' her father said, and with a final kick that left the ball lying in the corner, by the bike with no wheels that was propped on the wall, he turned towards the house. As he did so, her mum appeared behind her.

'Come in, Jake,' she called. 'Come and have a drink of squash.'

'This is no son of mine,' Kit snarled as he pushed past his wife into the kitchen, sending her flying off balance. 'He's yellow and he's crap at everything. Are you sure you haven't palmed off some other fellow's yellow get on to me? At his age I would be down the park every Saturday, playing footie with me mates.'

'He's only six.' She defended Jake, who had run to her, crying. 'He's not big enough for that heavy ball.' She hugged him to her, but Kit snatched him away with a hand on his arm and shook him as a dog would a rat.

'Rubbish. He's yellow. I'll not waste my time on him again.' And with a final push that left Jake lying on the step, Kit turned to the fridge and took out a can of lager. He stopped with the fridge open, peered inside then slammed it shut. 'You need to do some shopping. We're nearly out of lager,' he said.

'I've been trying not to go to the shops too often,' her mum said.

'Well we can't run out. Get some crisps, and something decent for my supper too. Steak, or a pie. A decent one, none of your rubbish.'

'I haven't enough money,' she said nervously.

'What the hell you doing with it?' he bellowed. 'I gave you some only the other day.'

'Yes, but it's all gone. You're drinking at home now instead of down the pub, so the weekly shop costs more.'

'My fault, is it?' He held his hand up and she took an involuntary step back.

'I'm just saying, all of us at home all the time, we get through stuff quicker. The kids won't be having school meals now either, so that means more cost too.'

'Oh, for God's sake!' He put a hand in his jeans pocket, pulled out some crumpled notes and slammed them down on the table. 'Don't spend it all at once,' he said, and went upstairs.

Karen and her mum looked at the curled and grubby notes in silence.

'Forty pounds,' her mum said blankly. 'That's not going to last long.'

24

Down the Ant

Steve found the proprietor of Rivers Edge Marina daubing anti-fouling paint on the hull of a small Broads dayboat. Steve negotiated the muddy grass around the trailer with some care to approach the man in tattered green overalls. Waving his warrant card, he explained what he was doing there.

'Yes, Miss Gabrys and her mother do have a mooring here,' the man said, standing up and stretching to relieve the ache in his back. 'It's over there. At the far end of that wharf on the left as you face the river.'

'What's the name of the boat?' asked Steve.

'*The Jolly Jane*. She's a big cruiser with an orange superstructure. You can't miss her.'

'Do you know if Miss Gabrys is on board now?'

'Absolutely no idea, mate,' the man replied. 'They come and go as they like.' He craned his neck round the small dayboat to look at the car park. 'I think that's her car over there, so she might be.'

Steve walked over to look at the small, silver BMW. He checked the number against the one in his notebook, and it matched. Peering in through the windows, he noted that the Gabrys family were a tidy lot. There was no rubbish lying on the seats or in the footwells. No empty drink cartons or sandwich wrappers. Nothing.

Mindful of his instructions to be discreet, he walked a short way along the wharf. To his considerable disappointment, the mooring at the far end was empty and there was no sign of a big cruiser with an orange superstructure. He went back to the anti-fouling worker.

'It's not there,' he announced. 'Do you know where she'll have gone?'

'No idea, mate,' the man said again, pausing his brushstrokes. 'But I'd make an educated guess she'll have gone downriver. That boat's a bit big to negotiate the upper river at Dilham.'

Steve went back to his car and got in, scowling at the mud he'd just imported to his floor mat.

'She's not here,' he reported. 'Taken her boat on its travels.'

Greg looked at his watch and then out of the window at the darkening sky. 'It's a bit late to be chasing a boat down the river,' he said. 'It's close to dark already. Let's organise a search for tomorrow morning. She'll keep until then.'

'Police boat?' asked Steve. 'The Broadsbeat team don't normally patrol this early in the year, but they could probably help.'

'They may not be patrolling at all this year,' Greg pointed out. 'No, let's stick with the discreet approach for now. We don't want to spook her into making a run for it. We'll ask the Broads Authority if they can help out again.'

***

Early Saturday morning, Steve, Chris and Greg found themselves boarding the Broads Authority fast RIB in Wroxham..

The Broads Ranger in charge of the RIB, Alan, was a compact, powerful-looking man with dark hair sprouting vigorously under a Broads Authority cap.

'Sorry about having to start from here,' was his opening comment. 'I'm afraid we have a bit of a trek down to Ant Mouth before we can turn upriver towards Stalham. On the other hand, we can use the trip to check the boat you're looking for isn't moored somewhere in the Bure. From all accounts, she's fairly noticeable.' He pointed at a photo on the seat beside him. 'This is from her registration details.'

Greg found himself looking at a blurred photo of a long, low cruiser with, as everyone had said, a very noticeable bright orange cabin.

'Lifejackets on, please,' said Alan, and started the engine as they all donned the inflatable lifejackets and found themselves a seat.

Greg was surprised at the steady pace adopted by the fast-looking RIB.

Alan read his thoughts. 'She can go fast if needed,' he said, 'but unless we find ourselves with an emergency, I'd rather keep to the speed limits if it's all the same to you.'

Greg nodded, and resigned himself to a slow morning on the river.

'Do you want me to do a quick sweep round the Broads we'll pass on our way?' asked Alan.

'Yes, please,' said Greg. 'Any area not readily under scrutiny from the landward side. I've got someone ringing round to check if *The Jolly Jane* is on private moorings anywhere, so we don't need to worry about those. They'll ring me if they find anything.'

'In that case, we'll check out Wroxham, Horning, Salhouse and Ranworth on our way. Then turn up the Ant. If we draw a blank up there, we can turn south towards the Thurne and then Yarmouth, but hopefully your phone calls may have uncovered something useful by then. Otherwise, we're going to be at this for days!'

'You wouldn't have thought it would be too hard to find a big orange boat,' remarked Chris.

'There's a lot of water and a lot of small inlets,' said Alan. 'It may not be that easy.'

'Perhaps you need ANPR,' muttered Chris, but quietly. She was already beginning to feel cold, and wasn't greatly enamoured of a whole day in an open boat.

Turning into Wroxham Broad, the boat picked up speed in the more open water. They drew a blank there, and in Salhouse Broad. In Horning they got excited briefly when they spotted a cruiser with her superstructure covered in a tarpaulin, but it proved to be a rather battered old boat with a probably leaky roof and a wooden cabin badly in need of revarnishing.

'Oy!' someone shouted from the shore, as they pulled the tarpaulin back into position. 'Leave my boat alone!'

Alan introduced himself. 'Broads Authority. Just a routine check of registration letters.' The objector on the bank shut up, and Alan added in an aside, 'I suspect his toll hasn't been paid yet this year. I'll run a check later.'

There was nothing remotely like an orange cruiser in Ranworth either, nor on the moorings they could see from the water.

'Okay. Up the Ant?' asked Alan.

Greg was on the phone, so Alan idled his engine as he rejoined the Bure, waiting for Greg to complete his call.

'Nothing so far,' said Greg. 'So yes, let's try up the Ant towards Stalham.'

'Shall we just check out South Walsham first, as it's very close,' suggested Alan.

'Okay. Yes, thank you.'

But South Walsham, the Broad and dykes, was also a blank. Rejoining the Bure, Greg looked right, to admire the image of St Benet's Abbey, showing stark against a still slightly rosy sky.

Alan noticed the focus of his gaze. 'Picturesque, isn't it,' he said, 'even if it is just the gatehouse.'

'Imagine what the whole abbey must have looked like, right on the edge of the river,' replied Greg.

'Very handy for their Friday fish suppers,' answered Alan. As though to prove his point, a couple of petrels were skimming the water ahead of the RIB. Looking around him, Greg spotted most of the same bird species that regularly paddled past his riverside home, further down the Bure, with ducks, coots and pink-footed geese the most prominent.

As they turned into the Ant, Alan cut his speed still further. This river was much narrower than the Bure and heavily overhung by trees. Chris, rather bored by now, had recourse to her phone, but found the signal very poor. Steve was discussing fishing with Alan, and Greg was still spotting bird species as they passed the minor stately home of How Hill and caught a brief glimpse of its gardens.

'It's very quiet on the river, even for March,' remarked Alan. 'I'd normally expect to see a few boats on a Saturday. This is going to be a very odd year,' he added.

They continued upriver, following the twists and turns, avoiding the overhanging branches and trailing reeds. For most of the journey, they could see very little beyond the bank, their view impeded sometimes by tall reeds and the rest of the time by trees. When small inlets opened off the river, Alan cut their speed so they could peer up the narrow channels, but most were too narrow for a boat the size of *The Jolly Jane*, and Chris began to feel, rather appropriately given their location, that they were on a wild goose chase.

After more than half an hour they arrived at the village of Irstead with its pretty riverside cottages, almost all with private moorings.

'Now I wouldn't mind living here,' announced Chris, admiring a house with a particularly good view upriver to Barton Broad. 'Provided I could be guaranteed no flooding, of course.'

On the edge of the village was a Broads Authority mooring with launch in situ. Again, Alan throttled back just to run his eye over the launch, then accelerated as the RIB entered the open waters of Barton Broad.

'I can speed up here,' he said. 'We'll just do a quick sweep round, then we can check out the dyke to Neatishead before...' His voice tailed off. Halfway up the Broad towards the turning to Stalham, in the shallow waters beyond the rusty green guideposts, could be seen a bright orange superstructure. Water was lapping in at the windows and geese were standing on its roof.

'Looks like yours,' said Alan, and turned the RIB towards the sunken craft.

25

Barton Broad

'Can you take us alongside?' asked Greg, but Alan was already nosing the RIB up to the sunken cruiser. They did one circuit of the boat, as close as he dared, then cautiously he tied up to the rail around the bow. They all peered in through the windows to the half-drowned cabin. There was no one visible in the day cabin.

'On this model, there are sleeping quarters below,' said Alan. 'If anyone's in there, they're under water.' Greg looked around at the reed-covered bank a few yards away. There was no one in sight there either, but at one point, reeds were crushed and bent. Greg got on the phone to HQ.

'We need the police launch and a team of divers to check out the remainder of the boat,' he said, 'and a dog team to check the riverbank.' He turned to Alan. 'If someone had gone ashore here, where would they end up?' he asked.

'The nearest village on that side is Wood Street,' he replied. 'But it's not an easy walk. There are dykes criss-crossing and what's in between them is as much reed marsh as it is grass.'

'So, the possibilities are that either the occupants of the boat are still on board, or they were taken off by another boat, or they somehow scrambled away through the reeds. The divers can check the first, the dogs can check the last, that leaves the second possibility as the problem. No CCTV out here.'

'I can ask around,' offered Alan. 'There are a few folk who fish the river regularly. They might have seen something. I can ask fellow Rangers and wildlife experts too, but we'll be lucky if anyone saw anything.'

'When you say "regular" fishers, would that mean poachers?' asked Greg. Alan grinned.

'There may be a few who are, how can I put it, flexible in their judgements,' he said. 'But a few salmon or pheasants here or there are one thing. Major crime is another.'

'We'd appreciate you asking,' said Greg. His phone rang again. 'The police helicopter will be overhead shortly, to take a look around,' he reported. 'The launch should be here within the hour. Are you okay to stick it out till then?'

'Don't see I've got much choice,' said Alan. But he said it cheerfully.

By late Saturday afternoon, Barton Broad was buzzing with activity. Literally buzzing, as the police helicopter circled overhead in an attempt to spot anyone in the reed beds edging the Broad. At ground zero, what seemed a long wait for the divers had just ended with the arrival of the Broadsbeat patrol boat and a team of two divers.

'I know you, don't I?' Greg asked the one in the stern as she pulled on her hood and checked her air tank. She looked round.

'That's right,' she said. 'We met on the bank of the Yare in Yarmouth when I checked out a drainage channel for you. I'm Mandy. [1]

'Good to see you again,' said Greg, shaking her cold hand. 'More work in confined spaces, I fear.'

'So I see,' she said, looking over at the semi-submerged Broads cruiser. Despite the human disturbance, one pink-footed goose was still standing on its roof, clearly resentful of the interruption to its daily round. As Mandy watched, it waddled to the edge and launched itself into the water before swimming off with an irritated waggle of its tail. Greg followed her line of sight and saw the goose haul itself onto the bank where the reeds were already crushed.

'Looks like someone went that way,' said Mandy.

'That's what we thought,' agreed Greg. 'The helicopter is checking it out from above and a dog team is working its way towards us from Wood Street. But realistically, the dog handler won't have much time before they need to turn back. With luck, the infrared camera on the copter might spot something.'

'Meanwhile, let's see what we have here,' she replied.

After a quick word with the man at the tiller of their boat, the two divers slid slowly into the water. Watching, Greg saw them make their way around the upper deck of the cruiser, peering in at the windows. He shivered as the wind found its way down the back of his neck.

'Bloody cold, isn't it,' said Chris at his elbow. 'A nice, indoor, desk-based job is beginning to look even more attractive.'

---

1. See Glass Arrows

'Let me know if you find one. I never have,' replied Greg, his eyes still on the divers now pulling the cruiser cabin door open. They made their way carefully into the boat.

After a moment one appeared on the submerged deck and shouted, 'As we thought, there's no one in the cockpit. Going down into the cabin next.'

There was a pause as both figures disappeared, then Mandy reappeared on deck and pulled her mouthpiece out.

'The cabin door's locked. We can't see a key. I'm going to see if I can spot anything through the portholes, but the water's murky. Don't hold your breath.' The second black-clad figure reappeared as well, and watched closely as Mandy slid into the water by the cruiser. Another delay, then her black head, looking remarkably like a seal, popped up and was seen to chat with her colleague on the deck of *The Jolly Jane*.

'She can't see much,' he reported in another shout. 'Water's dirty, as we said. There's stuff floating about and the portholes are small. She can't say one way or the other, whether there's a body in there. Do we have authority to break the door in?'

Greg thought for a moment, then shouted back. 'Yes. Go ahead. We need to know, and we can't wait for the boat to be refloated. I assume there's definitely no key?'

'Not that we can find,' was the response, and after a moment rummaging through the kit bag they'd left on the roof of *The Jolly Jane*, the two black shapes disappeared again, one of them carrying what Greg surmised to be a jemmy.

As they all waited, the radio crackled with a message from the helicopter crew.

'Spotted the dog team,' it said. 'No one else visible in the reed beds between here and Wood Street.'

Over on *The Jolly Jane*, the two divers reappeared and waved the patrol boat over. Face to face with Greg, Mandy pulled off her wetsuit hood.

'No one in the cabin,' she said. 'It's hard to tell after being submerged, but there may be signs of a struggle. Your forensic team will be able to make a more considered assessment. All I can tell you is that the bedding and some other materials seem to be disturbed, there is a knife on the floor and the door was locked from the outside. No sign of a key.'

'Okaayy,' Greg said slowly and reflectively while he thought fast. 'Chris, get hold of the dog team and tell them what we know. It's likely they're looking for Helen Gabrys and or her mother. Tell the helicopter the same.' He turned to the Broads Ranger. 'Best way to refloat *The Jolly Jane*?' he asked.

'Get hold of a local boatyard. I'd try *Ultramarine* first. They could do the job,' he recommended. 'And they'll tow her wherever you want. I'd suggest our base at Irstead. We have a mooring and boathouse on the edge of the village. It's a safe and private location for a preliminary survey by the forensic team.'

'Thank you, sounds good. If you could organise *Ultramarine*, I'll let our Chief Super know and arrange for the CSIs to meet us at Irstead. Tomorrow, I imagine.'

'Too late for anything to happen today,' agreed Alan, looking at the darkening sky.

'In that case,' – Greg looked at his colleagues from Broadsbeat – 'you and your team will have to stand watch tonight to preserve the crime scene. Can I leave that to you?'

'Got it.' The man at the tiller nodded. 'I'll stay here for now, until the relief boat arrives. Can you drop our dive team back to base?'

'Done, and thank you,' said Greg with an eyebrow raised in the direction of Alan for agreement.

***

Out on the marsh, Jenny Warren and her springer spaniel partner, Turbo, had set off from the lane just outside the village of Wood Street. A quick survey up and down the road had revealed several places where paths emerged onto the verge, but none that seemed of any greater interest than the rest. Jenny feared the search was doomed to failure. She'd called at Rivers Edge Marina to allow Turbo a sniff round the Gabrys car, where she'd found a glove down the side of the driver's seat. Given its location, she'd taken a gamble it had belonged to Helen Gabrys, but she had no certainty either of its provenance, nor when it had last been handled. She felt she was asking a lot of Turbo.

After a few minutes' fruitless searching along the road edge, she got out her Ordnance Survey map and decided on her route to the edge of Barton Broad. The path she chose very swiftly dwindled into a rough track and then the faintest possible tracing through the rough grass. Before long it had disappeared altogether, and she found herself alternately stumbling over tussocks and wading ankle deep in water. The reeds, by now, were taller than she was. With a sigh she got out her compass, and after a long half hour following Turbo's enthusiastically wagging bottom through the reeds, she eventually burst through the last barrier to find herself on the edge of the Broad. The two RIBs moored to the semi-submerged cruiser were off to her left, while the helicopter was rumbling overhead.

As Turbo scoured the water's edge, flushing a trio of geese as he did so, her radio crackled and emitted a message from her colleagues in the sky.

'You're about thirty-five metres from the track we can see leading away from the water,' he reported. 'Head south and you'll find it. Out.'

'Noted. Thank you. Out,' replied Jenny, and turned in accordance with the instructions. She called Turbo away from his ambitious eyeballing of an irritated swan, and the two of them returned to their scramble over the unpleasant ground.

After a considerably longer wade through more water than mud, Jenny arrived at her destination, out of breath and soaked to the elbows after tripping over an unseen branch. She noted that Turbo's enthusiasm was undented by being coated liberally in silt, and he set to quartering the ground where the reeds were undoubtedly trodden down by the recent passage of someone.

After a few moments, he sat and wagged his tail at Jenny, then pointed his nose along the route apparently taken by an interesting scent.

'Well, well,' muttered Jenny. 'Good dog, Turbo.'

To avoid his dashing off faster than she could follow, she called him to her and put him on his long, tracking lead, then allowed him to take her along the faint trail of disturbed foliage. She reached for her phone with the other hand to report her whereabouts and progress to Chris.

'Take care,' said Chris. 'The copter has had to return to base to refuel. I'm not comfortable with you out there unsupported. Why isn't Steve with you?'

'He's checking Wood Street with the local team,' said Jenny. 'He's not far away if needed. And I have Turbo.'

'He's not far as the crow flies, but he's a devil of a long way off as the human stumbles through that territory,' said Chris. 'Keep in touch and don't engage. If you think you are getting close to Gabrys, keep away and call for back-up. Her father used to go around armed, don't forget.'

This warning ringing in her ears, Jenny did proceed with caution. But equally she was very conscious that a woman and a dog cannot move silently through reed beds, whatever Hollywood might have you think. Especially when the light is fading fast, and a slow creep is impractical. With Turbo's panting ringing in her ears and the dog himself straining at the leash, she moved as quietly as she could over the crushed reeds.

Before she reached the drier land of the rough pastures behind the reed beds, Turbo stopped suddenly and signalled. Then, as Jenny moved forwards to see what had attracted his attention, he growled softly. She froze in place, then listened. The night's noises suddenly seemed sharper, clearer. The bark of a muntjac in the distance made her jump and she distinctly heard the soft sweep of wings just before she caught the *kee-wick* of a tawny owl almost directly overhead. Turbo maintained his soft growl until she patted his back. Then he fell silent. She could still hear nothing up ahead. She debated with herself whether to call for back-up, but dismissed the idea as likely to signal her position. She had to do something soon or be stranded out on the marsh in the dark.

The tawny owl called again and was answered by the scream of a vixen. The hair bristled on Turbo's neck, but his focus was still on something up ahead. Making her mind up, Jenny silently released him from the leash. He bounded forwards, then started barking. There was no response from his quarry, and Jenny decided to take the risk.

Taking out her baton, she readied herself for combat and crept forwards as quietly as she could. In the fading light she saw Turbo circling a body on the ground. It was making no movement, even in response to the dog.

She approached cautiously and immediately realised why the copter's infrared cameras hadn't picked it up. The body of a woman was lying face down on a particularly wet patch of reed bed, semi-submerged in the icy waters. Still carefully, Jenny felt the woman's neck for a pulse, and found one, weak and thready. The woman was poorly dressed for a chilly scramble across a marsh, in thin jeans and a t-shirt. The shoes on her feet were fashion trainers rather than heavy-duty boots like those Jenny was wearing. Everything she had on was soaked and muddy. Jenny reached for her phone.

'I've found her,' she reported to Chris. 'Helen that is. She's alive, but only just. I'm guessing hypothermia and possibly a sprained or broken ankle. We're going to need an ambulance asap.' She checked her phone. 'I can give my coordinates using *what3words*,' she added, 'so they should find me okay. The problem will be the terrain.'

'Leave it with me,' said Chris. 'I'll get Steve to you asap and I'll keep you updated on progress re the ambulance. Well done, Jenny. Any sign of the mother?'

'Not here, no. And no signs of a second person having been around or carried on through the reeds.'

With darkness well established, Jenny took her jacket off to cover Helen Gabrys as best she could, then settled down to wait. She was surprised how soon she heard Steve crashing through the undergrowth and calling.

'Here,' she said, turning on her torch and standing up from where she had been cuddling Turbo for warmth. Within minutes he was with her, out of breath, wiping sweat from his brow and accompanied by someone Jenny recognised from a modern slavery case of the year before.

'Hi Ben,' she said, and thankfully relinquished responsibility for the casualty into the hands of first responder, ex-policeman and ex-nurse, Ben Asheton.

26

Retrieval

Ben swiftly assessed his casualty.

'Unconscious but breathing,' he reported on his radio. 'Definitely hypothermic, and I suspect a fractured ankle. I'll get a collar on and immobilise the ankle, but the sooner we get her out of here the better. No, I don't think the air ambulance can land any closer than Wood Street. The ground is too boggy.'

Putting his radio away, he looked at Jenny and Steve. 'Can one of you show the paramedics the way here?' he asked. 'An ambulance will be at the roadside within ten minutes.'

As he spoke, he was fixing an immobilising collar on Helen Gabrys's neck. 'Just to be on the safe side,' he muttered, then inflated a splint on her right ankle. 'Right, give me a hand getting her out of this water, then you can scoot off to the road.'

Ben and Steve pulled Helen gently out of the wet area and onto the thermal blanket Ben had laid out on the drier ground, while Jenny illuminated the scene with her torch. Turbo watched with interest, then gave a small *wuff* of apparent approbation once she was wrapped in the silver foil.

'Now we wait,' said Ben, his fingers on her carotid pulse. Jenny was flashing her torch around the disturbed ground as Steve set off to guide the paramedics.

'Looking for something?' asked Ben.

'A phone mainly,' replied Jenny. 'But also checking she wasn't armed. Ahh...' She breathed a sigh of satisfaction as she picked an iPhone out of the shallow water. 'Dead, of course,' she said, putting it into an evidence bag. 'We'll see what the tech experts can do with it.' She too moved onto the drier ground, putting her jacket back on now it was no longer needed to act as a blanket. 'Is she going to be all right?' she asked.

'I hope so,' said Ben. 'The ankle is nothing to worry about, but the hypothermia needs sorting asap. I can't see any other injuries.'

'What puzzles me,' said Jenny, 'is how she got from the cruiser to the bank. She's clearly wet from falling in the marsh, and it may be that she swam or waded from the cruiser to the bank. But that would be a pretty desperate move in these temperatures. I didn't see any other boat. Hang on, I'll ask Chris if the cruiser has a tender.'

'No,' replied Chris. 'Would you expect one?'

Jenny explained the conundrum and her phone went silent. When Chris rang back it was evident from the background noise that they were now underway.

'We're heading back to Wroxham,' she said. 'The marina at Stalham seems to have shut up shop for the night, so we'll have to postpone questions about a tender to the morning. Once

Gabrys is in the ambulance, get yourself and Turbo home, Jenny, and well done. Steve can follow the ambulance, and we'll have a team from uniform to keep an eye on her while she's at the hospital.'

She was interrupted by the arrival of two paramedics, with a further two hot on their heels. Suddenly the quiet marshland was a flurry of activity, and the owl was heard no more. Torches flashed, orders were given, and advice sought. In a remarkably short space of time, Helen Gabrys, braced and wrapped like a turkey for the oven, was being carried across the marsh by four men, stumbling and swearing as they went. Jenny and Turbo followed tiredly behind, with Ben bringing up the rear.

By the time Jenny made it to the roadside, Helen was being loaded into the first ambulance, and it set off, blue lights reflecting off the dark clouded sky, just as Steve reappeared.

'Want a lift back to your car?' he asked Jenny.

She surveyed her clothes and Turbo's fur. 'We're a bit muddy,' she said doubtfully.

'So's the car,' said Steve cheerfully. 'Come on. I'm parked just behind the second ambulance and Ben's car.'

Ben was just winding up a discussion with the last two paramedics, as they loaded equipment back into their vehicle and prepared to set off. He waved as he turned back to his first-responder liveried car.

'Got another shout,' he said cheerfully to Steve and Jenny. 'Difficulty breathing, in Barton. Never a dull moment.'

'Have you seen any Covid patients yet?' asked Jenny.

'Not yet. But I admit, I think about it, especially when I get a shout like this one. Sounds like it could be Covid, doesn't it?'

'Aren't you scared?' asked Jenny bluntly.

'A bit,' he admitted, pausing with one hand on the roof of his car. 'But I take all the precautions I can. I'm masked, gloved, and keep in well-ventilated spaces as much as possible. Apart from that, and I'd do that for any respiratory infection, what else can I do? Until there's a vaccine, that is.' He shrugged, got into his car and drove off.

'Time for us to go too,' said Steve. 'I'll drop you off then get after the ambulance.' Jenny got into the front passenger seat with Turbo between her feet.

'Thanks,' she said. 'Yomping across that marsh was exhausting. I hope I don't have to do that again any time soon.'

'Turbo doesn't seem to mind,' replied Steve, checking over his shoulder before pulling out.

'Turbo doesn't mind anything,' said Jenny. 'Except donkeys. He's not so keen on them. I think it's the bray. He met one when he was a pup, and he's never got over it.' Steve was already pulling up behind her car. 'That was quick,' she remarked. 'But very much appreciated, thank you.'

She waved him off and turned to look at Turbo. He was standing by the tailgate, waiting for the command to jump up into his crate in the back. 'You are a star,' she said. 'Well done today, Turbo.' He wagged his tail in acknowledgement, turned around twice and settled down to watch the road behind the car unwind as Jenny drove them both home.

***

Over at Wroxham, Chris was shivering on the riverbank as Greg agreed the final arrangements for the next morning with the Broadsbeat officers. With a final farewell wave, he joined her at the car.

'I've arranged that they raise *The Jolly Jane* first thing in the morning and tow her to the Broads Authority mooring in Irstead. We'll meet Ned's team there at 11.00. Hopefully we'll have a boat to examine by then.'

'And Helen Gabrys?' asked Chris.

'There'll be someone by her bed when she wakes up, and they'll alert us. Ben reckons she should be okay to interview tomorrow unless a new problem rears its head, but the team at the Norfolk and Norwich Hospital will have the final say, obviously. Jim is on standby to talk to her tomorrow, while we see what we can find on *The Jolly Jane*. And I've asked the Broadsbeat team to resolve the issue of the cruiser tender. Was there one, and, if so, where is it now?'

There was an exclamation from Chris, and she looked up from where she was flicking through her emails on her phone. 'I've got it,' she said.

'Got what?' Greg was concentrating on the road, not really giving her his full attention.

'The job. The job in Suffolk. I've got it.' That got his attention.

'And the promotion?'

'Yes. The whole package. They want me to start next month. On the sixth of April.'

'But that's only three weeks away. Sorry,' he caught himself up. 'I mean, I'm thrilled for you, Chris. It's no more than you deserve. Just, I wasn't expecting it so soon.'

'I know. I'm sorry to leave when you're so busy, but...'

'But, of course you must. And we must celebrate tonight.' Greg swerved to the side of the road and pulled up so suddenly Chris was jerked forwards against her seat belt.

'What the...?'

'Champagne,' said Greg. 'Nothing else will do.' And dashed into the off-licence that had caught his eye at just the right moment.

27

By the Bure – Sunday 22 March 2020

After an evening celebrating with champagne and not much else – the shopping had been neglected and the best they could manage for supper was bread and Camembert – Chris was not best pleased to be wakened by the pronounced shrilling of the landline. Somehow, that phone ringing at the wrong time of day always seemed a portent of doom. Generally, a work emergency arrived via one or the other of their mobile phones. Greg reached out a lazy arm – the one she wasn't lying on – to the phone and glanced at the clock as he did so.

'Who the hell is ringing us at 6am on a Sunday?' he asked rhetorically as he picked up the receiver.

All Chris could hear was a high-pitched and apparently panicky voice going on and on.

'Hang on,' said Greg. 'Calm down, Mother. Slow down a bit and say that again.' There was a pause, and then Greg asked, 'Which hospital? Why on earth Hinchingbrooke? What are you doing in Huntingdon? Why aren't you at home?' Another pause, then he added, 'I'm going to ring off now, and see what I can find out. Then I'll ring you back.'

He put the phone down and sighed heavily. 'You're not going to believe this,' he said.

'If it's your mother, I'm pretty sure I will,' said Chris. 'Go on. What's she done now?'

'First and foremost, my father is in Hinchingbrooke Hospital in Huntingdon with Covid. He was taken in last night with breathing problems, and Mother's in a panic because she can't visit.'

'No one can visit in hospitals at the moment,' said Chris. 'It's been all over the news.'

'Yes, I know.'

'Hang on, what were they doing in Huntingdon?'

'My question precisely. It seems that my parents, together with a few other people who apparently think that movement restrictions don't apply to them, decided to have a country house party for someone's birthday last week. Now several of the guests have gone down with Covid. Mother is still a, no doubt unwelcome, guest in the country house, and father is in hospital.'

'What a mess,' said Chris. 'But what does she want you to do about it?'

'I think what she'd like is for me to drive over to Huntingdon and bulldoze my way into the hospital. Which I am definitely not going to do. I'll ring the hospital now and see how he's doing. Then I'm going to work as planned.'

'Do you need me at Irstead?'

'On balance, I think it would be best if you meet Jim at the Norfolk and Norwich later this morning for a chat with Helen Gabrys. I'll ring you with any news from the boat.'

'In that case, I'll fit in a quick trip to the office before I meet up with Jim. If I can get ahead with clearing my desk of routine stuff, I can prioritise this enquiry for the next three weeks.'

'Agreed.' Greg kissed her and turned back to the phone. 'I'll make the call to Hinchingbrooke. After you with the shower.'

When Chris came out of the bathroom, rubbing her hair with a towel, Greg was just putting the phone down.

'It's not as bad as she was making it sound,' he said with an expression of relief on his face. 'Dad is on a main ward, on oxygen, and they say it was as well he didn't delay any longer coming in for treatment. But he's responding well at the moment, and they don't anticipate him having to go into the high-dependency unit.'

'That's a relief,' said Chris. 'So what about your mother?'

'She's going to have to stay where she is for the moment. As someone exposed to Covid, she most definitely can't travel yet.'

'Bit rough on her hosts,' remarked Chris. 'I don't suppose they anticipated their guests having to stay on for days.'

'Then they shouldn't have arranged a house party in the middle of a pandemic,' said Greg heartlessly. 'Frankly, I think a little inconvenience is the least they deserve. From the sounds of it, the house is big enough for them all to isolate within its walls.

'I'll pass the good news about Dad on to her, and the bad news about her having to stay put, then I'll get myself over to Irstead, where I hope *The Jolly Jane* will soon be arriving.'

'I'll be off then,' said Chris. 'See you later. And if I can find a shop open, I'll get some food in, otherwise we'll be reduced to baked beans and Ryvita tonight.'

Greg shuddered at the prospect, and got into the shower, much relieved that his mother's worst imaginings appeared unfounded.

By the time he had made his way to the Broads Authority mooring in Irstead, *The Jolly Jane*, bedraggled and listing somewhat, was being towed by the Broadsbeat RIB across Barton Broad and into the River Ant. As the RIB pulled level with the mouth of the mooring, an officer appeared on the deck of *The Jolly Jane* and threw a line to the Broads Authority warden standing ready on the bank. Greg joined him as he pulled gently on the line, until she bumped the bank with a quiet thud. The officer on the deck jumped ashore with a second line and secured the newly refloated boat astern, then looked up at Greg.

'No sign of a body on board, as the divers said,' he reported.

'That leaves us with the question, where is Mrs Gabrys?' said Greg. 'Any update on the putative tender?'

'We checked with the Rivers Edge Marina,' said the constable. 'According to them, *The Jolly Jane* did have a small tender in the form of an inflatable rowboat, and it's not at the marina.'

'Anybody out looking for the tender?' asked Greg.

'Yes, sir, but the chances of finding it quickly are small. It could even have been punctured and sunk, in which case, we might not find it for years!'

'Okay. Keep me posted.' Then glancing over his shoulder, Greg added, 'And here is Ned.'

A man in white overalls, gloved and booted, was fast approaching over the damp grass, accompanied by two others weighed down with cameras and equipment bags. 'Left the van in the road. Hope it's okay there,' he said briskly. 'Okay, let's see what we've got.' He pulled the hood over his head and stepped aboard the gently rocking boat. The two assistants put their bags down on the bank and started sorting through the tools of their trade.

Ned stuck his head out of the cabin door. 'Come on,' he said, his words slightly muffled through his mask. 'Just remember,' he said to the two figures, anonymous behind their surgical masks, 'keep at least two metres from each other, and ideally don't go in the cabin together. Rule of thumb – don't go into enclosed spaces with anyone. Okay?' They nodded their assent and followed Ned onto the boat.

'Even more good reason for me to keep out of the way,' thought Greg, and stepped over to a bench on the bank with a good view of the Broad. His phone rang as he sat down.

'Hi Chris,' he said. 'Any news from Jim?'

'He's just rung,' she said. 'He says Helen Gabrys is conscious and about to have surgery on her broken ankle. We can interview her after the operation. Jim says he's getting a clear message that the sooner we can remove her from the hospital, the happier they'll be. They need all the beds they have for Covid patients.'

'Ned's just arrived here,' replied Greg. 'I'll let you know as soon as we have anything. Broadsbeat are looking for the tender, but we really need Helen to tell us if we need to be looking for her mother as well.'

'I'll get myself over to the N and N. Speak later.'

Greg looked up to see Ned approaching over the grass. He sat down at the far end of the bench and pulled his mask off with a sigh.

'This one's going to be a problem,' he said. 'Submerging a crime scene under water is not what I'd recommend. However, all is not lost. It just takes longer. If you don't mind a brief tutorial… We can generally get fingerprints after submersion from any material we would normally get fingerprints from. That's what the lads are up to now. They're also bagging items of clothing and other materials to see if we can get any DNA from them. That should give us some evidence of who has been in various parts of the boat. Obviously we've got the knife the diver mentioned, and I can tell you it's an ordinary kitchen knife. Nothing special. The only other fact I can give you at this point, is that the seacocks were open, so the boat was sunk on purpose.'

'Any indication of who had been living on the boat?' asked Greg.

'No paperwork that we've found so far. No passports, bank cards or letters, for example, which is a little odd. There's a family group photo in the cabin, of Gabrys with his daughter, son and wife, and that's about it.'

'Okay. So, all we know for sure is that Helen Gabrys left the boat by some means so far unascertained, and the boat was deliberately sunk by person or persons unknown. We don't know who was on the boat, where Mrs Gabrys is, or what happened to the tender.'

'You've got it,' agreed Ned.

***

Jim was sitting in the corridor, ear glued to his mobile phone, when Chris arrived at the Norfolk and Norwich Hospital. He looked up as she cantered down the corridor towards him, slopping coffee out of the two cups balanced on her iPad.

'Whoops,' she said, sitting down on the next chair to his, a precise two metres further down the wall. 'Here's yours. Sorry, I spilled a bit on the way.'

'So I noticed,' said Jim, observing the brown trickle staining the corridor floor. 'I don't suppose you have a bacon butty tucked into your pocket?'

'Sorry, no,' said Chris. 'But I do have a couple of these.' She produced two KitKats from her shoulder bag.

'Better than nothing,' agreed Jim. 'I gather congratulations are in order,' he added, biting into his chocolate bar.

'That was quick,' observed Chris. 'Even for you. Go on, tell me how you know. I know you're dying to.'

'The Suffolk Police secretary at Lowestoft happens to be going out with my cleaning lady's brother-in-law, who also works for us in the carpool. Easy,' he said with a grin. 'Seriously, well done, Chris. It's well deserved, but we're really going to miss you.' He was interrupted by an exhausted-looking doctor emerging from the door across the corridor.

'You can go in now,' he said to Jim, addressing him from several feet away. 'And the sooner you can take her into custody, if that's what you plan, the better for all of us. We can't afford a bed for someone with nothing worse than a broken ankle.'

'We don't want to leave her here any longer than we have to, not least because we don't want to import Covid into our cells!'

'Quite,' said the doctor, rubbing his hand over his face before replacing his mask. 'She's clear at the moment, so get her out of here asap is my recommendation.'

Jim nodded and picked up his coffee. 'Ready?' he asked Chris, and they went into the small private room opposite.

Chris recognised Helen Gabrys from their last meeting, when she had given evidence in court against her father, Constantin, but was surprised at how much she had changed. She looked ten years older, with a thin face and shadows under her eyes. Admittedly, having her hair scraped back in an unbecoming ponytail was doing her no favours, but even so! She was resting on the bed with a plastered ankle raised on a pillow.

'Helen, you may remember me,' began Jim. 'I'm Detective Inspector Jim Henning and this is Detective Sergeant Chris Mathews. How are you feeling?'

'Rough,' said Helen, pulling herself up a little against her pillows. 'How soon can I get out of here?'

'We'll come to that,' said Jim. 'In the meantime, I need to interview you under caution. Helen Gabrys, you do not have to say anything...' As he went through the familiar words, Chris was watching Helen. She had closed her eyes, and her fingers were fiddling with the fabric of her hospital gown.

'Yes, I understand,' she said in answer to Jim's question. 'What now?'

'First, can you explain to us what went on last night in Barton Broad?'

'Starting when?' she asked.

'How about you start with why you went there in the first place,' replied Jim.

'I had a phone call in the afternoon that frightened me. It was a threat, and whoever it was said they knew where I was, at Rivers Edge Marina. It seemed a good idea to move our boat from there, at least temporarily.'

'Who made the threat?' asked Jim.

'I don't know. It was a man's voice, that's all I can tell you.'

'Any distinguishing accent?' asked Jim.

'Very slightly east European, I would say. But very slight.'

'High pitch or low?' chipped in Chris.

'Just average, I guess.'

'What precisely was the threat?'

'I don't really remember. Something vague about making me pay, or else. Sorry, it feels like a lot has happened since then.'

'So, you upped sticks and moved *The Jolly Jane* from Stalham to Barton Broad. Who was on board?'

'Myself and my mother. Have you found her?' asked Helen.

Jim didn't answer. 'Did you go there directly?' he asked.

'Yes.'

'The hospital told me my mother couldn't come here to see me. No visitors they said. Do you know where she is?'

For the first time, Chris felt something wasn't ringing true in Helen's voice. Nor was she meeting their eyes. Her focus seemed to be on her hands, and their restlessness seemed to be increasing.

'Why did you leave *The Jolly Jane* last night?' asked Jim, changing tack.

'I got another phone call, and this time he said they were close. I thought I'd better leave the boat and draw the danger away from my mother.' The hands stopped moving and the knuckles whitened.

She's lying, thought Chris.

'How did you get ashore?' asked Jim.

'In the tender.'

'And why didn't you take your mother with you?'

'She's not good in small boats, and, as I said, I thought she'd be safer away from me.'

The fingers clenched still harder, the white knuckles showing clear.

'I'm sorry to have to tell you,' said Jim, 'that when we found her, *The Jolly Jane* had sunk at her mooring. Or to be more accurate, had been sunk at her mooring. There was no one else on board and the tender is missing. Is there any reason why whoever threatened you would have taken your mother?' Helen swallowed as though trying to deal with a giant lump in her throat.

'I don't know,' she said. 'I don't know. How could I know?' Slow tears were trickling down her face.

'Perhaps now you'd like to tell us exactly what has been happening since you left Horses Mill House?' As Helen remained silent Jim added, 'You obviously left the boat in a hurry. You were inappropriately dressed for a cold evening crossing a marsh. Moreover, your mother and the boat's tender have disappeared. Come on, Helen. Whatever else you've been up to, you've been the victim of a crime, and your mother would seem to have been kidnapped, if not worse. Time to come clean.'

Another long pause, then Helen took a deep breath, sighed, and looked Jim in the eyes.

'I'll talk,' she said. 'But I want a lawyer present.'

28

Sunday evening

By Sunday evening, Greg was beginning to feel that some of his ducks, if not yet exactly in a row, were now nicely grouped in an orderly flock. With the hospital on the verge of tipping Helen Gabrys onto the street and no other option presenting itself, he had stretched a point and authorised Jim to take her into protective custody. She was now safely, in every sense of the word, tucked away in one of their cells and, if anything, seemed relieved to be there. A solicitor had been identified and booked to arrive in the morning to see Helen, so he had reasonable confidence that he would be able to interview her under caution before lunchtime Monday.

The source and route of the leaks from Norfolk police had been found, stopped and charged.

According to Hinchingbrooke Hospital his father was improving and would probably be discharged within days.

He just wished he knew what had happened to Mrs Gabrys. So far, an assiduous search of Barton Broad and the Ant had revealed exactly nothing. The frustrated Broadsbeat team had now widened their search to embrace the Bure and the Thurne, but so far made no progress.

All in all, he'd had worse Sundays, and he was looking forward to a peaceful evening with Chris and their menagerie. He turned on the TV in time to catch a repeat of the depressing Covid update and sipped his wine with his wellbeing relatively undented.

Hearing Chris's car pull up in the drive with the usual scatter of gravel, he leaned forwards to pour a second glass of wine just as the landline rang. He picked it up and announced his name, nodding to Chris and waving at the glass of wine as he did so.

She sat down beside him, joined by both Bobby and Tally, as a strange voice announced in a cut-glass accent, 'Detective Chief Inspector Geldard? I am Lady Grace. I'm afraid I have some bad news about your mother.'

'My mother?' he asked, putting his wine glass down with a presentiment of disaster.

'Yes. Both your parents were staying with us last weekend when your father was taken ill. I'm afraid your mother has now gone down with this virus too, and has just been taken to Hinchingbrooke Hospital.' There was a slightly aggrieved tone in the voice which implied that falling ill during a pandemic was at the least a breach of etiquette, if not downright middle class.

'Do you know which ward she was taken to?' asked Greg.

'I'm afraid not. The paramedics did seem quite concerned about her breathing when they put her in the ambulance.'

Questions such as *How long has she been ill?* rose in his mind and were as swiftly dismissed. He had a sense that he'd learned all he was going to. 'Thank you for letting me know,' he said formally, and rang off.

'Your mother's got it too?' said Chris.

'Yes.' Greg had looked up Hinchingbrooke on his mobile and rung the number. He had a long wait before someone answered.

'Just a moment, while I look up our records for you,' said the weary voice on the other end of the line. A pause, and then the voice said, 'I'm sorry to say that Mrs Geldard has been admitted to the high-dependency unit. I'll put you through if I can, but you may need to try again later. The staff there are very busy.'

After another long wait with irritating electronic music occupying the line, another voice said, 'High-dependency unit. How may I help?'

Greg explained again, and this time there was a shorter pause, before the voice said, 'I'm going to pass you over to one of our doctors.'

The third voice also sounded tired and wasted no time getting to the point. 'I'm afraid that Mrs Geldard is very ill. We've had to place her into an induced coma and intubate her. The next few hours will be crucial.'

'Does your "no visitors" policy still apply,' asked Greg with little hope.

'Yes, it does, I'm afraid. We simply can't risk any further exposure to this virus.'

'My father already has it and is also a patient in your hospital,' said Greg. 'Has he been told, and can he see her?'

'I will ask the nurses to see to it,' said the doctor, rather ambiguously as Greg later realised.

He put the phone down and looked at Chris. 'It's not sounding very good,' he said. 'She's in the HDU and in a coma. I'm not even sure if my father knows.'

Chris took his hand. 'I'm sorry,' she said. 'What can I do?'

'Nothing. Nothing either of us can do, that's what's so frustrating. I'll ring and ask if I can speak to my father.'

This time, he couldn't get through to the relevant ward at all, and calls to his father's mobile phone went straight to the answering service.

'Probably turned off or out of battery,' Chris reassured him. 'Don't assume it's sinister. Those poor devils at the hospital must be rushed off their feet. Try again in the morning.'

29

School at home – 23 March 2020

Monday brought their first attempt at schoolwork online. Karen tried her best to stay connected on her mother's old phone, but it was hard. She kept finding that when the signal strength dropped she would be logged out and by the time she got connected again, she'd missed stuff. She looked longingly at the family laptop, but her father was using it for gaming. She opened her mouth to ask if she could use it for school, but her mum shook her head warningly, and Karen gave up on that idea. At least if her father was gaming, he wasn't bothering Jake.

In the end she settled down at the kitchen table with the workbook Miss Grain had given them all, and tried to work through some exercises. Even there she wasn't left in peace for long. Her mother started chopping veg at the other end of the table and the onions made her eyes water, while Jake was playing formula one with his toy cars under the table and making engine noises all the time.

'Don't you have work to do too,' her mum asked Jake after a while. He interrupted the revving sounds for long enough to say no, then carried on.

'He's lying,' said Karen. 'Everyone has work to do. He just isn't doing it.' She waited for her mum to insist on the schoolwork, but she said nothing. 'You have to make him,' said Karen in the end. 'Otherwise he'll get left behind.'

'Rubbish,' her father said, interrupting his game for a moment. 'It's all rubbish anyway. I've never used anything I learned at school.'

You didn't learn anything, Karen wanted to say. *And if you had learned something, maybe you'd have a better job now.* But she knew better than to speak up.

'Come on, Jake,' she said. 'Come upstairs with me and let's see what you've got in your school bag.'

'It's cold up there,' whined Jake.

'We can sit on my bed, under the duvet,' said Karen. 'Come on.'

Once upstairs and snuggled under the quilt, she found some books in the old shoulder bag Jake used for school.

'Look,' she said, 'we can read this together. This is fun.'

'Reading's no fun,' grumbled Jake.

'Yes, it is. Look, it's all about a naughty dog and his friends.' And she started to read the story aloud, pointing at the words as she'd seen teachers do. After a bit, Jake got interested in the story, but he wouldn't look at the words. From downstairs came a crash and loud voices. Karen sighed and kept on reading.

30

Not a good start

Monday did not start well. Greg cut himself shaving, and went down for his breakfast muttering about growing a beard. Chris took no notice and put a plate of toast in front of him.

'No milk, so no cereal,' she said.

'Thanks,' he muttered, trying to eat toast and ring the hospital for the third time that morning. After a few moments hanging on, he rang off irritably and swallowed the last of his toast. 'You coming in with me?' he asked, when he was interrupted by another phone call. When he rang off, he looked energised. 'Broadsbeat think they've found the tender.'

'Where?'

'Horning of all places. Not far from the Swan Inn. They're currently trying to knock up the landlord to see if they have any CCTV footage that might be useful. I'm going to get myself over there.'

'I thought I'd go straight into the office and make sure everything's ready for Ella Pentney's appearance in front of the magistrates. Do you want me for the interview with Helen Gabrys?'

'I'll check with Jim and get back to you. See you later, Chris.' Greg kissed her then ran out to his car, flinging his bag onto the back seat even as he rang the hospital again. He was put through to his father's ward after another long wait. His father sounded hoarse and was audibly wheezing, but claimed he was making good progress.

'Have you been able to see Mother?' asked Greg, navigating the roundabout near Acle with exaggerated care. Given how the day had started, he didn't need any more disasters.

'No. They won't let me leave the ward, but they did tell me she was still intubated.'

'Okay. Look Dad, I've got a busy day ahead, but I'll catch up with you later and see if they'll tell us any more then. Stay strong.'

'Same to you,' said his father, and rang off.

As ever when following the circuitous routes necessary in Norfolk to get around rivers and Broads, Greg found himself wishing the county had just a little less water. There wasn't any straight route from Acle to Horning, except by river. There was also a distinctly patchy mobile-phone service, which did not help him get hold of Ned. In all, he was a little hot and bothered by the time he parked, illegally, in front of the Swan Inn and behind the blue flashing lights of a liveried police car. A small crowd was starting to gather behind the crime-scene tape strung along the bank, albeit much smaller than would have been the case pre Covid.

Two uniformed officers were standing near what Greg could now see was a small inflatable, moored stern on to the bank.

'Morning,' he said. 'DCI Geldard. What have we here?'

'Sergeant Yelling,' replied the taller of the two. 'Your tender, I believe.' He looked rightly pleased with himself but added, 'The credit goes to the sharp eyes of Constable Jones here,' indicating the younger man beside him still wearing his lifejacket. 'He spotted the dinghy from our patrol boat.'

'How do you know it's the one we're looking for?' asked Greg, slightly dubiously.

'Well, we don't know for sure until the forensic team have been over it,' replied Constable Jones, 'but it's got *The Jolly Jane*'s registration mark on it.'

'Good answer! Bright as well as sharp-eyed,' Greg complimented him, but was interrupted by a burly man approaching from the pub behind him.

'Hey,' he shouted from beyond the crime-scene tape. 'I believe you've been looking for me? I'm landlord of the Inn.'

Moments later, Tom Harris, as he introduced himself, was wielding a huge bunch of keys to unlock the front door of the silent pub. 'Just let me turn the alarm off,' he said, over a loud beeping noise, to the officers standing behind him, and went to a small office near the entrance. The beeps fell silent and Tom, shedding a heavy jacket to reveal a navy fleece and polo shirt, beckoned them to follow him into the small room. 'The video recordings are in here too,' he said. 'What do you want to see?'

As he spoke, Greg's phone rang and he saw Ned pull up near the riverbank. 'Good, Forensic Science are here,' he said aloud as he turned his phone to silent. 'Right. The CCTV. The time we're most interested in is from Friday morning, and ideally we'd like to see the arrival of the dinghy on the mooring out there.'

'I doubt you'll see much of the boat,' replied Tom, busy with the controls of the video. 'She's a bit small to be caught on the one camera we have facing that way. You're more likely to see people on the bank than a small dinghy below it. But let's have a look.' He waved to Greg to sit beside him in front of the monitor. Constable Jones stood behind, while Sergeant Yelling muttered something and went out for a word with Ned.

Numbers flashed on the monitor as Tom wound the recording back, then started playing the images caught from the early morning of the 20th of March. Greg immediately saw that the landlord was right. That camera caught people moving on the bank – rather fewer than usual because of the pandemic – and the river from the centre to the far bank, but not the area of water closest to them. That was obscured by the slope of the bank. He was about to ask Tom to fast forward between glimpses of people, when Constable Jones shot an arm towards the screen and pointed.

'There! Look there!' he exclaimed. 'Isn't that *The Jolly Jane*?'

Greg peered but the image had already been fast forwarded. 'Go back,' he urged.

In a moment, Tom had wound back again, then froze the picture.

'It is,' asserted the young constable.

'It certainly is,' agreed Greg. 'Even I can recognise that superstructure. Forwards slowly, please,' he said to Tom.

In silence they watched as two figures got into *The Jolly Jane*'s tender and it was rowed across the river. They couldn't see it reaching the near bank, but they did see a smudgy figure that looked like Helen Gabrys help a second woman out of the dinghy and onto the riverbank. Then they both disappeared out of shot, walking towards the main village car park. Some five minutes or so later, Helen reappeared, this time alone, retrieved a bag from the dinghy and again disappeared out of shot.

'That's interesting,' murmured Greg. 'Now fast forward until *The Jolly Jane* disappears. We know she went to Barton Broad that afternoon or evening.'

The three of them watched the flashing images in silence, until the mooring on the other side of the river was suddenly vacant. A few moments fiddling forward and back, and they spotted the exact time when one figure boarded *The Jolly Jane* and cast her off, before turning downriver towards its junction with the Ant and the route to Barton Broad. Tom froze the picture at the moment when the cruiser was boarded.

'12.09 precisely,' he said. The sharp-eyed constable pointed again.

'Isn't that a taxi on the bank near *The Jolly Jane*?' he asked.

'I'd been wondering how she got back to the cruiser if she didn't use the tender,' said Greg. 'I take it there's a road near the mooring on that side too?'

'Yes,' said Tom and the constable together, and Tom added, 'If she got the taxi out the front, our other camera might have caught it.'

'Better and better,' said Greg, then caught a glimpse of the clock. 'I need to be getting back to Wymondham. Can I take these recordings and those from your other camera with me?'

Returning to his car, complete with recordings, he paused to bring Ned up to date and put his phone back on. It rang almost immediately.

'Hinchingbrooke Hospital HDU,' said an unknown voice. 'Is that Mr Greg Geldard?'

'DCI Geldard,' said Greg, not so much because of pedantry but rather to postpone, with his correction, what he guessed was coming.

'I'm very sorry to have to tell you, DCI Geldard, that your mother died just over an hour ago. Your father has been told, but we have had some difficulty getting hold of you.'

31

Back in Wymondham – same day

The first thing Greg did on arrival at Wymondham was to dump the recordings on Jill's desk and explain what she was looking for.

'I've got some uniforms looking round Horning to see if they can find out where Mrs Gabrys went, just in case you don't see her getting into a taxi as well. Thing is,' he added, 'with most places closed because of Covid, it's hard to see where she could have gone.'

'Have you asked anyone to check with the hospitals, or should we launch a missing person enquiry?' asked Jill. 'I think she could be said to be vulnerable.'

Greg smacked himself in the head. 'Of course. Sorry, I've got too much to think about it seems, and I'm missing the obvious. Truth is, I've just been told my mother has died of Covid.'

Jill looked up, aghast. 'Oh my God, I'm so sorry, Boss. Should you be here? Shouldn't you be taking some time off?'

'It's okay. I mean, it's not, of course, but I'm okay, and I'd rather be at work.' He looked round and saw Bill. 'Can you check with the hospitals Bill, as a first step?' he asked. Then went to find Chris.

'I came in here, partly because I didn't know what else to do,' Greg told Chris. 'All the normal things you'd do in these circumstances – visit my mother in the hospital chapel, sit with my father, start arranging the funeral – it seems I can't do any of that. Dad is still too ill to be moved, and I can't visit. Mother's body will go to an undertaker, and any funeral arrangements will probably have to be made by phone or on the internet. At some point, hopefully, Dad will need to come out of hospital and into some sort of care facility. I doubt he'll be well enough to look after himself, even in the best-case scenario. In the meantime, Mother's probable executor is out of commission, and I don't know who else can step in. In short, there's lots I don't know but, for now, I'm needed here and here I at least know what to do.'

'How about I make some phone calls,' suggested Chris. 'I can at least find out what's possible and what's not. And I can organise a funeral director, if you'd like. The one my family use have a branch in Cambridge, I think. Would you like me to sort that? And do you know who your parents' solicitors are?'

'Yes, please. I imagine I'll need to talk to the funeral director at some point, but if you could get it set up, that would be great. As for the family solicitor, they always used a firm in Muswell Hill. You'll find it in my contacts list on my iPad.'

'Leave it with me,' said Chris. 'I'll find out what your options are, and you can concentrate on Helen Gabrys.'

By the time Helen had met with her solicitor, it was lunchtime.

'How about we send some sandwiches in, and start the interview at one?' Jim suggested. 'People don't get any more amenable for being hungry.'

'Fine with me,' said Greg. 'Gives us chance to go over what we think we know and agree tactics. I also want to check with the CPS precisely what we can charge her with.' They retired to Greg's office, where they were joined by some packs of sandwiches and Frank Parker of the CPS.

'I've been looking at what you have on her so far. As a starting point, I think you can run with conspiracy to commit blackmail and conspiracy to commit murder. Expect her brief to argue that Tyson was only told to cut Nathan Standish and therefore that is, at worst, conspiracy to commit GBH. I'd like to say charge her with supply of controlled drugs as well, but at the moment you only have the link to her brother, Mica. Am I right?

'As to her mother, there's nothing illegal about taking your mother for a boat trip then dropping her off in Horning, even if you do lie about it. The question is, what happened to Mrs Gabrys after that?'

'And that we don't yet know. I have every intention of asking Helen what she did with her mother and why she lied about her being on *The Jolly Jane* in Barton Broad. As to the other charges, it's true we don't yet have any evidence of her being in possession of controlled drugs,' said Greg. 'We didn't find anything on the boat, but then I wouldn't expect to. If she has got into the old family business, I'd expect that to be run from a house in Yarmouth or a lock-up of some kind. Jim has people out looking as we speak. To be honest, I'm pinning my hopes on this interview. The Helen Gabrys I met last year didn't look like a prime candidate for organised crime. I think she's got sucked into something she never intended and may be looking for a way out. And that's how I plan to run the interview.'

'And if she isn't amenable?' asked Frank.

'Then we probably have to let her go and keep plugging away until we find more evidence. But I think all this has shaken her. Let's go see, shall we?'

Over in a quiet corner of the main office, Chris had been having a frustrating hour. Every time she thought she was making progress, she ran up against officialdom and its dislike of any enquiries made by 'those without status'. She could understand where they were coming from, but that didn't make it any easier to be on the receiving end. 'Fiancée', it appeared, just didn't cut it either with solicitors or hospitals.

The first, the family solicitors in Muswell Hill, were solicitous but unhelpful.

'If I can just summarise what I think you've told me,' said Chris in a painfully patient tone. 'You do hold a copy of Mrs Geldard's will but you can't tell me what's in it. Her husband is one of her executors, but he, as I have explained to you, is currently unable to perform the role because he is seriously ill in hospital with Covid. The other executor is a member of your firm, but she can't help because she too has Covid. Because *she* was named, rather than your firm, you cannot assist with a different partner. In the circumstances that both executors are unable or unwilling to perform their duties, the role can be taken by the principal beneficiary. As you won't tell me what's in the will, I can only make an educated guess that is her widower, who, as I've already said, is incapacitated. The words *Catch 22* do come to mind!' She breathed heavily for a moment, then added, 'So what do you advise the son of the marriage, DCI Geldard, to do?'

After a few moments' squawking from the phone, she said, 'So in essence, you're suggesting that he waits until his father dies, at which point he would be the main beneficiary of his estate; or gets better, at which point he can take instruction from him and help him apply for probate with regard to his mother's estate. Well, I suppose that's clear, if a little stark. Thank you.'

She looked up just in time to catch Jill's sympathetic eye.

'No easy solution?' she asked.

'No. But on the other hand, no desperate rush to act either. Perhaps it's no bad thing if it's all put on the back burner until the Gabrys case is resolved.' She looked at Jill a bit harder and added, 'You don't look particularly happy either. Have you got a problem?'

'Just had a call from my partner, Diana,' said Jill. 'It's probably nothing, but she's bothered about some of her pupils and how they're coping with lockdown. One of them has to share a laptop with two siblings and is missing classes as a result. Another looks as though they've been in a scrap, and she's concerned about abuse, while a third, normally really keen on school, has only logged in once, very briefly. And that's just on day one. She's really concerned about how she's going to monitor welfare.'

'It bothers me too,' said Chris. 'It's hard enough to keep abreast of domestic cases under normal circumstances. Under a lockdown, it's going to be next to impossible. I assume she'll report her safeguarding concerns to the headteacher or the local council, but tell her to let us know if she gets really worried, and we'll have to do our best to help.'

'Will do,' said Jill, turning back to her twin screens. 'But for now, I need a closer look at the material I got on the Gabrys bank accounts.'

32

Proceeds of crime

When Greg and Jim went into the interview room, the table was littered with all the signs that the sandwich lunch had been appreciated. Crumpled wrappers, crumbs and a stray slice or two of cucumber were scattered about. Jim picked up the waste basket and swept the detritus into it as Greg sat down and primed the recording equipment.

'Interview under caution with Helen Gabrys, at 13.45, 23rd of March 2020. Present in the room are Detective Chief Inspector Geldard, Detective Inspector Henning, Helen Gabrys and...' He raised a quizzical eyebrow at the dark-suited solicitor.

'Jeremy Wallis of Lacon and Kivell, Norwich.'

'Thank you,' replied Greg, and he administered the caution then sat back and looked hard at Helen Gabrys.

She was pale, her short, wavy hair brushed but unstyled, and her face free of make-up. She was now wearing a dark blue shirt over denims and a fleece the colour of sour cream. Greg wondered where the clothes had come from. *Her solicitor perhaps?* Her hands now were still and relaxed in her lap and she was sitting back in her chair, not leaning nervously forwards. *Very calm,* he thought. *Very composed. I wonder what's changed?*

The silence had run on for some moments. Jim waited quietly and Helen seemed unmoved, but Mr Wallis was more impatient.

'I assume you have some questions for my client,' he charged in. 'But before we begin, we have a question for you.'

A slight frown appeared on Helen's brow, and Greg wondered if she would have preferred a different approach or, left to herself, she would have waited for Greg to break the silence. He chose to ignore the solicitor and addressed himself to Helen.

'When we met last year,' he said in a measured tone, 'I never expected to be facing you like this. I thought you were the sane one, Helen. The honest one.'

'Circumstances change cases,' she said. 'The question Mr Wallis is so keen to ask you is, can you provide me with witness protection?' The question was not wholly unexpected.

Greg regarded her in silence for a long minute. Long enough that Mr Wallis was shifting in his seat again. 'That would depend on the information you can give us,' he replied. 'If it's sufficiently valuable, and if you are fully prepared to comply with the terms, then it's possible. I would need to take advice. But you should be aware, it's not a soft option. Starting a new life with a new identity and no contact with the old life – that's not easy.'

'Living my old life isn't easy either,' she replied. 'I'll be straight with you, DCI Geldard. I didn't expect to find myself here either. I thought I was better than the rest of my family.

Smarter and more honest. But forced into a corner, I found I responded in exactly the same way. Sadly, the moral high ground is as foreign to me as to them.'

'What corner?' asked Greg.

'You really don't know? Tell me, Geldard, what did you think would happen when my mother and I were forced out of our home, forced to sell the house, the cars, the horses, the boat, and left with nothing? How did you think my mother would react, after being looked after and cosseted all her life? Well, I'll tell you. She looked to me. She dumped everything in my lap and waited for me to solve all the problems, to deal with the demands for money, to find us somewhere to live and to carry on looking after her.

'Then, after the official demands were met, after all the "proceeds of crime" had been collected, the other demands began. The ones from my father's old associates. The ones who said he owed them money and if I didn't find a way to pay them, either with cash or with help, we'd both regret it.' Her voice was starting to rise a little now. 'And believe me, I knew all too well just how much we'd regret disappointing them. So, what would you do in those circumstances, Geldard? You needn't answer, but I'll tell you what I did, and perhaps you wouldn't have been so very different. I started small. I hoped that if I helped them with something minor, something that wouldn't do too much harm, then maybe they'd leave me alone and I could start to rebuild my life. That's when I discovered I could be stupid too. Stupidly hopeful. Because of course, once you give way to these people, you're in and there's no way out.'

She stopped, and reached for her paper cup of water. Greg noticed that despite her apparent control, her hand shook, just a little, as she put the cup down.

'So, what exactly are you offering?' asked Greg, determined to hide his underlying sense of sympathy.

Helen sighed. 'I'm offering all the information I have on my father's associates. I'm offering to spell out for you the routes that money takes, the locations of drug factories and storage, the network of county lines and the businesses that launder the cash. But only if I get a fresh start. I have no reason to want to stay connected with anyone from my old life. In fact, the further I can get from my father, the better. I want a chance to be the Helen I could have been if I'd been born into a different family, even if that means a new name and a new career.'

'Do you have that information?' asked Jim sceptically. 'More than we already know, I mean.'

'There's lots you don't know,' said Helen. 'If you did, I wouldn't have been able to pick up where my brother and father left off.'

Jim and Greg exchanged glances, then Greg started shuffling his paperwork together.

'Okay, you've almost convinced me you have a reasonable argument,' he said. 'But only almost.' He paused and looked at Helen, long and hard. 'I might have been convinced, just for one unfortunate discrepancy. Unfortunate from your point of view, that is.' Wallis opened his mouth but Greg talked over him. 'You see, we have hard evidence that a lot of what you've told us is a lie. We know your mother wasn't on *The Jolly Jane* last night. We know you didn't go straight from Stalham to Barton Broad. We have *The Jolly Jane,* clearly on CCTV, moored opposite the inn in Horning on Friday morning. We have you, also on CCTV, taking your mother across the river in *The Jolly Jane*'s tender, escorting her up the bank and round the side of the inn towards the village.

'My forensic team have been over the tender with enormous care. Whose fingerprints and DNA do you think they will find on the dinghy and its oars?'

Wallis rallied his forces. 'And if you think my client took the tender across the river, how do you imagine she got back to the cruiser without it?' he asked.

'I'm glad you asked me that,' said Greg. 'Although I am reminded of the old advice that an advocate should never ask a question to which he doesn't know the answer. Because, you see, we not only have your client on CCTV getting into a taxi outside the inn, but we have the same taxi turning up a little later on the other side of the river and dropping your client off by her cruiser. And before you tell me that the CCTV can't be that good, we also have the taxi driver.'

Another long pause, which Greg interrupted by asking quietly, 'Where is your mother now, Helen?'

'I don't know,' she said.

And Wallis, pulling his wits together, pronounced, 'I wish to speak to my client, alone.'

'Interview suspended at,' – Greg looked at the clock on the wall – '14.12. We'll be back,' he said, and the two detectives left the room.

Jim opened his mouth as soon as the door closed behind them, but Greg stopped him. 'Not here. Come to my office,' he said, 'and we'll collect Chris and Jill on the way.'

Sitting in Greg's office with the window open wide but the door firmly closed, both women were agog to know what had gone on. Greg outlined what they had learned so far, then added, 'This stays between the four of us. If there is a chance of getting some useful intelligence from Helen in exchange for witness protection, then we need to keep this tight.

'I'm going to have a chat with Margaret now and, assuming I have her agreement, I'll talk to the Protected Persons Service.'

'What about Mrs Gabrys?' asked Chris. 'We have no idea yet whether she's been kidnapped, or just got out of the way by Helen. She may even have gone on holiday! Surely we need to know what's happened to her before we take anything Helen says at face value.'

'Ideally, yes,' replied Greg. 'It's my view that we need to be able to test everything she says to us against what we know already or can find out independently. I believe she wants a fresh start. I'm just very doubtful of what she's offering in payment, especially after the lies so far.

'We'll restart the interview tomorrow. That gives you time to go over everything we've learned already, and maybe Bill will come up with something too. I agree, she's a smart cookie and we don't take anything at face value. We cross-check everything she tells us.

'Jill, you cover banks and bank accounts. Jim, drugs and county lines. Chris, chase Ned for an update on *The Jolly Jane* and her tender and what Forensics can tell us about the events of the weekend. Okay, everyone? See you back here just before four.'

Margaret was in a Zoom meeting chaired by the Deputy Chief Constable when Greg went looking for her. One look at the short note he put in front of her, and she made her excuses, muted her mike and rose from her seat.

'This better be good,' she said. 'He carries a grudge that one, and I'm not his favourite person as it is.'

Mindful of the porosity to sound of the door into the secretary's room, he kept his voice down as he spelled out what Helen Gabrys had said.

'Do I have your go ahead?' he asked.

'It's a qualified yes,' she replied slowly. 'This could be the breakthrough we've needed, but I think she'll try to hold back as much as she can.'

'I thought that too,' said Greg. 'We can put her in a safe house for now, but I'll be clear that a full new identity etc will be dependent on us being satisfied we're getting the full story. And we'll check everything, I promise you.'

'I know you will. Thanks, Greg. Go ahead then. Sorry, I should have asked... How's your father doing?'

Greg realised immediately that the news of his mother's death had not yet reached Margaret. 'Father's improving a bit,' he said, and made haste to leave the room.

33

Lockdown impacts – Tuesday 24 March 2020

Over in Great Yarmouth, Jill's partner, Diana, was scuttling from street to street, trying to catch up with pupils now studying from home. Most of her class had shown up on Zoom, and she was reasonably happy not only that *they* knew what they were doing, but that *she* knew what they were doing too. But there were a few, maybe eight to ten, whom she worried about. After dithering about for the best part of an hour, she had decided that safeguarding was a justifiable reason for travelling, and got into her car.

The main problem, she very rapidly discovered, was discouraging excited children from rushing up to her. After taking refuge behind her car at the first two houses, she developed a methodology that allowed her to talk to the parents and children from a safe distance.

At the home of the boy who was sharing a laptop with his siblings, she dropped off an ancient iPad and charger. It was so old it had one of the old-style chargers, but it still worked and would do for homework and Zoom calls. Further across town, the child with the bruises had come to the door and seemed reasonably happy. She herself was not entirely happy with the mother's explanation and the father seemed needlessly antagonistic. She made a note to keep an eye on developments and to report it to her headteacher if a problem seemed to be developing.

The one home at which she failed altogether was that of Karen, the school enthusiast who had struggled to stay logged on. Her mother came to the door, but stood back in its shadow, her face hidden in the gloom of the unlit passageway. There was no sign of Karen. From the far side of the pavement, Diana explained.

'I was worried when Karen didn't join the class. I thought I'd better check that she was okay and there were no problems with IT or wi-fi that I could help with.' As she spoke, a small boy appeared behind his mother and pushed to the fore.

'Karen's in bed,' he announced. 'She's being naughty. She—'

His mother pushed him behind her skirts. 'Hush, Jake,' she said. 'You are talking rubbish.' She looked up again at Diana and said, with a slightly forced smile, 'Karen's just not very well today. I think perhaps she's eaten something that's disagreed with her. She will be in the class tomorrow, I'm sure.'

'I'm sorry to hear she's not well,' said Diana. 'It's not Covid is it? I believe that can cause stomach upsets too.' She was talking to hide her immediate thoughts, which were that Karen's mother had the beginnings of a very nasty black eye. And if she was getting knocked about, what had happened to Karen?

'I don't think so,' said her mother. 'She has no coughs or cold. I'm sure she'll be fine soon.'

'Well, I hope I see her online tomorrow,' said Diana. 'If not, I'll need to report it. Would another iPad help? I know it can be difficult when there is more than one child trying to access lessons.'

Unseen by either woman, Kit had come up behind his wife. Now he pushed forwards. 'We don't need charity,' he said.

'It's not charity,' said Diana quickly. 'Your children are entitled to school lessons and if online is the only way, then they need the tools to access them.' She rummaged in her capacious tote and pulled out a slightly battered iPad and lead. 'It will probably need charging up,' she said. 'I'll look forward to seeing Karen tomorrow.'

At the window upstairs, unseen by Diana, Karen turned away and slid down to sit on the floor. Tears came to her eyes. *I wish it was Covid*, she thought. *I wish I was really ill. I could go to hospital if it was Covid.* She remembered the non-stop rows of the evening before. The shouting, the broken crockery, the threats to her mum that, in the end, had sent her running upstairs to take refuge in her bedroom.

And she would have cried some more, except she seemed to be running out of tears. The ones in her eyes stayed there, fogging her sight.

34

Tuesday 24 March –
picking up the threads

After a frustrating evening of no news from anywhere, Greg intended to start the new day by sorting everything out. Back in Wymondham, he had his hand on the phone to ring the hospital, the solicitor, the funeral director – but he took it away without ringing any of them.

'I'm a coward,' he said aloud, 'clinging to what I can control rather than dealing with what I can't.'

Chris had come into his office behind him, without him noticing. 'No, you're not,' she said briskly. 'You're focussing on where you can make a difference, rather than wasting time on stuff you can do nothing about. That's good sense, not cowardice.'

'Even if it plays to my preferences,' he asked with a wry smile.

'Even then. The fact you'd rather do the right thing than the expected thing is more evidence of courage than the opposite.'

'I think you're making excuses for me – very effectively, admittedly,' he said, but his heart felt lighter nonetheless. 'In that case, I'll ring and ask about my father, then I'll prepare for the next interview with Helen Gabrys.'

'Good,' she said, and would have said more, when Bill burst in through the door.

'Sorry to interrupt,' he said, 'but I've found Mrs Gabrys. She's at the Norfolk and Norwich. She was found wandering around Horning, no idea where she was nor why. Some Good Samaritan called an ambulance and she was taken to the N&N for assessment, but it seems that, in the judgement of the paramedics, she's suffering from dementia and will need care in a specialist home.'

There was a long silence.

'Well, well, well,' said Greg reflectively. 'That *is* very interesting, Bill. Chris, can you and Bill get over there and see how much you can get out of Mrs Gabrys that might be usable in interview, even if it's useless in court? I'll have a chat with Jim and Jill, then we'll get started. Get a message through to me as soon as you have anything.'

A night in the cells hadn't changed Helen's appearance for the better. Her hair looked flatter and danker, her complexion paler and her clothes were the same as yesterday's. Mr Wallis, by contrast, looked well-rested, freshly shaved, and recently breakfasted. The preliminaries out of the way, Greg sat back and let Jim start the questioning.

'Yesterday,' said Jim, 'you offered us information on sites involved with drug production and distribution, money laundering, bank accounts and recent associates of your father's. Let's start with the drug production.'

'Where do you want me to begin?' asked Helen.

'A list of addresses would be a good place,' replied Jim, and poised his fingers over his laptop.

Helen took a deep breath. 'I know some addresses; others, I can point to the locations on a map.'

'I have a map,' said Jill, and placed a detailed map of Great Yarmouth on the table before them. 'You give me the first addresses and I'll mark them on here. Anywhere you're not sure of the details, you point, and I'll mark those too.'

It didn't take long. Helen gave three detailed addresses, including the one from which a police team had rescued their colleague, Sarah Laurence, the previous year, then pointed to two more. No one made any comments as the few red dots accumulated on the map.

'Okay,' said Jim. 'That's a start. Now bank details.'

'I don't have those memorised. For those I need my phone,' said Helen.

'If they're on your phone, then we already have them,' remarked Jill.

'Yes, but they're in a personal code,' said Helen. 'I'll give them to you if you bring me my phone.'

Jill looked at Greg, who nodded, then she produced the phone in an evidence bag from the tote at her feet.

'I thought you might need it,' she said. 'Here.' And proffered the phone to Helen. She happened to glance at Mr Wallis as she did so. He was scribbling notes but looked rather bored.

'Might we perhaps take a short break?' he asked, noticing Jill looking at him.

'After we have the bank account details,' said Greg.

Helen was flicking through the phone and opened the Notes app. She scrolled through several documents, then paused. 'Here,' she said. And pushed the phone over to Jill. Jill looked at the list of names and addresses, then back at Helen.

'It's quite simple when you know,' she said. 'It's a substitution code. The first six letters of alternate names are the bank sort codes. The first eight of the associated addresses are the account numbers, ignoring any letter past 'J'.'

'Is 'A' zero or one?' asked Jill, catching on quickly.

'Zero,' replied Helen.

'And the account name?'

'The next name in the list.'

'So, for example, the first name in the list: C.A. De Guares has a sort code, 30-45-70, and the account name is,' – she looked down the list – 'Gorleston Enterprises Ltd.'

'That's right.'

'We'll take that break now,' announced Greg, looking at Mr Wallis, who heaved a sigh of relief.

'Before we do,' interrupted Helen, 'have you found my mother yet?'

'I'm still waiting to hear,' said Greg ambiguously, and he led the way out of the room. Wallis headed for the gents at a trot, and Jim for the offices.

'This won't take me above a few minutes,' said Jill, looking at the phone list. 'But I can tell you now—'

'We already know about the first one,' said Jim. 'Yes, I thought I recognised it.'

'Let's take a break ourselves and regroup in half an hour,' said Greg. 'I'll see if Chris has anything for me about Mrs

Gabrys.' *And fit in a call to Hinchingbrooke*, he added to himself.

The call to the hospital was reassuring and worrying in equal measure. His father had improved to the point he could leave, but, on the other hand, was certainly not well enough to go home to an empty house. They recommended a care home.

'Okay,' said Greg. 'Can he travel to Norfolk? If I can find one near me, I would feel better about it.'

He was assured that was possible, and he put the phone down, wondering how he was going to find a care-home place at short notice in the current circumstances.

35

Tuesday afternoon – Great Yarmouth

After things went quiet, Karen waited for her mum to shout them down for lunch. She waited and waited, and after a lot of complaining from Jake about how hungry he was, she led him quietly down the stairs. She listened carefully at the kitchen door and was about to open it as silently as possible, when Jake said in a loud voice, 'Why are we hanging about out here? I want some lunch. I'm hungry.'

Karen whipped round and scowled at him. 'I told you to be quiet, you stupid boy,' she hissed, then heard the door open behind her. Her mum stood in the doorway and summoned up an attempt at a smile.

'Is it that time already?' she said. 'Come on. I'll open a tin of soup and you can have some toast with it.'

'Tomato?' asked Jake hopefully and he went to the cupboard. Karen was looking at her mother, then glanced round the kitchen. She noticed immediately that the kitchen clock was missing and there were some bits of plastic and glass in the dustpan on the floor by the back door.

'The clock's broken,' she said. 'That's why you didn't know what time it was.'

'That's right,' said her mother with another weak smile. 'It fell off the wall.' Karen's eyes had moved to the table and her mother's phone. It had a long crack across the screen.

'Oh no,' said Karen. 'Your phone's broken too. How are we going to log on for school if we can't use your phone?'

'It's still working,' her mum said. 'Don't panic.' She reached over Jake's head for the can of tomato soup, and winced as she stretched up.

'Are you all right, Mum?' asked Karen. 'Are you hurt?'

'I'm fine,' said her mum, and poured the soup into a bowl before placing it in the microwave. 'Lunch will be ready in a tick. Set the table, Karen, and wash your hands, Jake. They're filthy.'

'Where's Dad?' asked Karen. 'I heard…' She stopped, not wanting to say what she'd heard. Somehow, talking about it made it all too real.

'He's gone out,' said her mum, her back turned as she fussed with the soup. Over the ritual complaints from Jake at the sink, Karen heard a knocking at the back door.

'There's someone at the back door,' she said.

'Sit down and eat your soup while it's hot,' said her mum. 'I'll see who it is.' She glanced through the kitchen window, gasped, and hurried to open the door, then closed it behind her.

'What are you doing here?' Karen heard. 'You're mad. He won't be gone long.'

Karen heard Uncle Tim's voice in reply. 'I was worried when you didn't get back to me. I know how he is and—'

Jake piped up in a loud voice, 'Mum forgot to put the bread in the toaster,' and Karen missed the next few words.

'Shush, Jake,' she said, and went to fill the toaster just to keep him quiet. That brought her close to the kitchen window, and, looking out, she saw her Uncle Tim reach out a hand to her mum, just as the yard gate flew open and her father stood in the entrance, his hands on his hips.

Even through the glass she could hear his growl and his face was all screwed up and red. Then he reached down, picked up a piece of fence post that was leaning on the wall, and swung it viciously. Tim stepped forwards to shield her mum, and threw up an arm to deflect the post.

As Karen cried out and Jake asked, 'What's happening, what's the matter?' Uncle Tim fell back against the kitchen door, one arm hanging limply across his chest and blood beginning to trickle from his fingers. Karen saw her father throw the wood to the ground, a nail stained with blood protruding from the end. Her mother seemed to be frozen to the spot.

Jake had joined Karen at the kitchen window, but couldn't see a lot, being much shorter.

'What's happening?' he kept demanding, but Karen ignored him, wholly focussed on the scene in their yard.

'Get out and don't come back, unless you want that round your head next time,' her father said, pointing first at Uncle Tim and then at the post. 'And you...' Now he was pointing at her mum. 'You get in the house. I'll deal with you later.'

By the time Kit came in from the yard, the children had been sent upstairs, out of harm's way. Anne looked at him but kept quiet. He said nothing too. Just walked over to her, quite slowly, and quite deliberately punched her in the stomach. She folded up with fierce gasp, losing all the air in her lungs, and he landed a second punch on her right shoulder. Even as she fought for oxygen, she realised he was trying to avoid leaving marks in visible places. Far from being out of control, this attack was premeditated.

She collapsed to the floor, holding her shoulder, and trying not to pant – trying not to do anything that would provoke more blows.

'How dare you cheat on me,' he said in a whisper that was, if anything, more terrifying than a shout. 'And with that useless wimp. I don't think he'll be back, do you? Why would he risk another beating for a fat, slovenly, stupid, lazy cow like you.' With each word he prodded her chest with a hard finger.

Opening her mouth to deny any involvement with Tim was a mistake. It prompted another punch to her chest, and this time, for a moment, it felt like her heart had stopped. By the time she could breathe again, Kit had stood up and moved away to the fridge to get himself, she assumed, another beer. She seized her chance to stand and make a break for the door and the hall. Whether she was heading for the stairs or the front door, she didn't know and never found out. Throwing his can of beer to the floor, Kit was after her, and catching one arm he swung her round to hit her again. Only this time, the end of the swing brought her head into contact with the large round knob on the top of the newel post. Suddenly there was no noise in the hall except the echo of the crunch of skull and the sound of Kit's breath.

36

Assessing the evidence

Just as the half hour was up, Jill came into Greg's office with a piece of paper at the ready.

'Nothing new here,' she said. 'We knew about all but one of these last year, and the other is the one we found recently thanks to Nathan Standish.'

Jim had come in behind her. 'Nothing new on the drug locations either,' he said. 'Only one was new since last year, and we found that in February when one of our brighter and more observant colleagues noticed that one house in a terrace had no snow on it, while all the rest did, and that it seemed to be a preferred resting place for a large flock of seagulls. It turned out to be leaking a lot of heat through its poorly insulated roof, from a load of lamps creating greenhouse-type conditions on the floors below. In short, it was a grow-house.'

'Let's just have a chat with Chris, then get back to Helen and see if she can do any better with the names of associates,' remarked Greg.

Chris's voice on speaker phone was soon filling the office. 'We've been lucky to catch a word with the paramedics who brought her in,' she said, and after this, I think Bill should pop over to Horning and interview the people who found her and dialled 999. We've tried to speak to Mrs Gabrys, but we've only been allowed a few minutes, then she started to get distressed, or to be more accurate, more distressed. She is very confused. At one point she thought she was at home and confused Bill with her butler. She did keep asking for Helen, but on the other hand, she kept asking for Mica too, and got very upset when we reminded her he was dead. I don't think we're going to get anything useful out of her, but I think there's little doubt she has dementia. I don't think she's a good enough actress to be faking it. What will be interesting is why Helen chose to dump her vulnerable mother on the streets of Horning.'

***

When they restarted the interview, Jim began by asking Helen for the names and locations of the associates she considered a threat. She listed four names in Lithuania, mentioned Bakalov in passing while acknowledging he was, of course, already in gaol, and wound up with the man who had threatened her and got her involved in the first place.

'He calls himself Red,' she said. Jim made a note, then looked at Greg, but Helen interrupted before he could say anything. 'I still want to know where my mother is. And what you're doing to find her,' she said. 'And some reaction to all the information I've just given you would be good as well.'

Greg leaned back in his chair and regarded her for a long moment. 'I'll come back to your mother,' he said. 'First of all, you've told us little we didn't know already, so that data is of limited value. It confirms what we have on file, and goes some way to convincing me you're on the level. But only so far.

'As for your mother. She's in the Norfolk and Norwich Hospital suffering from dementia. I'm sure you knew the latter, and fully intended the former.' Helen held his eyes for a moment, then flushed and looked down.

'Perhaps now, you'd like to give me an honest explanation of precisely what happened last Saturday,' said Greg. As he anticipated, he was immediately interrupted by the wrong-footed solicitor.

'I'd like to talk to my client,' he said.

The door safely closed behind them, Greg turned to Jim. 'What do we know about this Red?' he asked.

'Only that he's mentioned in connection with the attack on Nathan Standish, and that there are some forensic traces that suggest he was involved with the earlier stabbing in Yarmouth. What we know so far suggests he may have been moving in Mica Gabrys's circles, and given what's happened recently, he may have shared some of Mica's nastier tendencies.'

'No known link with Lithuania?'

'No. Not that we've uncovered to date. What's puzzling me, is why the Lithuanian gang would have used him to put pressure on Helen Gabrys rather than one of their own. They usually keep stuff like that close,' added Jim.

'What's puzzling me,' replied Greg, 'is why they wanted to put pressure on her at all. What value could she add to their schemes? There must have been other people much better placed to pick up where her father left off. Was it some information she had, and they wanted? Something we haven't uncovered yet? Or have we completely misread Ms Gabrys?

'Grab a coffee, Jim. I'll have a chat with Hinchingbrooke to see how things are going on there, and then we'll go back in. Half an hour do you? It shouldn't take much longer than that for Mr Wallis to convince her that keeping him in the dark does her no favours.'

'One other thing,' said Jim. 'I'd like a chat with our friends already in witness protection – Menton and Shinfield. See what they know about this Red.'

'Good idea. Set it up and we can at least talk to them on this Zoom thing.'

When they went back into the interview suite, it was apparent that the solicitor had been reading the riot act. Helen looked simultaneously mulish and chastened.

'My client has something to say,' said Mr Wallis, and all but gave her a nudge with his elbow.

With Greg and Jim looking at her expectantly, Helen cleared her throat and said, 'I took my mother to Horning by boat on Friday morning, as you have said. I left her on a bench near the car park and said I'd be back soon. Then I took a taxi back to *The Jolly Jane* on the other side of the river, made an anonymous 999 call, told them there was a vulnerable woman sitting in the car park in Horning, apparently confused and lost. Then I sailed to Barton Broad on my own.

'And before you all condemn me for abandoning my mother,' she added with a bitter tone in her voice, 'I suggest you try living on a small boat with a woman who doesn't remember who you are, doesn't remember who she is, doesn't remember to eat or drink unless prompted, and quite often doesn't remember to go to the toilet when she needs to.'

'That sounds as though the dementia is quite advanced,' said Greg. 'Couldn't you get any help from the authorities?'

'You try,' she said.

Greg winced. Even in a few hours he'd already discovered how hard it was to find a place in a care home, even for a man who had all his faculties and just needed time to get over Covid.

'With hindsight, I realise that my father had covered up her deterioration, if indeed he even noticed it, given how he'd surrounded her with servants and didn't actually spend much time with her. Once there was only me, it soon became clear there was more at play than just stupidity or absent-mindedness. Carers were out of the question once we were living on the boat. I tried to find a place in a care home but found nothing but long waiting lists. I once drove her to the Norfolk and Norwich Hospital and planned to leave her in A&E, but chickened out at the last minute. Now you can't get near a hospital because of Covid, so a safe village and a 999 call seemed the best bet.'

'And the threats you told us about?' asked Greg.

'The first ones were real, the threats from the man calling himself Red. Those were real. Sometimes he sounded like my brother reincarnated, and that is not what you want to hear when you're alone with no company but a woman with dementia. You met Mica, didn't you? You know what I mean.'

'No, I never met him,' said Greg. 'At least, not until he was dead. But I heard all about his enthusiasm for playing with knives from other people, DI Laurence for one. But explain to me exactly what Red wanted. The demands from your father's old associates just don't ring true.'

'I'm not lying,' she said heatedly. 'He did say he was working on behalf of the Lithuanian gang.'

'But what exactly did he want?'

'More or less what I've just given you. Bank account details and money-laundering stuff. The production locations and the routes for distribution, those they already knew.'

'Where did you get them from?'

'My father, mainly. At least, he told me where to find them hidden at Horses Mill House.'

'We searched the house,' said Jim. 'We took away everything there was.'

'So you did,' agreed Helen. 'But you didn't do a very good job of searching the garden. My father told me where to find a mobile phone hidden under the statue of the Green Man. All the information I needed was on the phone once I charged it up.'

'Do you still have it?' asked Greg.

She hesitated, then said, 'It's in the bilge of *The Jolly Jane*. It's probably not working now, but the SIM card should be okay.'

'Which takes us to who sank the boat,' said Greg, and he raised an eyebrow.

'I did,' said Helen after a pause.

'Why? What were you trying to cover up? It was a rather over-elaborate way of getting rid of a phone. You could have just lobbed it over the side anywhere between Horning and Barton Broad.'

'True, but this way, I could get the phone back if I needed to, or more to the point, I could retrieve the SIM card. No, I sank the boat to get your attention. If you were going to give me witness protection, I needed to convince you the threat was serious.'

37

Great Yarmouth – from bad to worse

When Karen did eventually venture downstairs, her father was out in the yard. He'd pulled the kitchen table and chairs out through the door and was sitting talking to two of his mates from work. She went to the sink for a glass of water and listened at the window. The conversation in the yard seemed to be mostly about work at the abattoir. She watched as they all popped another can of beer each and drank some.

One of them, the one with a beard said, 'You're not coming back anytime soon then? Lucky dog. Most of your pay and no work to do. It's not a bad deal, is it?'

'Not so bad,' her father replied, 'although I wouldn't mind some work on the side, if you know what I mean.' He tapped the side of his nose. 'Let me know if you hear of anything.' He belched, stood up, and said, 'Just need a slash. I'll bring out some crisps or something when I come back.' He shouldered past Karen, ignoring her, and went to the stairs.

She risked the question. 'Where's Mum?'

'Gone shopping,' he said, and disappeared towards the bathroom.

Out in the yard, the two men were still talking. 'Not surprised they took the opportunity to get rid,' one said. 'He's a lazy sod and he's got a nasty temper. Not good.'

'Seen Anne recently?' asked the other. 'Can't be doing with a man who hits women.'

'What we doin' here then?' asked the first.

'Drinkin' his beer,' said the other, then added, 'Watch out, he's coming back.'

Her father pushed past Karen, opened the cupboard door and snatched up the last few packets of crisps.

'What are we having for lunch?' asked Karen, plucking up her courage again.

'Don't know,' her father said over his shoulder, then looked back and tossed her two packets of crisps. 'Start with these.' And he went outside.

Karen foraged through the cupboards and found a sliced loaf, some margarine and jam.

'Jake,' she called. 'Come on. Come and get your toast and jam.'

That afternoon, she logged on to the school call using the tablet Miss Grain had left. Jake was still refusing to do anything connected with homework but had tired of his toy cars and spent most of the afternoon whining that he was bored. Karen tried to ignore him and focus on the lesson on screen. Her mum still hadn't come home, and her father seemed to have gone out.

She was concentrating so hard she didn't hear him come back. She didn't hear his opening comment properly either.

Something about getting supper, but she was struggling with the sums she'd been set and didn't take any notice, until a hand came over her shoulder, snatched up the iPad and hurled it at the wall opposite.

'I said,' her father bellowed, 'if your mother's not back you need to be doing something about tea. You're old enough now.'

Jake started crying, shocked by the sudden noise, and his father pounced on him, shook him like a rat and threw him after the iPad.

'And I've had enough of that snivelling,' he shouted, 'you useless yellow girl. Get him out of my sight,' he snapped to Karen where she sat, open-mouthed with horror, at the table she had, with considerable difficulty, retrieved from the yard. She ran to Jake and, pulling him by the hand, got him out of the room and up the stairs.

He was white with shock and there was a big bump on the back of his head, but there didn't seem to be any other damage. They both sat on the floor in her bedroom and she hugged him close.

'I'm hungry,' said Jake after a while.

'I know,' she said. 'So am I.'

38

Wednesday 25 March – virtual interviews

It was quickly apparent that Ralph Menton, Constantin Gabrys's ex-butler, had little to contribute on the subject of 'Red'. He was, however, quite the character witness for Helen Gabrys, expressing himself astonished that she'd been caught up in what he termed 'the family business', and strongly of the opinion that she had been the straight and honest member of the family, with her sights firmly set on a career as a solicitor.

'She told me she wanted to specialise in family law,' he said. 'And I think she'd have been good at it. She was good at picking up on how people were feeling.'

'Except her mother,' remarked Greg, as the screen went blank.

'I think she just got overwhelmed by the whole situation,' said Jim. 'I don't think it's possible to understand the strains of living with someone with dementia unless you've done it. It's not just the forgetfulness. Their whole personality can change.

Sometimes they can be really nasty to the people caring for them. Even violent.'

'That sounds like personal experience,' said Greg.

'Not directly. Only second-hand. My father-in-law got it, and he was downright dangerous to my mother-in-law on occasion. She didn't want to give up on him, but he was still a powerful man and she was a small, frail woman. Something had to be done.'

'Okay, I get the message,' said Greg. 'I'll ease up on the judgement of Helen Gabrys. I'm aware I've been lucky so far. I haven't had to go through anything like that.

'Ah, I've got a text Peter Shinfield is in our virtual waiting room. Let's see if he can help.'

Shinfield looked distinctly different from when they had seen him last. His once fair hair was now dark and cut much shorter. He was clean-shaven and seemed to have been working out, judging by the his general air of good health and the muscles in his forearms.

'How are things going for you?' asked Greg. Then interrupted himself to say, 'But don't tell me details that would give away information about your new identity or location. I don't want to know. And we'll keep using your old name, if you don't mind.'

Peter grinned and said, 'I'm good, thanks. I will tell you I'm training to be a plumber. I'm enjoying it and it's good money.'

'You don't miss your old life then?'

'Not a bit.' It was said cheerfully and convincingly.

'Sorry to take you back there, in your mind at least,' said Greg. 'But we're looking for information about someone you may have known back then. He seems to call himself 'Red'.'

'Red, yes I knew Red,' said Peter. 'If he's in trouble, I bet it's knives.'

'Now that's interesting,' said Greg. 'Why do you say that?'

'Because he was one of Mica's crowd, and if Mica was bad, Red was very keen to copy him.'

'What role did he play in the Gabrys organisation?' asked Greg.

'Nothing much really. He fancied himself as a big man, but he didn't have the brains or the contacts. He'd boast about knowing the boss, but I never saw any evidence of that.'

'You mean Constantin Gabrys? You're saying he ignored this "Red"?'

'Red was much too small fry for Gabrys senior. He only got in at all because he was a mate of Mica's. I suppose he was an enforcer in a small way, but I don't recall him ever being let loose on his own, or allowed to use his initiative. I think the boss used him for what he was good for, which was bullying, but basically, everyone thought he was a bit of a thicko.'

'So you wouldn't have seen him as a natural heir to the Gabrys empire? Or a go-between to the Lithuanian end?'

'God, no!' exclaimed Peter. 'Never in this world. I told you, Red thought he was the bee's knees, but that just goes to show he was too thick to know how thick he was!'

'Any idea what his real name is?' asked Jim.

'Never heard him called anything but Red, sorry,' replied Peter.

'Do you know anything else about him?' asked Jim.

'No, I don't think so. The Gabrys empire didn't work like that. Mostly everyone was kept apart unless you really needed to work together. That way, no one could know too much.'

'Thank you for your time,' started Greg, but Peter interrupted him.

'Hang on, before you end this call,' he said. 'Now I think about it, I did meet his sister once. She worked in an office in Gorleston. I think her name was Ella, and I seem to remember something about a lake, but that's all.'

After the call, Greg leaned back and looked at Jim.

'It couldn't be, could it?' he said. 'Ella Pentney?'

'Worth a look,' said Jim.

39

That morning in Great Yarmouth

When Karen woke in the morning, she found Jake asleep beside her.

'Come on,' she said, giving him a nudge. 'Get up, get dressed and let's see what Mum's got for breakfast.'

Jake was drowsy and inclined to be whiny but did as he was told. When Karen got downstairs it was to find her father sitting at the kitchen table, the TV on and showing the news. He took a swig from his mug as she entered, but said nothing. She looked round for her mother and went to the window to see if she was out in the yard. No sign of anyone else.

'Where's Mum?' she asked.

'Not here,' was her father's uninformative reply.

Karen ventured to look in the fridge and found some milk, close to its use-by date. She put it on the far end of the table from her father and added a couple of bowls and a packet of cereal. When Jake came in, she put a finger to her lips, with a side-long look at her father, and pointed to the cereal. For once, Jake took the hint, filled a bowl with cornflakes, added milk and sugar and started eating, all in silence.

'Is she coming back soon?' Karen ventured.

'No idea,' her father said. He tipped the remains of his coffee in the sink and left the room.

That day, at a loss for what else to do, Karen concentrated on her schoolwork while Jake played dungeons and dragons under the kitchen table. At lunchtime she got Jake and herself toast and marmite. As evening approached, she searched the cupboards and fridge for something they might have for supper and found a tin of beans with sausages. They had that with some more toast. There was not much left of the loaf, and the milk was almost gone too.

When her father came home, later in the evening, she summoned up the courage to say, 'We need some food shopping. There's nothing left.'

Her father grunted, felt in his pocket and came up with a couple of crumpled notes. 'Go and get whatever you want from the corner shop.'

It was too late that evening, so she put the money safely away in her pocket until the morning, when she took Jake with her down the road to the small corner shop. The shopkeeper moaned about there being two of them in his shop, but she ignored him. *What else can I do with Jake?* She bought milk, sliced bread, margarine, cheese, bacon and some Cornish pasties and pies. She ignored Jake's requests for chocolate. The shopping took slightly more money than she had. She looked at the shopkeeper in silence and he sighed heavily but let her take the food.

'Tell your mum she owes me,' he said. Karen nodded and headed for home before he could change his mind.

'Where's the beer?' her father asked when she got home.

'I'm not old enough to buy beer,' she said. 'And there wasn't enough money anyway.' She thought for a moment she'd taken one risk too many, but her father didn't say anything. 'When's Mum coming home?' she asked again.

'I've told you, I don't know,' was the reply. 'Maybe never.'

Back upstairs, Karen said to Jake, 'She will be back, you'll see. She'd never just leave us. She'll come and fetch us soon.' She hoped she was right.

40

Red or dead?

After the call, Greg leaned back and looked at Jim. 'It couldn't be that simple, could it?' he said. 'Ella Pentney? And what about Red's contacts with Helen Gabrys. Assuming for a moment that she's telling the truth about the threats and what he wanted from her. What was he really up to, do you think?'

'I think,' said Jim, 'that he had ambitions to take over the Gabrys empire but had too little information, no contacts and no real clout. He conned Helen into thinking he was something he wasn't, and used her. She, or at least the Gabrys name, became a front for him. And the stuff that's started to go wrong for them since is, at least partly, down to him being what Shinfield calls "a thicko".'

'That's what I think too,' said Greg. 'Which means that if we can mop up this Red character, we can put a stop to a lot of the drug sales and production in this county.'

'At least until the next hoodlum moves in. Nature abhors a vacuum, my dad used to say.'

'Don't be so cheerful,' replied Greg. 'It might become a habit. Okay, the priority is to catch Red, and his real name would be a good start. Let's begin with Ella Pentney, but we'd better not neglect other possibilities either.'

'Can I set Chris on Pentney?' asked Jim.

'Of course. Let's make good use of her while we can.'

As Jim left the office, Greg picked up his phone again with an inner sigh. Back to what looked like being the more intractable problem: his father's welfare.

Before dialling, he ran his eye down the list of options Chris had put together for him.

1. Move him to a care home near us – so far, no luck with finding a space, except for that rather dodgy one we looked at.

2. Move him in with us and find a carer to come in. Mum's cousin might know someone.

3. I've run out of ideas.

'Looks like two,' he muttered to himself, feeling guilty that he didn't feel more enthusiastic about it. Once through to his father though, he was quick to extol all the advantages. 'It would be great to see more of you,' he said. 'You and Chris get on well, and my cottage is quiet. A good place to convalesce. We have a spare room so that's no problem, and Chris's mother thinks she knows someone who could come in and look after you while we're working.'

'Absolutely not,' replied his father in as firm a voice as he could manage. 'You both have jobs to do, and I don't want to be in the way, which, at the moment, I would be. I do still need some help if I'm being realistic.'

'Then what do you suggest, Dad?' asked Greg. 'It's a struggle finding a convalescent place round here that has any vacancies.' He was careful to avoid the phrase 'care home'. 'I do think it would be best if you came to us. I've told you, we can get some help in—'

'No,' his father said again. 'It's a kind offer, but I want to keep my independence as long as I can. There's a place near here that's almost a hotel with care staff. It has a coffee bar, cinema and everything. And en-suite rooms, which I'm pretty sure your cottage doesn't. It has a vacancy, and I've taken it. Sorry, Greg,' he added, 'but I had to move fast before it went. I hope you're not offended.'

'I'm just relieved at how much better you sound,' said Greg. 'Almost like your old self.'

'If I could stop coughing and didn't feel so tired all the time, I'd go home, but as it is, this is a good solution. And Greg, when I'm settled in, I'll ring you about your mother's funeral.'

'Okay, Dad. I arranged—'

'Not now. When I'm in St Ives. Then I'll ring again. Bye, son.'

Greg put the phone down, torn between relief that everything was working out so well, guilt that he felt like that, and a strong feeling that he'd just been put in his place.

In the general office, Jill was dealing with a tricky phone conversation too. 'You don't usually ring me at work,' she said into her personal mobile. 'What's wrong?'

'I know. I'm sorry,' said Diana. 'I'm really worried about one of my pupils. Karen Mirren. She's normally one of the keenest in my class, but her attendance on Zoom calls is not good, and I think her mother had bruises to her face the last time I saw her.

And on that occasion, I didn't see Karen at all. I waited until today's Zoom to see if she attended, and she didn't. She hasn't responded to any direct messages either. I think I'd better go round there.'

'To her home, you mean?' asked Jill.

'Yes.'

Jill thought quickly, trying not to be distracted by the messages flashing on her screen with Red-related data. 'How about you try again to contact her by text or email,' she said, 'and if there's no response, go round in the morning. I could get someone to go with you then.'

'Oh, would you? Thanks, Jill. I hope I'm worrying about nothing, but I'm afraid I'm not. I'll do that.'

41

The great escape

By evening, Karen was losing hope that her mum would return for them. She alternated between a fear that she had been hurt and was in hospital somewhere, and the worse fear that she didn't love them after all and had chosen to run away with Tim. She would have tried to contact Uncle Tim to see if she was with him, but after the fight in the yard, she didn't dare. Anyway, every news item she saw or heard stressed that no one was to go out. Everyone was to stay home. Even her father was staying home now. Mostly.

Then she noticed the bolt and padlock on the door to the understairs cupboard. She might not have noticed it at all, except she'd left her satchel in there and wanted a book for her schoolwork. She tried to open the door, but the padlock wouldn't let her. Then she looked for a key, but none of the bunch hanging in the kitchen fitted the lock. Her father caught her trying the last few, and was angry. But then, he was always angry, so no change there.

'I wanted a book out of my bag,' she tried to explain, but he wouldn't listen.

'Too bad,' he said. 'I have some of my things in there and I don't want you meddling.'

'I only want—' began Karen.

'I don't care what you only want,' he said. 'Just leave things alone.'

'There's a funny smell too,' she muttered rebelliously. 'Of Brussels sprouts cooked for too long, like the mouse that died inside the old sofa. If you let me get my book, I could check for the dead mouse as well.'

'Just mind your own business,' he snapped, and walked off. She let the subject drop, but she kept going back to the stairs, and sniffing. By the time she went to bed, she was beginning to entertain a terrible idea. That night she smuggled the emergency torch from the kitchen, the one hanging there in case of power cuts, into her dressing-gown pocket. When her father went out on one of his mysterious errands, she started to peel back the stair carpet from the eighth step up, then she turned the landing light off and, using the torch, tried to peer through the gap in the stairs to the cupboard beneath. It didn't work as well as she'd hoped. The one thing she *was* sure of was that the cooked-sprout smell was getting stronger. Then her father burst in through the front door and demanded to know what the hell she was doing.

For the first time in her life, he thrashed her using his leather belt. And she screamed to beat the band until there was a knock at the front door, from a neighbour wanting to know what was happening.

'Just a game,' her father explained. 'Nothing to worry about.' And he closed the door firmly on the well-meaning neighbour.

Very early next morning, while her father was still slumped in beer-sodden sleep, she went to Jake and shook him awake, her hand over his mouth.

'Get dressed,' she whispered. 'We're leaving.'

'What?'

She clamped her hand over his mouth and shook her head violently. 'Don't wake him,' she warned, 'or I'll leave you behind!'

'Where're we going?' Jake whispered.

'To see Uncle Tim. I think he'll know where Mum is.' She didn't voice the fear that had begun to fester in her head. 'We can't stay here. Come on. Hurry up before he wakes up. Put your warmest things on, and two coats.'

'Two!' he started to exclaim, and she clamped a hand over his mouth again.

'Two coats,' she whispered. 'And hurry up.'

A few minutes later they were creeping down the stairs. 'Tread by the wall,' she whispered, 'then they won't creak.' Jake did as he was told.

In the kitchen Karen filled an old shopping bag with bread, cheese and margarine and packets of biscuits. Jake picked up his school bag and put his favourite toy car in. She opened her mouth to object, then shrugged and added a book she was reading. Finally she filled a bottle with water at the sink, then stopped, terrified she'd heard a sound from upstairs. After a moment she had a sudden thought and slid a hand into the vase on the windowsill where her mother kept a little stash of cash. To her surprise there was some in it, and she emptied it into her pocket.

Moments later, and she was opening the backdoor as silently as she could before leading Jake down the yard and out into the ginnel. Once out of sight of the house, they ran as fast as they could and headed for the Market Square.

42

Morning of 26 March 2020 – in Caister

According to the HR records, Ella Pentney lived in a bungalow in Caister, overlooking the marshland. As they pulled up outside, Bill noted the location and remarked, 'This wasn't bought on the part-time earnings of a secretary at Norfolk Constabulary. I wonder if it qualifies as "proceeds of crime".'

'I suggest you don't mention that just yet,' commented Chris, ringing the doorbell.

When she saw who it was, Ella's face changed from welcoming to surly so fast that Chris wondered if she had cramp in her cheek muscles.

'You,' exclaimed Ella. 'Now what?'

'Can we come in, or would you rather do this down at the station?' asked Chris.

Ella stood to one side to allow them access. Bill followed Chris through the small porch into an open-plan living room. The large TV on the wall above the fireplace was on but silent, showing, so far as Bill could see, an old film. Ella sat herself down at the dining table at the far end of the room and waved them to seats at the other end.

'No need to get too comfortable,' she said. 'Hopefully this won't take too long. I'm about to go out.'

'Then I'm sure you were also planning to be back soon, bearing in mind your curfew and the Covid rules,' replied Chris, taking a recorder out of her bag. 'You know the next bit, Ella.' And she delivered the caution. 'Okay,' she went on, 'we'd like to ask you some questions about your brother.'

'Which one?' asked Ella.

'How many do you have?' enquired Chris, knowing that Jill's quick exploration of birth records had turned up only one.

'Two. One full brother, and one stepbrother.'

'I see,' said Chris making a note. 'And their names, please?'

'Do I need my solicitor present?' asked Ella.

'If you want one, of course you may have one,' replied Chris, 'but at the moment I'm just looking for a conversation about some of your family. How about I ask a couple more questions, then you can see if you want your solicitor.' Taking silence as consent, she went on. 'I was asking for their names.'

'John Edwin Galway and Eddie Fisher,' she said.

'And your maiden name was Fisher, I think,' said Chris. 'It must have been confusing having two brothers in the same family with the same name. Edwin and Eddie, I mean.'

'Not really,' said Ella. 'Eddie was short for Edward, and anyway—' She stopped herself.

'Were you about to tell me that Eddie used a nickname?' asked Chris. Ella was silent for a moment, so Chris added, 'You realise that we have your DNA on file, Ella, and can check samples from relevant crime scenes for a familial match. If your brother has been involved, we will find out.'

'Why do you need me then?' asked Ella, rallying her resistance.

'Speed and efficiency,' replied Chris. 'That's from our perspective. From yours, it will play in your favour when you come to trial, if you have been cooperative.'

Another short pause, then Ella said, 'His nickname was Red. From when he was a boy.'

'Why?' asked Bill.

'Because as a child he had a terrible temper. My gran used to say a red mist would descend. After a bit, it caught on. Every time he had a tantrum someone would say *Oh-oh, more red mist.* Then someone took to calling him Red, and it stuck.'

'Where is he now?' asked Chris.

'No idea,' said Ella. 'He turns up when he wants, and I don't see him in between.'

'Where does he live?'

'No idea,' was the answer again. 'Last I heard he was sofa surfing.'

'Anything else you could tell us that might help us find him?'

'No.'

Another pause, as Chris decided to change direction. 'How did he get involved with Mica Gabrys?' she asked. 'Did you introduce him? Or was it the other way round? Did he get you involved?'

'No comment,' said Ella firmly. 'You get nothing else from me without my solicitor present.'

'Okay.' Chris rose and Bill followed. 'In that case, we'll leave it for now, but we may well want a further interview down at the station. Bye for now, Ella.'

'She's lying,' said Bill as soon as they got into the car.

'Yes, I think so too. We need a warrant to monitor her phone. Shouldn't be a problem. I'll ring Greg asap.'

'But, in the meantime, she's probably going to rush to tell Red we've been asking about him,' said Bill.

'Yes. I think so too. Which is why we're going to lurk around the corner here until we can get someone to take over from us. If we're lucky, she may lead us straight to him.'

43

On the run

Across the Market Square was the bus station, tucked under a shopping arcade.

'I thought we were going to find Tim,' complained Jake.

'We are,' said Karen. 'But I don't know exactly where he lives. Only the village.'

'So how are we going to find him?' whined Jake. 'It's cold and we haven't had breakfast, and...'

'We're going to go to the village. And then we'll ask someone. In the post office, say. Or the pub,' said Karen, forgetting the pubs were closed. 'Come on. We'll take a bus to Ormesby, then look around. It won't take long.'

They got a funny look from the bus driver when they got on board. 'Out early, aren't you?' he asked. 'Where's your mum?'

'Meeting us in Ormesby,' said Karen, drawing on her knowledge of the complicated family arrangements of divorced couples. 'The arrangement was my dad would put us on the bus, and she'd meet us off it. But he's had to dash off. An emergency.'

'Oh.' The driver didn't look satisfied, but he made no further objection.

'Look, he gave me the fare,' said Karen, holding out some change.

'Okay. Sit down then, and we'll be off.'

There were almost no other passengers, and it stayed that way as they progressed through the villages. Karen's plan had been to get off amid a crowd of others, but there were no others. Once they passed the sign saying 'Ormesby St Margaret' on the outskirts of the village, she made her mind up.

'Come on, Jake, next stop's ours,' she said loud enough for the driver to hear. The bus passed the village green and pulled up beside a pub converted into apartments. Karen peered through the window by the door and suddenly pointed. 'Look, there she is,' she said, pointing again, down a narrow road that led between the old pub and a little row of shops.

'Where?' asked the bus driver as the door folded open.

'Right there,' said Karen. 'Thank you.' And pulling Jake by the hand, she dragged him as fast as she could, off down the narrow lane. Behind them, after a brief hesitation, the bus signalled and drove off.

'Where's Mum?' asked Jake, confused.

'I don't know,' said Karen impatiently. 'That was just to get us off the bus. Come on.'

She dragged him back up towards the main road, then past another, smaller green and across to a garage with a shop attached.

'We'll get something to eat here,' she said, 'and ask after Tim.'

The man at the garage gave them a funny look too, but sold them a large, hot sausage roll and a carton of milk without asking any questions. When Karen asked about Tim, he shook his head, but when she described his van, he did say he thought he might have seen it about.

They went round the corner to eat their sausage roll and drink their milk, sitting on a low wall by a village hall.

'Why don't we ring Tim?' asked Jake.

'Duh,' said Karen, through a mouthful of sausage meat and puff pastry. 'Because we don't have a phone, stupid.'

'Yes, we do,' contradicted Jake. 'I brought Mum's, so I could play games on it.'

'You...' Words failed Karen for a moment. 'Where is it?'

'In my bag.' Karen snatched up the bag from where it was lying at their feet and rummaged through it.

'You're a genius, Jake,' she said. 'If you weren't so horrid I could kiss you.' She found the phone, entered the familiar password, and checked the calls list.

'Oh,' she said, disappointed. 'I can't see Tim in this list.'

'Let me see,' said Jake. Karen was minded to ignore him, but in view of the stroke of genius that was the phone, she changed her mind and showed him the calls list.

'That one,' said Jake, pointing. 'Try that one.'

'Why that one?' asked Karen, mindful that they had no way to recharge the phone and unwilling to waste its remaining charge on random calls.

'It was our joke,' said Jake. 'When we went to the amusement place and I won that tiny teddy bear, Jake called it MiniBear and said he would use it as his call sign to celebrate my huge prize.' The phone number he was pointing at had an emoji next to it. A bear.

'Okay,' said Karen, and rang the number. After the excitement, it was disappointing that there was no answer. 'We'll try again later,' she said. 'Meantime, let's take a look around for Tim's van.'

44

Following on

After all the Red-related excitement, it was disappointing for Chris and Bill to be led straight from the Ella household to Caister's Lidl.

'Damn. She's going shopping,' said Bill as Chris parked by the church opposite the supermarket entrance.

'Or, she's going to the gym,' said Chris, pointing to the 'Hotel, Gym and Spa' sign on the other side of the car park. 'Take a wander down there, Bill, and see if you can see which way she went. Try not to be spotted.' As Bill waited for a gap in the traffic, to cross the road, she got on the phone to Greg again.

'Any luck with the warrant?' she asked.

'Not yet,' he replied. 'I'll chase it again. Good news from Forensics though. They tested various materials connected with the two stabbings in Great Yarmouth. You know, Nathan Standish and the other one. You remember Jim managed to get hold of the hoodie that was found discarded and marked with blood... That blood matches the victim. But there was other DNA on the hoodie, and it's a familial match to Ella Pentney.'

'So Red *is* her brother,' said Chris.

'Related to her, certainly,' said Greg.

'Speaking of Nathan, have you had a chat with him yet?'

'Not yet.'

It was on the tip of Greg's tongue to say he'd had just a few other things to do, when Chris said, 'Sorry. Got to go. Bill's coming back in a rush.'

Bill was panting when he jumped into the car. 'Get ready to go,' he said. 'Pentney's heading back to her car from Lidl. Looks like she did go shopping.'

Chris started the car and got ready to rejoin the traffic. To her annoyance a car pulled alongside her as the lights changed to red, and she saw Ella's car come out of the supermarket entrance and turn right, away from her home.

'Where's she going now?' she asked rhetorically, banging her hands on the steering wheel in frustration. It seemed an age before the lights changed to green again, and then she had to wait for the car beside her to get out of the way, before she barged into the traffic – to the two-fingered annoyance of the driver behind.

'Did you see which way she went?' she asked Bill, driving down the high street.

'No. She could have gone on towards Yarmouth or have turned off at any of these junctions.'

'Okay. We'll go towards Yarmouth, and hope for the best. Get on the radio and put out an APB on her number plate, but tell anyone who spots her to hang back and watch where she goes.'

Past Tesco, round the roundabout and still no sight of Ella Pentney's little runabout. Chris ignored the 40mph speed limit and the irritated drivers she was passing. Just as she went through the lights near the BP garage, Bill said, 'She's gone left, down towards the racecourse.'

'Damn.' Chris took the next left, and then left again to get back to Jellicoe Road. Turning towards the sea, they both kept a lookout for the small red car.

Lost her again, was on Chris's lips, when Bill said, 'There, parked on the roadside, near that bus shelter.'

Chris jammed the brakes on and pulled into a side road running parallel to the main coast road. 'Hand me the radio,' she said tersely, then demanded to know if there were any units anywhere near the North Dene dunes.

'Car near the Imperial Hotel, south of your location,' said Despatch.

'Good. Have them come north along North Drive and stop just before the bus shelter. The woman we're following has parked there and is probably either in the shelter or walking on the dunes. They need to block her car in, then see if they can spot her. Bill and I will join them. Between us, we should be able to find her. If there's a man with her, warn them to approach with caution,' she added. 'If he's who we think he is, he's known to be handy with a knife.

'I'll hand you to Bill for some descriptions.'

While Bill passed on his description of Ella and what she was wearing, together with the rough description they had of Red, Chris rang Greg with one hand, getting into her stab vest with the other. His number was engaged, so she left a message, then joined Bill at the front of the car.

'Okay, let's go,' she said as she saw a marked car pull across the access to the dunes where Ella Pentney's car was parked.

From the elevation provided by the road, they could see a mile or two to left and right, and straight ahead as far as the final ridge before the dunes dropped to sea level. The beach itself was out of sight. Towards the horizon, the wind-farm turbines were turning briskly and a ship with large derricks was waiting outside the new harbour for the tide to change and entry to be granted.

'Thanks for coming quickly,' said Chris to the two uniformed officers from the squad car. One was a grizzled older man with a beard partially hiding a scar across his right cheek. His partner was young, female and sturdy in build with her brown hair in a tight bun at the nape of her neck. Both were in stab vests, as advised.

The older man introduced them to Chris. 'Constable Drake and Sergeant Briscoe. Do you have a photo of the man we're after?'

'Only a photofit,' replied Chris, proffering the image on her phone. 'I do have a photo of his sister, though.' And she swiped the screen to change the image. Both nodded.

'Got it,' said the woman.

They all turned to survey the dunes. They could see at least four sets of dog walkers accompanied by a variety of canine companions.

'Don't assume they're in the clear,' cautioned Chris. 'It's just possible he asked to meet her here because he's walking a dog.'

'Do we know he has one?' asked Constable Drake.

'We don't know he doesn't,' replied Bill, still surveying the dunes within sight.

'Okay,' said Chris. 'Two of us go down onto the dunes and head towards the sea. Two stay closer to the road, in case anyone makes a run for it. Both pairs check out any grouping that includes a man and a woman. I suggest Bill and I head down towards the sea, and you two start checking nearer the road. Let's go.'

The first three pairs of walkers Chris and Bill checked looked nothing like Ella and Red, and they passed by at a distance, with a friendly wave. As they breasted the rise towards the sea, they were passed by a single man with a retriever heading back towards the road. They gave him a close scrutiny.

'No, I don't think so,' said Chris. 'Too old and too fat.' From the height of the dune they could now see to where the waves were lapping on the sand. Turning they checked north and south, but there were fewer walkers on this side of the dunes than there were towards the road.

'Let's head south towards town,' said Chris. 'There are more people in that direction and more that look likely.'

Bill pulled out a small pair of binoculars. 'These might help,' he said, and used them to survey the ranks of dunes to north and south. 'There are several pairs that look worth a check,' he said, his eyes still glued to his binoculars. Then, as he swept the horizon to the north, he suddenly stopped and froze, his focus on a section of the road leading towards the holiday camp.

'Take a look at these two,' he said, and handed the glasses to Chris.

'Where'm I looking?' she asked, sweeping her amplified gaze along the road.

'Roughly where Jellicoe Road joins North Drive,' he replied. 'On the dunes, below road level and walking south towards where there's a van parked.' Chris adjusted the direction of her gaze, paused and then adjusted the focus of the binoculars a little.

'Got them,' she said. 'Yes, I see what you mean. That does look like Ella, and the man with her fits the description of Red.'

Bill got out his radio. 'Briscoe,' he said. 'We have eyes on possible targets, roughly five hundred metres north of you, on the edge of the dunes near the road.'

From their vantage point, they saw the two police officers almost due west of them separate and walk north, one on the road and one on the dunes. Switching her gaze to the probable Ella and Red, Chris noted they were engrossed in conversation, with Red waving his arms about to reinforce some point or other. As she watched, he broke off to look around, apparently for his dog, which ran up to him. From this distance it looked like a Norfolk terrier, but she couldn't be sure. As the man called the dog to him, he bent down to pat it, then straightening up, seemed to catch sight of the two uniformed police walking towards them.

Chris started off down the dune, still using the binoculars, and stepped straight in a hole in the sand, wrenching her ankle and falling heavily.

'Damn,' she exclaimed, then as Bill came towards her to assist, she waved him away. 'No, go and help the other two. We can worry about me later. Just make sure we don't lose Red.'

Bill sped off as instructed, and Chris got to her feet cautiously. Nothing broken as far as she could tell, but her ankle hurt like the devil. Standing more or less on one leg, she refocussed the binoculars again and saw that brother and sister had parted. Ella seemed to be waiting for the police to catch up with her. Red, on the other hand, hotly pursued by his dog, was running to the north and the next available ramp to the road. Constable Drake, with a turn of speed Chris would have admired under any circumstances, was gaining on him as he ran up the slope onto the road. At that moment, everything changed. Grabbing a bike which they had all overlooked, Red stooped to unlock a chain, picked up his dog and almost threw it into the basket on the handlebars, then set off back towards town at a speed that even Drake could not match.

By the time Chris had limped back to the roadside, Drake and Briscoe in the squad car were already in hot pursuit, with Bill monitoring progress on the radio. She slumped into the passenger seat with a sigh and massaged her ankle. Ella was waiting sulkily in the back seat.

Bill bent to talk to Chris through the open window. 'Think they've lost him,' he said. 'He cut down a narrow alley where the car couldn't follow. Want me to drive?' he added.

'Yes, please,' said Chris.

'What about her?' asked Bill, indicating Ella with a flick of his thumb over his shoulder. 'Take her in?'

'Oh yes, I think so, don't you?' said Chris, and buckled up for the journey back to Wymondham.

45

Great Yarmouth – early 26 March

Diana began her working day on a Zoom to Karen's class, from which Karen was absent. After hesitating for some minutes, she made a phone call to her headteacher, the designated safeguarding lead for the school.

'I'm worried about Karen Mirren,' she began, and explained the circumstances. The Head's response was swift and clear.

'Contact the county council children's team and tell them what you've told me,' he said. 'It may be nothing, or it may be serious. Better we err on the side of caution. Keep me in the loop, will you?'

Diana rang off, took a deep breath and rang Norfolk County Council, as instructed. 'Hi, my name's Diana Grain,' she said. 'I teach at a primary school in Yarmouth, and I seem to be losing contact with a particular pupil. She's not attending class Zooms, and when I called round a couple of days ago, I didn't get to see her.'

'Not unusual, surely, in these strange times,' said the voice on the end of the line. 'Do you have a specific reason for concern? Maybe they're just struggling with schoolwork from home?'

Diana hesitated. *Explaining to the Head was easy, but how can I explain to someone outside the school?*

'It basically comes down to the fact that this behaviour doesn't fit what I know of Karen, and that I wasn't comfortable with the explanations I was offered when I spoke to the parents,' she admitted. 'Look, I'm going to call round again today, and if I'm still unhappy, I'll get back to you.'

'That seems sensible,' the voice agreed, and rang off.

Diana set off for Yarmouth feeling that at least she'd put a marker down that all might not be well with the child. Turning into the street where Karen lived, she spotted a parking space a little short of her destination. As on her previous visit, it seemed that more people than usual were either staying home or working from home. She closed the car door behind her, and heard the lock click as she walked away towards the terraced house where Karen lived with her brother and parents. She noted, with some resignation, there was a space much nearer that she could have used to park, and reached up to the old-fashioned knocker on the slightly battered front door. She lifted it and let it fall several times but got no response. After a few moments, she moved to the front window to see if she could spot any movement in the house. At first, she thought there was nothing, then something caught her eye and she turned back to peer again through the curtains.

There was a flicker of something by the door from the front room into the hall. She reached up to tap on the window, then realised that the movement was elemental. It was the movement of flames flickering in the hall. She opened her mouth to shout for help, and even as she did so the flames grew until they were taking over the front room.

Without conscious thought she screamed for help and scrabbled in her bag for her phone, to dial 999 and ask for the fire service. Then she went back to banging on the front door with all her strength, still shouting and screaming. It seemed ages although it was only minutes before neighbours started to emerge from houses nearby. They began by asking what was wrong, then rushed to help. Two men ran through the ginnel to see if they could access the house from the backyard. They soon returned to say that the fire had taken hold in the kitchen, and they couldn't get in. Other neighbours started evacuating the houses to either side.

'The children...' Diana was gasping. 'There are two children in there. And possibly their parents.'

The two men who had tried round the back started to pull her away from the front door. 'You can't do anything here,' they were saying. 'We need to wait for the fire brigade.' Even as they spoke, a police car pulled into one end of the street, and the sound of sirens flagged the arrival of two fire engines from the other. Diana and the neighbours found themselves pushed away to a safe distance as the firemen took over with ladders and hoses.

Watching, frustrated, Diana tried again and again to get some news of the children, but no one knew anything. An ambulance arrived on the scene, but for the moment the paramedics had nothing to do. The firefighters seemed to have stopped the fire spreading to the neighbouring properties, but as far as Diana could see, no one had gone into the burning house and no one had come out. In the end, she retired to her car to await developments and to ring Jill.

***

It was afternoon when Jill arrived. Still no one had come out of the house and no casualties had been treated. Another police car had arrived, and the firefighters were in deep conversation with the officers. Diana continued to watch, thirsty, hungry, and frustrated, but determined not to leave until she knew something of the fate of Karen and her brother. She was so focussed on the scene before her, that a sharp rap on the passenger window almost made her jump out of her skin. To her enormous relief, it was Jill. She flicked the button that released the lock, and Jill got in wrapping her in a warm embrace.

'Got your message. Sorry I couldn't get here sooner. What's going on? What's happening?' she asked.

'I wish I knew,' said Diana. 'But no one will tell me anything. Perhaps they'll talk to you.'

'I'll go and see,' said Jill. 'Wait in the car. I'll be back soon.'

Diana watched her walk towards the fire engine and the two uniformed men conversing near it. She saw Jill take out her warrant card as she neared them and introduce herself. Then she saw Jill point at the car, and assumed she was explaining why Diana was there.

There was a pause while Jill seemed to be listening intently to the police officer , then she turned to speak to the fireman.

Finally, she turned and walked with him towards the still smoking remains of the terraced house, and there was more conversation. She had her concentrating face on, Diana noted. Jill nodded sharply at something and turned to walk back towards Diana. Behind her, a couple more police officers started to unroll crime-scene tape, and one took up position outside the burned house.

Jill got back into the car and twisted in the seat to talk to Diana. 'You need to know you can't pass this on to anyone,' she said. 'It's just between us, and my job's on the line if this leaks.'

Diana nodded. 'Okay,' she said. 'Understood.'

Jill nodded too. 'First,' she said, 'there are no signs of any children in the house. No, hang on,' she said as Diana opened her mouth. 'Let me finish before you start asking questions. Second, the fire service thinks the fire was started deliberately. Third, the remains of an adult have been found in what's left of the cupboard under the stairs. Which makes this a murder enquiry and why the next thing I need to do is speak to my boss, Greg Geldard.'

46

Round the village

Ormesby was, Karen realised, a much larger village than she'd imagined. After an hour or two walking streets, avenues, roads, gardens and crescents, they were tired, cold and hungry. She realised something else as well. On these largely empty streets they were starting to attract attention.

Jake was lagging behind with an expression on his face that said a whine was on the way. Karen felt guilty. He was, after all, much younger and he'd done very well so far.

'Okay, Jake,' she said, trying to sound confidant. 'We'll find somewhere cosy to hide away for a bit and have something to eat.'

She looked round, but nothing immediately recommended itself as a safe harbour. They walked on a little further, and she realised they had come full circle. In front of her was the village hall she had seen when they left the bus, and, near it, the petrol station and the shop. She was about to suggest trying the doors of the village hall, when Jake dragged at her hand and pointed.

'How about that?' he asked.

She looked where he was pointing and saw a small boat on a trailer in a nearby driveway. It had a canvas roof and, as far as she could tell, appeared to be waterproof.

'Possibly,' she said, looking round to see if there was anyone about, and whether they were overlooked. The house opposite was hidden behind a tall hedge, and there were trees between the boat in the drive and the nearest neighbour. The bungalow it belonged to had blinds down in the nearest windows, and, as far as she could see, no one was moving.

'Come on,' said Jake. 'We could play pirates. Bags I be Black Jake, the captain!'

Karen gave in to his enthusiasm, and with a still wary eye for anyone who might spot them, she followed Jake towards the boat.

'Shush, though,' she warned him. 'We need to be quiet.' Then, as inspiration struck, 'Otherwise, the Excise will get us.' Jake immediately adopted an exaggerated tiptoe movement and put his finger to his lips, nodding agreement.

The interior was accessed by a zip in the waxed fabric canopy. With one last look around, Karen pushed the zip up. Sitting on its trailer, the boat was quite high off the ground, but the nearby garden wall provided a route to climb in. She pushed Captain Black Jake up first, then followed and pulled the zip down again behind her.

It seemed the boat had been cleared out for winter storage. It was empty except for a padded bench seat the full width of the stern, and two swivelling bucket seats. Jake instantly appropriated the one by the wheel and took command of his vessel.

'Quietly remember,' cautioned Karen as she sorted through their remaining food and drink and decided what they would eat for tea.

47

Divided resources

Putting down his phone after the conversation with Jill, Greg was startled to see Chris enter his office, leaning heavily on an umbrella as a makeshift walking stick.

'What in heaven's name have you done to yourself?' he asked, hiding concern with mock humour.

'Put my foot in a hole on the beach,' replied Chris, sagging into a chair. 'And it hurts like buggery.'

'Have you had it checked out?' asked Greg.

'Not yet. Been too busy. Anyway, I don't think a hospital is a very good idea, just at present, do you? I'd go in with a busted ankle and come out with the plague! Anyway, I didn't come in to discuss my ankle. I've brought Ella Pentney back in with me. We're going to have to interview her again under caution and she's demanding a solicitor. She's just met her brother, the so-called Red, on the dunes in Yarmouth.'

'So I heard. Tell me you got him too,' urged Greg without much hope.

'Sorry, no. He got away on a bike and has gone to ground, probably somewhere in Yarmouth. Uniform are looking for him. It can surely be only a matter of time.'

'We've got another problem,' interrupted Greg. 'Arson, also in Yarmouth, and there's a body, so it's landing in my lap.'

'That's an image I could have done without,' remarked Chris, rubbing her ankle.

'There may be children involved as well. Jill's partner teaches one of them and was already concerned about her non-attendance in Zoom classes.'

'Were they in the fire?' asked Chris.

'The Fire Service haven't found any children's bodies so far, although I gather they've not been able to access the cellar yet. I'm just off to see Margaret to ask for more resources. While I'm gone, get that ankle looked at.'

'And how do you suggest I do that?' asked Chris.

'Dr Paisley is in the office. I saw her a few minutes ago. I'm sure she won't mind making an exception for a live victim, just this once.'

'Oh thanks,' said Chris.

Greg's discussions with Margaret were short and unsatisfactory. *Yes, the arson case must definitely fall to him, and no, he couldn't have any more resources.*

'Sorry, Greg, there are none,' she said. 'I have several officers down with Covid, so I'm short-handed already. And if this thing is as infectious as they say, that's only going to get worse. I gather there's a problem among the Bure prison staff too.'

Greg left feeling distinctly grumpy and went to find Jim.

'Just to be clear on the scale of our challenge,' he said, 'we have to organise the capture of a knife-wielding nutter, investigate a murder-slash-arson, probably launch a search for two missing children, tie up the loose ends on Helen Gabrys's fantastical attempt to get witness protection and make sure the Ella Pentney case is watertight. All with just you, me, Jill, Bill, Jenny and Steve.'

'Plus whatever help we can drum up from uniform,' said Jim optimistically. 'At least lockdown means they have a lot less to do catching speeding cars, drug dealers and rounding up drunks. And we have Chris of course.'

'Of course, you don't know yet,' said Greg. 'Chris has managed to sprain an ankle, assuming it's no worse than that, so we can take her off the active list for the rest of her time before she buggers off to Lowestoft. Which isn't far off.'

'She can still use her head,' said Jim. 'Assuming it's not broken. Her ankle that is, not her head. Sorry, I'm getting confused. Is she getting the ankle checked out?'

'Dr Paisley's taking a look,' said Greg. 'At least I assume that's what Chris means in this note she left on my desk.'

Gone to see Dr Death. Back soon, on one leg or two.

'Jim, I think Chris and Steve had better interview Pentney. She can do that sitting down. Can you, Bill and Jenny focus on catching Red? I'll join Jill in Yarmouth. We may need to regroup when we know more about what's happened to the children.'

'Leave it with me,' said Jim.

'Good. I'll speak to Chris before I go. And for God's sake, don't catch Covid! Any of you!'

Half an hour later, Greg was parking behind Jill's car in the still blocked street, with the burned house leaving a gap in the roof-line of the terrace like a missing tooth. A quick glance around and he spotted Jill by the one remaining fire engine. The Forensic Service van was just beyond that, and as he walked towards the group, he saw Dr Paisley's car pulling up as well.

'I see the troops have gathered,' he said to Jill, and looking at the fire officer he recognised one of the men he'd last seen at the site of a burned-out laboratory near Norwich. 'I recognise you, don't I?' he said.

'That's right,' said the man. 'Norwich Science Park – the terrorist attack.[1] Good afternoon, DCI Geldard.'

'Greg, please,' said Greg. 'And if I remember correctly Commander Fisher. What have we here?'

'One partly burned body found in the cupboard under the stairs. The cupboard was padlocked from the outside. From what remains of the clothes I would say female, but I'm sure the pathologist will give us a definitive answer.

'Signs of an accelerant having been used in the hall, on the cupboard door and in the kitchen. If the intention was to dispose of the body, then the attempt was amateurish. On the other hand, it was a pretty good try at burning the house down. The flames, once established, roared up the stairwell and there was plenty of combustible material both in the hall and on the stairs.'

'How long would it have taken the fire to get going?' asked Greg.

---

1. see Fires of Hate

'Not long. The witness who raised the alarm said she saw flames leaping in the hall through an open door, but at that point the room at the front of the house was unaffected.'

'Would there have been much of a delay between the arsonist setting the first flames and the fire taking off?'

'No. A matter of minutes, I'd say. He, or she, used what seems to have been firelighters and petrol.'

'So, if we're working on the assumption it wasn't the person in the cupboard, where are they?'

'My theory would be that as the alarm was being raised in front of the house, they were legging it out the back and down the ginnel behind the terrace until they escaped into the road that runs at right angles to this.' He pointed.

Dr Paisley passed by at that moment. 'Hi, Greg,' she said, and pulled the hood of her coveralls over her head. 'The usual?'

'Yes, that's right. Especially anything that will help me ID the victim.' He was talking to her back as it disappeared into the house, but she turned suddenly.

'Sorry, message for you from Sergeant Mathews. Said to tell you it's a sprain and she'll be getting on with the interviews.'

'Thank you. Jill, let's take a look at the back of the house while we wait for Ned and Dr Paisley.'

The ginnel stank of smoke and when Greg put his hand on the wall, it was still warm. He surveyed in silence the ruin of the backyard, running with water and blackened by soot, noting the open garden gate and the route someone running away could have taken to the road beyond.

'Any CCTV down there?' he asked.

'I'll check,' said Jill.

'I believe it was your partner who raised the alarm,' said Greg, walking back to the front of the house. 'Why was she here?'

'She already had concerns about the family,' said Jill. 'Apparently, the daughter is in her class and one of the brightest and best. Very hard-working and very committed. When she didn't join in class Zooms, Diana checked to see if there was a problem. You know, lack of hardware, no wi-fi, that kind of thing. When she came round here, she didn't get to see the girl at all, which was the first red flag, and she found the father aggressive. She thought the mother may have had a black eye too, all of which added up to a potential safeguarding problem. Trouble was, she couldn't be sure about any of it; she had no proof, and none of the neighbours had expressed any concerns. When she spoke to Norfolk Children's Services they were a bit lukewarm, so she said she'd visit the family again today and get back to them if she was still worried.'

'And instead, she finds a fire.'

'That's right. I've had chance for a quick word with some of the neighbours. They say the father would normally work long hours, but recently, like a lot of people, he'd been furloughed. Mother generally stayed home. The children, a boy and a girl, were described as happy and in the girl's case, "always had her nose in a book".'

'What was, or is, the father's job?' asked Greg.

'Works in a slaughterhouse.' They were interrupted by the sight of Dr Paisley emerging from the front door, taking care to avoid the piles of charred bricks lying in the road.

'Anything for me?' asked Greg.

'The body under the stairs is female. Around five foot five or six in height. And I'd say she was dead before the fire started. There is absolutely no indication that she was moving or attempting to get out of the cupboard when the flames reached her. And I think cause of death was blunt force trauma to the head, on the left temple. But I'll know more when I've had a better look, in the mortuary. That do you for now?'

'Yes. Thank you,' said Greg. 'Let's catch up with Ned, then check out the CCTV at the end of the road,' he said to Jill. 'Unless the fire service turn up another body, the missing father looks like being our number one suspect.'

'And the children?' asked Jill.

'Maybe he took them with him. That's the first thing to find out.'

48

Lost pirates

Karen tried to contact Tim on the mobile phone several times that afternoon. Only the last call, late in the evening, was answered.

'I'm sorry,' a strange voice said, 'but Tim Simmons is in hospital and can't take any calls. Who did you say was calling?'

Karen said nothing and rang off.

'What's Tim say?' asked Jake, who was beginning to tire of being a pirate captain.

'Nothing. That wasn't Tim,' said Karen. 'Tim's in hospital.'

'Is he going to die?' asked Jake.

'No, I'm sure he's not,' said Karen. 'Perhaps he's got Covid.'

'P'raps it's because Dad hit him,' said Jake more practically, and started running his toy car round the bench seat, with accompanying engine noises.

'Shush, Jake,' said Karen. 'I told you we mustn't make a noise.'

Jake was protesting, still too noisily for Karen's satisfaction, when there came a sharp rap on the hull of the little boat.

'Come out, whoever you are,' said a sharp voice. 'Come out at once. I know you're there. Come out, or I call the police.'

49

Déjà vu

Chris surveyed Ella Pentney across the table. Flanked by her, rather fed-up-looking, solicitor, she seemed in turns sulky and bored. Steve's notebook rustled as he turned the pages. He was old school and preferred to make his notes with biro and paper.

'Am I the only one experiencing a strong sense of déjà vu?' asked Chris. 'Here we are again, warning administered, tape running, everyone introduced and identified. All quite needlessly because we could have settled all this last time around.'

The, recalled, duty solicitor looked as though he agreed but forbore to say anything. Ella just shuffled in her seat.

'Let's see if we can get it right this time,' said Chris. 'No more evasions, lies or silences. Now's the time to come clean, Ella, if you want to come out of prison before the menopause.

'Tell me about your brother Eddie or Edward Pentney, also known as Red.'

'What do you want to know?' asked Ella.

'Where he lives would be a start,' said Chris.

'I've told you, I don't know,' replied Ella.

'You also told me you couldn't contact him, yet you were meeting him less than an hour after Detective Constable Street and I paid you a call. So that doesn't wash.' Suddenly Chris banged her hand on the table. 'Where does he live, Ella?'

'I've told you, I don't know.' Ella raised her voice too. 'I really don't know. I don't. It's somewhere in Yarmouth I think, but that's a guess. All I have is a mobile phone number. I rang it, said you'd been asking questions, and he said to meet him while he was walking Freddie.'

'The dog?'

'Yes, of course the dog.'

Chris put a printed list of phone numbers on the table. 'For the sake of the recording,' she said, 'I'm showing Ella Pentney a list of phone numbers taken from the contacts on her mobile phone.' Then to Ella, 'Which one is Red's? Point for me!'

Ella glanced at her solicitor, who moved not a muscle, then sighed and pointed to a number part way down the list. 'That's Red's,' she said.

'Let the record show that Ms Pentney has indicated a number which her phone records have displayed as the last number she rang today,' said Chris. She nodded at Steve, who got up from the table and left the room.

'We'll wait until he returns,' said Chris, and leaned back in her chair, sipping at a glass of water.

When Steve re-entered the room, he nodded and took his seat again.

'Interview resumed,' said Chris. 'Let's try a slightly different angle. How often do you normally see Red?'

'About once every few weeks,' replied Ella. 'He has his life, I have mine. We don't live in each other's pockets.'

'And typically, why would you meet?'

'Usually because he wants me to do him a favour,' said Ella with a slight tone of bitterness.

'What sort of favour?' The solicitor stirred in his seat but remained silent.

'Sometimes, would I look after Freddie, because he's travelling. Sometimes because he wants me to do something for him.'

'What sort of something?' Ella hesitated, and Chris added, 'Come on, Ella, you've already admitted passing information from here to the Gabryses. How much worse can things get? Be honest with me now, and at least you'll get some credit for helping us with our enquiries.'

'What sort of credit?' asked the solicitor, waking from an apparent doze. 'Is a plea bargain on the table?'

'Now, you know we don't go in for that sort of discussion in England,' reproved Chris. 'Have you been watching too many American TV shows? But I think I could say that if Ms Pentney assists us with answers to our questions, then maybe the CPS might conclude that it wasn't in the public interest to pursue all the items on Ms Pentney's charge sheet.'

'Such as?' demanded the solicitor succinctly.

Ella was transferring her attention from Chris to the solicitor, like a spectator at a tennis match.

'As you know, that's up to the CPS. But, for the sake of argument,' replied Chris, 'possibly the charges relating to supply of drugs?'

'Leaving the unauthorised disclosure of information and aiding and abetting blackmail?' clarified the solicitor. Chris agreed. He whispered for a moment in Ella's ear. She looked undecided, then nodded.

'Okay, I'll help if I can,' she said.

'Then let's go back to the question I asked earlier,' said Chris. 'What did Red ask you to do?'

'He would ask, from time to time, what I knew about stuff that was happening in the office. Sometimes it was just gossip, nothing of importance. Sometimes he asked for specific info.'

'Like, when witnesses were being moved?'

'That was the only time he asked that,' Ella said defensively. 'He said that he would be in big trouble with the boss if he didn't come up with something. And he *is* my brother.'

'Was he involved in the attack on Shinfield?' asked Chris.

'I don't know,' she replied. 'I really don't know. Honest. But guns don't sound like Red. He likes a knife.' Chris had to concede there was a ring of truth in that.

'What about the blackmail of Anthony Tayler?' she asked.

'I don't know about that.'

'One thing I'm not clear about,' said Chris, 'is precisely what Red's role is in the organisation. What do you know about that?'

'Only what he told me,' said Ella. 'To start with, he was proud of being a Gabrys empire hard man, an enforcer. That happened because he was mates with Mica. Then after it all blew up, when Mica died and Mr Gabrys went to prison, suddenly he said he was in charge of the Norfolk business. You know,' she added, 'I never really believed that. It just didn't ring true. It sounded like Red bigging himself up. Then stuff started to go wrong.'

'What sort of stuff?'

'I think other people were moving in to the territory, and whatever Red did, it didn't work. And that's about when Helen Gabrys suddenly asked me to collect the money from Anthony Tayler.'

50

Fugitives

Jim and Bill were deep in conversation with their colleagues at the Yarmouth police station. Constable Drake seemed to harbour the conviction that using a bike in a getaway was distinctly unsporting.

'Where exactly did you lose him?' asked Jim.

Drake pointed a long finger with a bitten nail at the map in front of them. 'Somewhere in this network of roads between Barnard Road and Beaconsfield Avenue,' she said. 'We lost sight of him around here,' – she pointed again – 'and after that it was guesswork, which way we went. We guessed wrong.'

'Have you checked CCTV footage?' asked Bill.

'For a man on a bike in a hurry?' asked Briscoe with a wry smile. 'Yes, we have. And yes, we spotted several, but I'm not convinced any of them was our man. At least, if they were, he'd dumped the dog.'

'Okay, then I think we've exhausted that line of enquiry. We have to give him best on that. We do have a mobile number now though, and the latest on that pinpoints a location not in Yarmouth, but in Gorleston. Let's see if we have better luck there.'

Bill unrolled a second map and laid it on the table. Then it was his turn to point. 'Just half an hour ago, the phone was here, somewhere in these streets between Nile Road and Springfield Road. It's been there quite a lot according to the historical data, so I think there's a good chance this is an important location for this Red. May be even where he's living.'

'Surely he wouldn't be stupid enough to carry on using his phone, knowing we're on to his sister?' said Drake. The older and more experienced police officers exchanged glances.

'Luckily,' replied Jim, 'as you will learn, there are few limits to the stupidity of the ordinary criminal. That's why we catch them. I recall one who thought that we wouldn't be able to track him through snow if he took his shoes off! And it would seem that Red is very ordinary, notwithstanding his grandiose ideas. It's worth checking out anyway.' He let go of the map, and it rolled itself up with a snap. 'We'll go in two cars,' he said. 'We'll start with the local businesses, asking if anyone recognises Red, or knows a man of his description that has a small Norfolk terrier named Freddie. Then take it from there.'

***

Over at the arson case, while Jill, joined by Jenny, checked out possible CCTV in the immediate vicinity, Greg snatched an opportunity to do some catching up. His first call was to his father, but when that went to answerphone, he tried Jim.

'That's good progress, Jim,' he said after listening to a succinct update.

'Thanks to Chris and the info she got from Ella Pentney,' replied Jim.

'One thing occurs to me,' went on Greg, still pursuing a line of thought. 'Have you checked with local vets for a man named Edward, Eddie or Red Pentney with a Norfolk terrier named Freddie. They might be able to give you an address.'

Jim smacked his head in frustration. 'Of course. Sorry. Next job,' he said, and rang off.

Greg grinned and tried his father again. This time the call was answered. His father sounded bored and tired, but his tone picked up markedly when Greg announced himself.

'How are you, Dad?' asked Greg. 'Have you settled in okay?'

'So far so good,' his father replied. 'My room is nice. Quite spacious and it has an en-suite. Which is just as well, as at the moment I'm being asked to isolate.'

'That sounds a bit grim,' exclaimed Greg. 'Why? I thought you were over the Covid.'

'As a precaution against me still being infectious,' his father replied. 'You can see their point. They have a lot of very vulnerable residents here, and the last thing they need is an in-house Covid outbreak. So they're being super careful. I'm isolated for the first week. I don't have much contact with the staff either, and the ones I do see are masked and gowned. It doesn't much matter,' he reassured Greg, 'because I'm still pretty tired, so I'm not exactly dashing around wanting to join dance classes or anything like that. No visitors permitted either, so I'm afraid we're stuck with phone calls.'

'We could do a video call,' said Greg. 'You've got your iPad there, haven't you? We could Zoom.'

'If I can work out how to do it,' his father replied. 'First, though, I need to talk to you about your mother's funeral.'

When Greg came off the phone and walked across the street to Jill, he was shaking his head.

'Something the matter, Boss?' she asked.

'Just the funeral arrangements,' he said. 'My mother's. It's going to be a weird one.'

'Lots of restrictions?' she asked.

'And then some. Only immediate family members, no singing, and we all have to keep two metres apart. In some ways, I think my father's relieved,' he added. 'He's never liked elaborate, set-piece ceremonies, so this would be his preference anyway, except for the two-metre thing. He's told me where he wants it, what he wants, and who he wants, and he's leaving the rest to me.'

'Can we help, Boss?' chipped in Jenny.

'Thanks, but I think we're okay,' he said. 'But it's kind of you to ask. Especially as we've enough to do here. Come on, gather round my car for a moment and let's compare notes. Ned,' he hailed the figure coming out of the blackened house. 'Quick catch-up, please.'

Greg leaned on the side of the car, while Jill, Jenny and Ned spaced themselves carefully in a socially-distanced semi-circle around him.

'Let's share what we know,' said Greg. 'Jill, describe the family who lived here, according to Diana's witness statement.'

'Diana taught one of the children and had visited,' explained Jill for Ned's benefit. 'I've been talking to the neighbours too.

Okay, the family, as far as we know, were father, Kit Mirren and mother, Anne Mirren, children, Karen aged nine and Jake aged six. Karen is described as a bright child, enthusiastic at school and always with her nose in a book. Jake is described as lively and not particularly interested in anything except cars and games, which isn't terribly unusual in a six-year-old boy. Diana had concerns that Karen wasn't engaging with online tuition, which she thought was out of character. When she visited, she wasn't able to see Karen and she thought the mother, Anne, had a black eye. She found the father abrasive and aggressive.

'Kit Mirren normally works in a slaughterhouse but is currently furloughed. I spoke to his employers a few moments ago and they said they had no plans to bring him off furlough any time soon. Something didn't ring quite right with me, so I plan to follow that up. The neighbours I've spoken to so far agree with Diana's assessment of the children.'

Jenny added, 'The neighbours in the house on the next road, the ones whose yard backs onto the Mirrens', they say there seemed to be a row going on yesterday and a visitor to the yard got hurt. Punched or kicked or something. I'm checking that out with local surgeries and the hospital. No one has seen any sign of any of the family for the last couple of days. But in the current circumstances, that's hardly surprising. No one has seen anyone at all, as far as I can make out.'

'Ned, what have you found?' asked Greg.

'Can't confirm it until the doc has done the post-mortem and, hopefully, found some viable DNA, but all the indications are that it was Anne Mirren locked in the understair cupboard and that she died of blunt force trauma to the head. There's no obvious weapon that I've found so far. There are no signs of any other casualties in the house, so the working hypothesis has to be that they all left the house before the fire took hold.'

Greg paused for thought. 'Priorities,' he said. 'Jenny, follow up the information you got from the neighbours, please. Check out the slaughterhouse for any information they have on Kit Mirren: what he's like, who he associates with, their view of him as a man. Also, please check the James Paget and any minor injuries units around here for anyone who may have been injured in that fight in the yard.

'Jill, can you organise uniform to give you a hand with a house-to-house? In particular we need to know when the children left the house and who with. See if anyone has any CCTV that might help, particularly in the streets at the end of the ginnel and then in the immediate vicinity. Also,' he added as an afterthought, 'do they know of any family members or friends who might have taken the children in?

'Ned, the main questions for you are what accelerant was used, any indication of where it might have come from and who used it. Also, can you find anything that might have been the blunt instrument that caused the victim's death. I'll look to Dr Paisley for anything further on ID.'

'Will do,' said Ned. 'We were lucky the fire didn't destroy the body completely, so she should be able to get some reasonable DNA. And fingerprints survive better than you'd think under the soot, so I may be able to lift some that will help us find the arsonist.'

'That would be good,' agreed Greg.

51

Thursday evening – sanctuary?

For a moment, Karen just froze. Jake looked at her open-mouthed and his hand was clenched so tightly round his toy car, his knuckles shone white.

'Did you hear what I said? Come out now, or else.'

'We'd better get out,' whispered Karen to Jake. She picked up the bag and lifted the corner of the oiled cloth roof. 'I'm coming out now,' she said, and was disgusted that her voice wobbled.

The person standing beside the boat was half in shadow, but, as Karen noted immediately, was a woman, an old woman. She immediately felt more confident.

'We need to climb down the wall,' she warned, and clambering over the side of the boat, felt for it with her feet. It was harder coming down than going up. Once she was at ground level, she clutched her bag to her chest and turned to the woman, waiting for her next move.

'How many are you?' she demanded.

'Just me and my little brother,' replied Karen, then raising her voice shouted, 'Jake, come on down.'

As Jake clambered down too, Karen surveyed the boat owner. She was indeed an old woman in Karen's eyes, probably at least fifty or sixty. She had dark hair speckled with white, and wrinkles round her mouth. Her jeans looked well-worn, and her jumper had seen better days too, in Karen's estimation. Jake jumped the last couple of feet off the wall and landed by her side with a thump.

'You'd better come into the light, so I can get a good look at you,' the woman said. 'Go on. Don't even think of running off, or I will call the police.' She held up her phone so they could see she meant what she said, and ushered them towards the open back door.

Once inside the house, she almost pushed them through the kitchen and into her living room. The lights in there were bright, and the children blinked in the glare.

'Not very old, are you?' said the woman, her hands on her hips as she surveyed her haul. 'Hungry?'

'Yes,' said Jake.

'Thought you might be,' said the woman. 'Sit there, don't move, and I'll be back with some sandwiches.' She pointed at a large sofa in front of the fire and went towards the kitchen. Suddenly she poked her head back into the sitting room. 'By the way, my name's Jo. You can call me Aunty Jo.' And she was off, back into the kitchen.

Jake looked at Karen. 'What do we do now?' he asked. 'Do you think she'll help us find our mum?'

'Shh,' warned Karen, looking at the door into the kitchen. 'Don't say anything just yet.'

The woman came back with a big plate of egg sandwiches and two packets of crisps. 'Egg is all I've got, so egg it is,' she said. 'I hope you're not fussy types.'

'We like egg,' said Karen, albeit her comment was somewhat unnecessary in the face of Jake's enthusiastic consumption. She took a sandwich rather more politely and accepted the packet of crisps offered.

'I have some cake as well,' Aunty Jo offered. 'Lemon drizzle. Want some?' Jake's affirmative was obscured by egg butty, but clear enough for all that. Aunty Jo retired to the kitchen again, and came back with the cake, already cut into thick slices.

Once the rate of consumption slowed, even Jake's, Aunty Jo said, 'Time you two told me what you're doing, wandering about on your own and hiding in my boat. You,' – she pointed at Karen – 'tell me where you came from and where you're going.'

Karen took her time over her last mouthful, then looked at Aunty Jo, considering what to say.

'Don't lie to me,' said Aunty Jo. 'I can see you considering what story to tell. Much easier to just tell me the truth.'

'Okay,' said Karen. 'Our father is violent and our mum disappeared, so we ran away. We know she has a friend in this village, and we were looking for him because we think that's where we'll find Mum.'

'Who's the friend?' asked Aunty Jo.

'Uncle Tim,' said Jake, interrupting what Karen had been going to say and earning a glare. 'But he's not answering his phone and we couldn't find him.'

'What's his phone number?' asked Aunty Jo. 'I could try.'

Karen took the mobile out of her bag and showed the old lady the last number she'd dialled. 'It's this one,' she said.

Aunty Jo picked up a phone from the table beside her, tapped three numbers then looked at the phone Karen was holding out. She dialled again, referring to the number in front of her, then held the phone to her ear. 'It's ringing,' she said. She was just about to ring off when it was answered.

'Hello,' she said, 'can I speak to Tim?' She listened for a bit, then said, 'Thank you,' and rang off.

'They said your Tim is in hospital,' she reported.

'That's what they told me,' agreed Karen.

'I think you'd better stay here tonight,' said Aunty Jo. 'Then we can decide what to do in the morning. Thirsty?' she asked. After crisps, egg butties and cake, they were.

'I'll get you a Coke each, then to bed.'

'I don't think we should stay here,' said Karen, feeling rather nervous.

'Nonsense,' said Aunty Jo, and went to fetch the drinks.

'Should we run away again?' asked Jake in a whisper.

'Let's wait and see,' said Karen as their hostess came back with the glasses of Coke.

Before she'd quite finished her glass, Karen was feeling odd: very sleepy and her eyes seemed fuzzy. She turned to look at Jake. He'd already finished his drink and had dropped the empty glass on the carpet.

'Sorry,' Karen managed to say, as she put her glass back on the table. Then both children were asleep.

Jo looked down at them. 'Sweet dreams,' she said, and collected the glasses to put in the dishwasher.

52

Friday 27 March – progress on all fronts

Jim punched the air with delight, startling the veterinary receptionist who had been addressing him from the prescribed distance of two metres.

'Sorry,' he said, aware that she now looked as though three metres were all too few between her and this apparent madman. 'That's good news. Thank you for your assistance.'

Outside the vet's surgery and heading for his car at something close to a run, he was barking orders into his radio.

'Converge on the following address,' he said. 'There's a good chance our suspect might be there. I want at least two officers round the back, approaching from either end of the ginnel. Constable Drake and Bill, meet me at the front. I'll be there in five minutes. No blues, no sirens. We don't want to startle our prey.'

Moments later, as Jim entered the west end of Cliff Road, he saw a liveried police car turn in from the east. There were sufficient cars parked along its length that the road was, effectively, reduced to single carriageway for much of the way.

'Fine, suits me,' muttered Jim, and parked in the middle of the road, thus neatly blocking passage to all traffic. He saw the police car at the other end do the same, boxing in all the houses in the immediate vicinity of No 14. A large BMW behind him hooted, and Jim reached for his warrant card as he walked towards the impatient driver.

'Sorry, madam,' he said to the back of the long-haired head that had turned away as he approached, in order to deal with a toddler tantrum going on in the front passenger seat. 'Sorry, sir,' he amended as the head turned back towards him, beard bristling with outrage. 'We have a police operation underway. I'm afraid you'll have to take another route.' And he waved the car away. As he walked towards No 14, he heard a lot of revving and grinding of gears, indicative of yet another SUV driver who struggled with reversing. He smothered a smile as he met Drake and Bill coming from the other direction, the uniformed constable burdened with a big red door key.

'Team in place at the back, sir,' said Bill.

'Good. They know what to do?' asked Jim.

'Yes. And I particularly warned them to watch out for the target escaping on a bike,' replied Bill. Constable Drake snorted but said nothing.

'Good. Let's do it.' Jim rapped smartly on the front door of No 14, and then rang the doorbell for good measure. When that got no response, he banged again and shouted, 'Police! Open up!' Still no response, so he stood back, beckoning for sterner measures to be employed.

If Jim was expecting Bill to deploy the enforcer, aka the big red door key, he was wrong. Constable Drake swung it with impressive and effective force, and the door was open. Even as they entered, they heard shouts from the rear of the property, a scuffle and the clang as something metallic fell into a sheet of corrugated iron, apparently forming part of a scruffy fence. A voice on the radio piped up, 'Got him, sir.'

Jim led the rush down the yard to where a gate stood open onto the ginnel. A figure in a dark sweatshirt and trackies was struggling on the ground under his bike, held down by one of the uniformed officers who had been guarding the rear exit. Bill stepped forwards to pick up an excitable Norfolk terrier, which immediately attempted to lick him to death.

'You were right about the bike,' said the constable sitting on top of it, apparently impervious to the struggles of the man in the hoodie, face pressed into the mud of the ginnel. 'He almost made it away again.'

'Edward, or Eddie or Red Pentney,' said Jim, catching his breath. 'I am arresting you for the murder of...' He turned to Bill. 'What was the first victim's name again?' he asked.

'Geoff Manners,' said Bill.

'...the murder of Geoff Manners and the attempted murder of Nathan Standish,' he said. 'That'll do for now. Cuff him and take him to Wymondham. We might as well have the whole conspiracy in the same set of cells.'

***

In Yarmouth, Jill had struck lucky with a neighbour's doorbell linked to a camera. Unfortunately, she'd had to wait an hour for said neighbour to return home from an early shift stacking shelves in Asda, but now, at last, she was sitting reviewing footage for the day before. The downside was, all it showed her was an unmoving and neglected front door, with no associated traffic whatsoever until her partner, Diana, was seen to arrive in the late morning.

'Drat,' she said. 'I still have no idea what happened to the children. It's clear the father left through the back door, maybe the kids did too. One last try, and I am truly grateful for your patience, but could we try going backwards through your recordings until we do spot something happening over the road. That will at least show us when the children and maybe their mother were out and about.'

'Okay,' said Mrs Tenent, a middle-aged lady in an Asda uniform. 'I can just flick to the moments when the camera picked up some movement, but there will be a lot of irrelevant stuff, like me coming and going, and people walking past.'

'That's fine,' said Jill. 'Don't worry, I spend my life sifting through irrelevant stuff. It's a pretty good definition of the job, come to think of it.' She smiled at her hostess and finished the mug of coffee she'd been given on arrival. 'Let's go backwards, starting from midday today and see what hits we get.'

'Okay,' said Mrs Tenent. 'More coffee?'

'Not just now,' replied Jill, and settled down to watch the tablet screen in front of her.

Front door battery low, was the first thing she saw. 'Drat,' she said again, but Mrs Tenent was reassuring.

'Don't worry, that won't affect the earlier recordings,' she said, and started winding time backwards.

She was right; there was a lot of irrelevant stuff, albeit considerably less than in a more normal year without the plague-related movement restrictions. At Jill's request, the recording was stopped a couple of times to check that people walking past the camera weren't obscuring something on the other side of the road, but she was unable to spot anything of interest.

The recording was moving quickly through the darker hours of the early morning, when Jill suddenly snapped, 'Wait!' and pointed. Two small figures left the house and walked over the road, before disappearing from the realms of the fisheye lens into the area in front of the alley to the next road.

'That's them,' she said. 'I'm sure of it.' She made a note of the time recorded on the camera: 05:55. 'So the two children left, on their own, just before six in the morning. I wonder where they went after that! Thank you, Mrs Tenent, you've been very helpful. I will need to take these recordings with me, but I can do that by copying them to my iPad. We'll be in touch if we need anything else.'

Back in her car, she reported to Greg, then followed up with a call to Jenny.

'Anything from the medical centres?' she asked.

'Not yet,' Jenny replied. 'But I'm going to have a chat with Mr Mirren's employers next, then chase up the hospitals and so on after that. Judging from what was said about the fight in the backyard, I think I might get a name from his workplace, and that will make the search easier.'

Jill nodded, forgetting that Jenny couldn't see her. 'Okay. Makes sense,' she said. 'Let's keep each other posted.'

53

Friday in Gorleston

Over at Great Yarmouth and Gorleston Meat Packers, Jenny was settled in a hard wooden chair facing a man with a similarly hard wooden expression.

'Forgive me for asking,' he was saying, 'but what does this have to do with us?'

'Nothing directly, as far as I'm aware,' replied Jill. 'I just need some information on your employee Kit Mirren, as I said. Normal stuff, like how long have you employed him, who are his colleagues or associates, what sort of man is he, and where might I find him?'

'And you're not seeking to dig up dirt on our operations here?' the man asked. According to the sign on his desk, he was Mr Hamilton, CEO of GYG Meat Packers. 'Sorry if I'm a bit suspicious,' he added, leaning back in his chair. 'It's only a couple of years since the previous company here was raided by animal rights activists, who filmed in the plant and caused all sorts of trouble. The previous company ended up bankrupt, which is when we moved in and took over. I don't want the same to happen to us.'

Jenny had a vague recollection of the trouble of a few years ago. 'Weren't they found guilty of all sorts of animal-welfare breaches?' she asked, with an innocent air. 'So perhaps the activists had a point.'

'Quite, no argument about that,' agreed Mr Hamilton hastily. 'But we've been very careful to keep on top of our procedures here, both hygiene and animal welfare. Our standards are very high, and we record our processes ourselves, just to make sure. But you've no idea how hard it is to shake off a bad reputation, even when we weren't here at the time. Although,' he hesitated, and flushed slightly, which was at odds with his normally sallow complexion, 'there are one or two men we re-employed from the old times. Kit Mirren is one of them.'

'I understand he's furloughed at present,' said Jenny. 'Were you planning on bringing him back to work soon?'

'As the workload picks up,' agreed Mr Hamilton.

'I thought it already had,' said Jenny, 'judging by your throughput statistics so proudly displayed in your outer office. But still no Kit Mirren?'

'The thing is,' admitted Mr Hamilton, 'he's a good enough worker, but he's a troublemaker. If I have a choice of men, he's not first on my list.'

'What sort of troublemaker?' asked Jenny. 'Union activist? Lazy?'

'No, nothing like that,' said Mr Hamilton. 'But he has a bad temper, and he gets into fights. The other men don't like him, and I think some of them are afraid of him.'

'Doesn't he have any mates here?' asked Jenny.

'A few. Mainly among the cutters rather than among the slaughter crew.'

'Could I have a word?'

Mr Hamilton looked dubious. 'They're a rough lot,' he said. 'Are you sure you want to walk through a hall full of men wielding sharp knives?'

'So long as I'm not their target, I think it'll be fine,' said Jenny. 'But perhaps I could have a look at his personnel file first, and anything he's got stored in his locker?'

In fact, in what Mr Hamilton called the cutting hall, where carcasses were being reduced to piles of joints and chops, Jenny's first thought was how much her usual partner, PD Turbo, would have enjoyed this visit. As a result, she had a smile on her face when she walked up to the first two men in the processing line, and they were disarmed by the friendly expression. In no time at all, she was in possession both of the information that Kit Mirren had beaten up, quite badly, a man named Tim that he suspected of sleeping with his wife, and of a packet of bones and trimmings for Turbo.

'Bring the dog next time,' said one of the men as she left, pursued by friendly waves. The bemused Mr Hamilton showed her out with a much friendlier expression than which he had greeted her.

'So,' she concluded her report back to Jill and Greg on a party call. 'I'm off to the James Paget in pursuit of a badly bruised Tim. Any news on those poor kids?'

'Only that they seem to have run away from the house in the early hours of the morning,' said Greg. 'On the plus side, they missed the fire, but where they are now is our next problem. The whole of the Yarmouth team is on the lookout now!'

'Perhaps this Tim might be able to cast some light,' said Jenny. 'I'll get over there as quickly as I can.'

Arriving at the James Paget Hospital, Jenny took one glance and realised that in the fuss and flurry of the moment, she'd forgotten all about Covid and its complications. If the car park was unusually empty, the ambulance parking spaces were not. There was a substantial queue of vehicles waiting to offload patients outside the new, temporary, Covid-positive entrance to A&E. Jenny parked close to the usual hospital entrance and attempted to walk in. She was very swiftly waved back by a masked security guard, who informed her that hospital visiting was not currently allowed. She found that communicating her role and the reason for her visit was not easy through two masks and two-plus metres of space, but eventually, after much waving of her warrant card, she managed to get the guard to understand that she needed to interview one of the hospitals patients.

'I understand he was brought in with injuries from a beating,' she repeated for the umpteenth time. 'Nothing to do with Covid at all.'

'Just wait here,' said the harassed guard, pointing at a spot a safe distance from the entrance. 'I'll go and consult.'

Waiting outside, Jenny noted with resignation that it had begun to rain, and hoped the guard would not be long. In fact, she was cold, wet and moderately bad-tempered by the time he reappeared with a man in mufti in tow.

'He'll explain,' he said, indicating his colleague, and returned to guarding duties.

The person in dark trousers and white shirt with blue jumper turned out to be a volunteer receptionist. 'I'm sorry,' he said, 'you can't come into the hospital, even for a formal interview. The person you wish to see is in a Covid ward.'

'But he came in after a fight,' said Jenny.

'And either had Covid already or caught it here. Quite probably the latter,' the man agreed. As far as Jenny could see round the edges of his mask, he was in his early thirties and looked tired. 'There's a lot of it about, which is why I'm filling in for a colleague. I'd normally be working in accounts!

'The best we can do, I'm afraid, is let you talk to him via an iPad. Do you have a mobile phone or similar to hand? If you can give me your number, I can get the ward to set up a call. Say in thirty minutes, provided they don't have a crisis in the meantime,' he added with belated caution.

'I suppose that will have to do,' said Jenny, conscious of rain now dripping down the back of her neck. She told him her phone number and watched him write it in biro on the back of his hand.

'Around half an hour,' he repeated, and disappeared back into the hospital. Jenny went to sit in her car, with a sigh.

Half an hour passed, then three quarters.

I'll give them an hour. Then... thought Jenny, albeit she couldn't think of a 'then' that didn't involve waiting patiently. She scrabbled round in her glove box for some mints, and jerked upright again as her phone rang with the irritating jingle she'd chosen in a foolish moment.

'DC Warren,' she said, and regarded the figure showing on the screen. A pale man with livid bruising showing under strapping on his head looked back at her, then coughed convulsively. 'I'm sorry to bother you when you're clearly not well,' said Jenny. 'But I need to talk to you urgently about

Kit and Anne Mirren, and more specifically about their two children, Karen and Jake. First of all, can you confirm your full name for me?'

'Tim Simmons. What's happened?' asked Tim hoarsely.

'Am I right in thinking you were a friend of Anne Mirren?' asked Jenny and realised, too late, what she'd said.

'I am a friend of Anne's. Hang on, what's happened to Anne? What's that maniac done now?' demanded Tim.

'I'm very sorry to have to tell you, Mr Simmons, that a body has been found at the home of Kit and Anne Mirren, and we have reason to believe it is Anne. I'm very sorry,' she repeated.

If anything, the man on the screen went paler, and one of the nurses, dimly visible in the background, took a step closer.

'Don't you know whether it's Anne?' he asked. 'What do you mean, have reason to believe? Where's Kit and where are the children?'

'That's what I wanted to talk to you about,' said Jenny, disregarding the question she didn't want to answer. 'Both Kit and the children are missing, but we don't think they're together. It seems likely the children ran away from home in the early hours of this morning. Do you know where they might have gone? Do they have family, for example, in the area?'

'No,' said Tim. 'They don't have any family I know of. Neither Kit nor Anne has brothers or sisters, and none of the parents live anywhere near. In fact, I don't think they were on speaking terms with Kit's parents. The kids might have gone looking for me I suppose, but I haven't been home.' He ended on a despairing note and started coughing again.

'Where do you live, Mr Simmons?' asked Jenny. 'Is it far?'

'Not far, but not walking distance, not by children. I live in Ormesby.'

'Do the children know where you live?'

'I think so. Yes, they do. At least, Karen does. She asked me once.' He coughed again, and had to stop talking. The nurse who'd moved before now stepped forwards to intervene.

'I think that's enough,' she said. Tim waved a hand to attract her attention and shook his head.

'Wait, I want to know what's happened to Anne.'

'I'm sorry, Tim,' said Jenny. 'I can't tell you any more until the next of kin has been informed. Do you know how I might contact Anne's parents?'

'All I know is, they live in Woodbridge and their surname is Brownsey.'

'That will help us find them,' said Jenny. 'Thank you, Tim, and I'm sorry for your loss. One last question,' she said, forestalling a further interruption from the nurse. 'Is there anyone at your home who might answer the door to two runaways?'

'No. I live alone,' said Tim. 'Hang on though, there was a call on my phone. One of the nurses here took the call, because I was a bit out of it at the time. They said they told whoever rang that I was in hospital.' He started to fumble on his bedside table.

'Can you tell who rang from your call records?' asked Jenny, without much hope the conversation would go on for much longer.

Indeed, Tim was interrupted by another bout of coughing, but continued to flick through screens on his phone. 'It was Anne's phone,' he said, 'at around 10.30 this morning. So she must have been okay. God, I wish I'd taken the call!' and he started coughing again.

'That is definitely that,' said the nurse, and ended the call.

54

Darkness visible

When Karen woke, it was to sounds of Jake crying.

'I don't like it. I don't like the dark. You know I don't like the dark. Put the lights on, Karen. Make them put the lights on.'

Once Karen got her eyes fully open and her brain in gear, she realised that although black enough to scare Jake, it was not completely dark. There was a little light flashing high up in one corner of the ceiling and, by its dim and intermittent glow, she could see just a little. She put her arms round Jake and hugged him close.

'It's okay, Jake,' she said. 'I expect the nice lady didn't know you were scared of the dark. Just wait a minute and I'll find the light switch.'

She got to her feet and almost fell over the duvet that had been covering them both. She sat down again and felt around her. She and Jake seemed to be sitting on a bed, in a corner of a room. She made a second attempt at standing up, and started to move cautiously round the walls, feeling for a light switch. She did a full circuit of the room but found nothing: no switches, and no window.

'Hurry up,' whined Jake. 'I don't like it.'

'I am trying,' replied Karen, thinking, *I don't like this either. Where are we?*

Suddenly, the room was flooded with a harsh light from a fitting in the ceiling. Karen blinked in the glare, blinked again and looked round the room. In addition to the bed, there was a small table, two wooden chairs, a bookcase and a short flight of steps leading up to a door in one corner. She turned to Jake as his sniffles subsided with the coming of the light, and then whipped back as she heard the door open.

The lady from the night before was standing in the doorway, a tray in her hands.

'Good morning,' she said cheerily. 'I've brought you some breakfast. And this.' She put the tray down on the small table and proffered his toy car to Jake. 'You left it upstairs last night,' she said.

'Where are we?' asked Karen.

'In my guest room,' said the lady. 'Don't you remember coming down here to sleep last night?'

'No,' said Karen. 'I don't remember anything after our supper.'

'You were very tired,' said the lady. 'And no wonder after all that worry and the wandering around. Just you enjoy your breakfast and relax a bit.'

'I want the loo,' announced Jake.

'Oh, of course,' said the lady. 'All that sort of thing is over there in the corner.' She pointed at the bookcase, and Karen noticed for the first time that it formed a sort of screen between the bedroom and a little space, not much larger than a cupboard, containing a toilet and a washbasin.

'It's very kind of you to do all this,' said Karen, 'but I think we should be on our way now.'

'Just enjoy your breakfast first,' said the lady, and went back up the stairs to the door. It closed behind her with a clang.

Karen followed her up the steps and tried to open the door, but it was locked. She shook the handle, but the door was firm in its frame and didn't budge even a millimetre. She banged on the door and shouted, 'We want to come out. Let us out!' and banged again, but there was no response.

Turning, she looked down at Jake, who was now tucking into buttered toast and marmalade. He had, typically, ignored the boiled eggs that were also on the tray.

'The door's locked,' she said. 'We can't get out.'

He shrugged. 'I expect she forgot,' he said. 'She'll be back.' He took another bite of toast.

55

Three days later – Monday 30 March 2020

It was the morning of his mother's funeral. Greg was feeling guilty at taking time off from his investigations, and feeling guilty that he was feeling guilty. When he expressed this to Chris, she snorted.

'Your trouble,' she said, dropping a kiss on his cheek that took the sting out of the words, 'is an overdeveloped conscience, combined with an assumption that everything will go to pot if you're not around. For goodness' sake, forget about work for today, and...' She just stopped herself from saying *enjoy yourself* and ended, '...focus on your father. Leave the rest to Jim and the team. They know what they're doing.'

'I'd feel a lot happier if we'd found those children and their father,' he replied. 'I don't know whether to hope they're together, or hope they're apart, but either way it terrifies me that they're still missing.'

'As far as we know, the children skedaddled for Ormesby, and the father disappeared somewhere in Yarmouth. We've no reason to believe they left together, and Jim's got a full-scale search underway. There's not much else you can do at the moment,' replied Chris.

'No, but Kit Mirren could have arranged to meet them later. It's very odd, how they just seem to have disappeared in what's not an enormous village after all. That bus driver was clear he saw them walking down into the centre of the village, but after that, nothing. The logic has to be that someone's taken them in, or taken them away. There's not much else that's possible.'

'Very little CCTV, that's the problem,' commented Chris. 'But this isn't focussing on your father, and that's the job for today. Come on, forget the Mirrens just for a few hours. What time are you due at the crematorium in Cambridge?'

'Ten,' Greg replied. 'I should be back early afternoon. This strange new world doesn't include provision for a wake. Just a short, socially distanced service, then goodbye.'

'I still think it's odd to have it in Cambridge,' said Chris. 'It's nowhere near your family home.'

'But it is near the home Dad's currently living in, and it's handy for the hospital where Mother died. Given that none of their friends can attend, but only watch it online, it didn't really matter where it was held.'

'True. But I'm sorry I can't come.'

'I know, but the numbers are difficult and it's your first day in your new job, so don't feel bad about that. Go on, time you were leaving. I'll ring you later to let you know how it went. Good luck.'

***

When he arrived at the Cambridge crematorium, the first thing Greg noticed was the plethora of Covid-related instructions. The second was the hearse.

He parked hurriedly in a space more than adequate for the tiny number of mourners permitted to attend in person and nodded to his aunt and uncle still sitting in their car.

'I'm so glad you could come,' he said to them through the closed car windows. 'My father will be very pleased.'

They nodded and his mother's sister wiped a hankie under her eye. 'We'll join you when your father arrives,' she mouthed at him.

Greg looked up at the sound of another car engine. 'I think that's him now,' he said. He watched as the car pulled up alongside the hearse, then walked over swiftly to join the father he hadn't seen in person since he had contracted Covid. The first person out of the car was a carer, who proceeded to unload a wheelchair from the boot and push it to the passenger door. His father emerged slowly, and, with caution, sank into the wheelchair. As Greg approached the carer looked up.

'Please don't make physical contact,' he was warned. 'Your father is still vulnerable to reinfection, and we have to protect the rest of our residents.' Greg stopped awkwardly, the prescribed two metres away, unsure how to proceed with all his natural instincts thwarted.

His father summoned up a smile. 'I'll take the hug as read,' he said, correctly interpreting his son's expression. 'There'll be time enough for all that when this damn virus is defeated.'

They both watched as the simple coffin, topped by white lilies, was unloaded from the hearse and wheeled into the crematorium.

'You go first, Dad,' said Greg. 'I'll follow.' Coffin was followed by wheelchair, then by son and after that by two couples from the car park, in a pathetically tiny, socially distanced procession.

Sitting, carefully spaced out in the large hall, well-ventilated to the point of frigidity, the family of Monica Leila Geldard said their isolated goodbyes with words and recorded music, then went their separate ways.

'As soon as I'm allowed, I'll come to see you, Dad,' were Greg's final words.

'Yes, do,' his father replied, then added to the carer, 'Don't hurry me away, please. I know we're due back soon, but I can have a chat with my son, can't I?'

She sighed heavily but smiled and nodded. 'But be quick,' she said.

'I'm sorry I haven't been able to do more,' Greg began, but his father interrupted.

'You do all you can,' said his father. 'I know that. I just wanted to tell you that I plan to sell the house, when I'm able, and move to sheltered accommodation nearer you. I don't want you to feel you have to nurse me,' he added, 'but I would like to be close enough to see you more often. I hope that's okay.'

'I'd like that, Dad,' said Greg. 'That would suit both Chris and me very well. I'm glad you want to do it.'

'Okay, that's sorted then. I'm going to need a hand organising the house for sale and eventually with moving, but that can all wait a bit. There's no hurry. But at least we're agreed on where we're aiming.'

'It's a plan,' agreed Greg and, feeling a bit silly, blew his father a kiss.

'Get off with you,' his father said. But he was smiling.

***

Greg considered the remainder of his hypothetical day off, the prospect of spending time at home, without Chris, worrying about the missing Mirren children, and turned his car resolutely to Wymondham. His arrival at Jim's desk had something of the whirlwind about it. Newly energised by both the clarity of his father's decision and the much-dreaded funeral being over, he was full of plans. The first was derailed immediately.

'Jim, can we have a meeting with the CPS to clarify where we're going with the Gabrys and Pentney cases?' were the words on his lips.

'Good, you're back,' was Jim's response. 'Margaret wants to see us about a press conference.'

Greg wondered whether the rest of the day off might not have been a good idea after all. 'The children?' he said with a sinking feeling.

'Yes. She says she can't sit on the press any longer without giving them something, so there's to be a press conference on Zoom in an hour,' – he checked his watch – 'and she wants a final catch-up before she goes live.'

'Trouble is, we've nothing to report except failure,' said Greg. 'Unless you've got anything new since last night?'

'No, just more of the same,' replied Jim.

If Margaret was pleased to see Greg, she hid it well. 'You were supposed to be at your mother's funeral today,' she said accusingly.

'I was. It's over,' he said, used, by now, to Margaret in this mood. 'Covid-era funerals don't last long.'

'And your father?' she asked.

'As well as you can expect. Better really. He's starting to sound like his old self and making plans.'

'Good. Now for the press conference,' she said. 'What's the latest news?'

Jim stepped up to the mark. 'In summary,' he said, 'we've blanketed the village where the children were last seen getting off a bus. We've posters all over the village and messages on social media asking for any sightings. We've also started a house-to-house down the street where the bus driver saw them walking, and the streets leading off, but that's been problematical.'

'In what way?'

'In every way really, and all down to Covid. First, there's next to no one out and about on the streets, so no sightings. Second, although there's a lot of people working from home, not everyone is willing to come to the door. On quite a few properties there are signs saying that someone inside is shielding, and not to bother them. In some cases, it's been possible to have a conversation at long distance, or through a window, but it's not very satisfactory. And for those who don't answer the doorbell at all, what can we do? We can't go using forcible means without good reason.'

'Hence me wanting this press conference,' said Margaret. 'I want an appeal for information on TV. It's the one thing you can be reasonably sure everyone is watching, even the technophobic.

'To sum up, we're confident the two children left Yarmouth on the bus and got off in Ormesby. We have the statement from the driver, backed up by the CCTV on the bus. No one else got off at that stop, so no help there. And no other sightings, that's what you're telling me?'

'That's right,' said Greg. 'It's as though they vanished into thin air.'

'What about the phone call they made to their mother's friend, this Tim?'

'We've tried to track the phone they used, which was their mother's. Unfortunately, the masts in the area don't triangulate the call very precisely. They put it in the middle of Ormesby, which we knew already.'

'And the location of the phone now?'

'Nothing.'

Margaret drummed her fingers on her desk, then ran them through her hair. 'What about the elephant in the room? The Trinity Broads? They're not far away.'

'But we've no evidence the children went near them, nor any reason to believe they would want to. Do we really want to start that hare running? Or incur the costs of dragging three large Broads for bodies?' asked Greg.

'What do you propose to do? The press are bound to ask.'

Greg sighed and scratched his head. 'Essentially, more of the same,' he admitted. 'I can't see what else we can do. We need more knocking on doors, more checking of outhouses and garages, more scrutiny of properties to see if they have any doorbells with cameras that may have spotted something useful, and we'll continue to monitor for the mobile phone, in case it comes back into use. But on top of that, what we most need to do is find Kit Mirren. I think we need a new focus on him. I'm proposing to revisit every last item of evidence we have. I refuse to accept he's disappeared as well. Someone must know something, and or someone's hiding him. If you plan a public appeal at the press conference, then I'd include something about that.'

Back in Greg's office, Jim looked at him and laughed. 'I thought you'd blown it then,' he said. 'I think she was within a whisker of telling you to join the conference.'

'So did I,' admitted Greg. 'Even as I heard the words leave my lips, I knew it was a mistake. However, as it seems I've been let off, let's make good use of the time. Get the team together and we'll go over what we know. Someone may come up with a new angle. And tomorrow, we'll have that meeting with the CPS to tie up the Gabrys and Pentney cases.'

'They're saying the delays in getting to court are getting longer and longer,' warned Jim. 'The last I heard it could be a year. Or even more.'

'Dear God,' said Greg. 'I'll have forgotten what it was all about by then! Okay, let's meet in fifteen minutes, and everyone bring their notes, formal and informal.'

56

Examining the evidence

Greg reinforced this message as he looked round the intent faces of Jim, Jenny, Jill, Bill and Steve. 'Right,' he said. 'This is about reviewing what we know, think or guess about Kit Mirren and coming up with new approaches to finding him, since the old ones seem to have run into the ground. I'll start, but everyone chip in if I miss something or you have a new idea.'

'What about Ned, shouldn't he be here?' asked Jill.

'He's out on another case, but I have some notes he made for me.

'Kit Mirren, aged thirty-four, has worked for Yarmouth and Gorleston Meat Packers for the last eight years, the first three under the old management. In those early years the company was targeted by animal rights activists and was subsequently the subject of several improvement orders from the Food Standards Agency's Meat Hygiene Service, relating to animal-welfare breaches. I think it's fair to conclude that his work experience in those years was probably pretty rough, if not brutal.

'He was kept on by the new management, but they're not too keen on him, describing him as bad-tempered and unpredictable.'

'In a violent sense,' added Jenny.

'Yes, that's right. There was mention of anger-management issues, and having put him on furlough, they've little appetite for bringing him back. On Tuesday, 24th of March there was an altercation in his backyard during which he inflicted serious injuries on a Tim Simmons, who he accused of being his wife's lover. Tim does indeed say he was a friend of Anne Mirren and had taken both her and her children out for day trips more than once; the last occasion being a few days earlier. As well as Tim himself, the fight was witnessed by neighbours. We have their statements.

'There is also some indication that he was violent to his wife prior to the events of this week. Two of his fellow workers claim he was known to be free with his fists and that he hit his wife, but there's no concrete evidence of that.'

'On the other hand,' chipped in Jill, 'Diana said she thought Anne Mirren had a black eye when she saw her on the morning of the twenty-fourth.'

'No one, neighbours, workmates, or anyone else, has accused Kit Mirren of assaulting his children, although several have commented that he seemed hard on the boy and dismissive of the achievements of the girl,' Greg pointed out. He took up the story again. 'That takes us to this Thursday, the 26th. Around 5.55 in the morning, the two children, each carrying a bag, were caught on a neighbour's doorbell camera, emerging from the ginnel by their home and crossing the road. They caught a bus from the bus station at 06.15, having convinced the driver they were meeting their mother in Ormesby and got off at the stop by the old Royal Oak. They were seen to walk down the street called Wapping and that was the last the bus driver saw of them.

'Subsequently, they were caught on camera at the village petrol station, buying a sausage roll and milk, which they ate while sitting on a low wall. They then walked away towards the centre of the village. After that, nothing.

'But to go back to the early hours in Yarmouth, Jill, you pick up the tale for this bit.'

'My partner, Diana,' said Jill with a faint flush, 'teaches the elder child, a girl named Karen. She was concerned that Karen hadn't attended recent online classes and that this was out of character. She had already made one visit to the home and had left an old iPad for the children's use, so she knew the problem wasn't lack of hardware. That morning, she arrived outside the family home at 11.10 and spotted flames leaping in the hallway, which rapidly spread to the sitting room. She and neighbours raised the alarm.'

'And to cut a long story short,' said Greg, taking up the tale again, 'when the fire service arrived, they found one casualty, subsequently identified by DNA analysis as Anne Mirren, locked in the understair cupboard. The body was charred but not completely consumed. Dr Paisley is of the opinion that cause of death was a blunt trauma to the head. There were no other bodies anywhere within the house or yard.

'Ned informs me that the fire was started deliberately using firelighters and petrol as accelerants. The firelighters were stacked against the cupboard door, suggesting that this was an attempt at getting rid of the body. Kit Mirren's fingerprints were found in multiple places in the house, as you'd expect, but, most importantly, on the cupboard door, the padlock and on a petrol can found in the yard, as though discarded in a hurry as Mirren exited the house. Footprints were also found in the yard, and more footprints down the ginnel. They match, in size, the shoes belonging to Kit Mirren that were at the slaughterhouse, indicating that he probably fled the burning house through the yard and down the ginnel towards the river. But we have no signs of him after that.'

'Transport?' said Jim.

'Yes, thanks for the reminder, Jim. We found a motorbike in the backyard. Neighbours don't think the Mirrens possessed a car. One other thing to add from Ned; he thinks there's a good chance that the murder weapon was the finial at the end of the staircase. Although charred, it is, in his and Dr Paisley's opinion, a good match for the injury to Anne Mirren's head. So, the original death may not have been deliberate.

'Anything else, anyone?' he asked.

There was a series of head shakes. 'Only negatives,' summed up Jim. 'All the things we've looked for and haven't found.'

'Any questions, anyone?' asked Greg. 'Any ideas at all? There's no such thing as a stupid suggestion at this point.'

A silence fell. Everyone studied their notes, then almost as though at a signal, gazed at the ceiling in a search for inspiration. Jill coughed.

'Where's the iPad?' she asked.

'The iPad?' queried Greg.

'Yes. The one Diana left for the children. It wouldn't burn too well, so, have we found any remains of it?'

'I don't know,' said Greg, making a note. 'I'd need to ask Ned. Why are you interested, Jill?'

'Because I think it's one of those iPads with a SIM card. I'm pretty sure Diana said she was loaning it to the children because it would operate without wi-fi, and that might be useful. Perhaps we could track it in the same way as a phone, whether it's with the father or the children.'

Really good suggestion,' said Greg. 'Well done. Anyone else?'

Bill had been thinking too. 'Have we checked ANPR for vehicles moving in the vicinity of the end of the ginnel that day?' he asked. 'Given he seems to have got away without showing on CCTV in the town centre, perhaps he was picked up by someone?'

'Or,' said Jim, 'even if he doesn't own a car, he might have driven himself away. Do we know if he has a driving licence? Apart from one for a bike, I mean.'

'Yes he does,' said Jenny. 'I remember seeing a copy on the HR file I was shown at the slaughterhouse. And I was told his duties sometimes included driving one of their vans...' Her voice trailed off as she realised what she'd said.

'I wonder if they're a van short,' said Jim.

'Both good suggestions to follow up,' said Greg. 'Let's get to it.'

57

Cribbed and cabined

Like every other day, the morning wore on slowly. With some idea of currying favour with their hostess, Karen stacked the used breakfast things neatly on the tray, then washed as thoroughly as she could in the little handbasin in the corner. The toilet, she discovered, was a camping-style unit with a cassette underneath. She hoped she wouldn't be using it for long. In fact, she still hoped they'd be out of there as soon as possible.

By mid-morning she was bored, so got out her study notes and the old iPad she'd been given by her teacher. The battery was flat, but she had the charger. After a brief search of the small room, she found a power point behind the bed, and plugged it in. The lead wasn't very long, so she left the iPad on the floor under the bed. With nothing else to occupy her, she decided to examine the contents of the bookcase. Jake was busy with his fleet of cars.

The shelves seemed to contain mainly children's books, some of them very old. There were four or five ancient hardbacks with orangey-red covers, their spines battered and splitting. On examination they proved to be a strange mixture of elderly books for girls, with unexciting titles like *Feud in the Fifth*, or *A Term of Trouble*, and some that looked more like books for boys. These had titles like *The Adventure Book for Boys*. Karen wondered why it was only boys who had adventures, and carried on looking.

There were some newer paperbacks with brighter covers. She recognised some from the school library. *The Borrowers* was among this batch, and a full set of the Narnia books by C. S. Lewis. She took some of these off the shelf and looked inside. All had a name written inside the cover. *Francis Chalmers*, she read, and put the books back, all except the first of the Narnia series, which she sat down on the bed to read.

She was interrupted by a noise at the door and leaped to her feet as it opened. This time the lady was carrying a bag and an iPad. I've brought you some lunch, and you need to see this. She was still standing at the foot of the stairs, blocking the route to the door, and proffering the iPad for the children to see.

It seemed to be a bit of the news, saying something about a fire at a house in Yarmouth. Karen didn't understand and looked at the woman in puzzlement. Jake wasn't interested at all. He carried on playing with his cars.

'It's in the papers as well,' said the woman, and handed Karen a copy of the *Eastern Daily Press*. 'See!' She pointed to a photo on the front cover.

'I don't understand,' said Karen, but even as she spoke, she recognised the photo of the burned-out house as being of their house.

'It's saying,' said the woman, 'that your father set light to the house, then made a run for it, and the police haven't found him yet. So you see, you're much safer here. You'd better stay hidden, in case he finds you before they find him.'

'But what about Mum?' asked Karen.

'Oh, didn't I say?' asked the woman, then looked sideways at Jake and dropped her voice. 'It says they found a body in the burned house. I'm sorry, but they think it's your mother. Like I say, you really are much safer here. Don't worry, I'll look after you.'

She picked up the tray and her iPad, and carried both back up the stairs. The door closed behind her, leaving Karen with a bag full of sandwiches, crisps and drinks, an uncomprehending brother, and a newspaper full of the worst news ever.

58

Turning threads into a net

Greg stared at the CPS adviser on the other end of the Zoom call in some disbelief.

'Over a year?' he repeated. 'When Jim told me that, I thought he was exaggerating.'

'He wasn't,' said Frank shortly. 'And that may be a conservative estimate. There was already a backlog of more than thirty-seven thousand Crown Court cases before Covid hit. Take into account that some courts are closed altogether, and others are having to operate in a very different way in order to preserve social distancing, and you have a recipe for total chaos.

'Take Norwich for example, which is where we'd expect these cases to come to trial, *eventually*. It's effectively taking two courtrooms to try each case, so, of the seven courtrooms, we can use only three at a time. And that's when we're up and running in the new layout and with the new restrictions. At present, no cases are being heard because screens, and I don't know what else, are being fitted around jurors' seats, the bench, etc, etc. There are similar problems in the magistrates' court, with the added issue that we're already seeing accused and witnesses failing to show up, claiming that they have Covid. My key message, therefore, is don't expect to see either Helen Gabrys or the Pentneys in court any time soon.

'My *advice* is make sure you've documented every action and decision you took, and then put it all to the back of your mind. I'm sure you've got plenty else to be getting on with.'

'But what do we do about bail?' asked Greg. 'We can't just lob them all into prison for over a year or those will be overflowing too. I believe the Bure already has a problem with Covid infections.'

'Quite,' agreed Frank. 'We've been instructed to review the cases already on remand and prioritise. It's likely that some of those originally thought to be too big a risk to be out on bail will now be released to make room for even higher-risk cases. Otherwise, the whole prison estate risks being completely overwhelmed. My instructions are to agree bail if at all possible, ie if there is little chance of the accused being a danger to the public or of absconding, and only remand the highest risk defendants.'

'Where does that leave my three?'

'Well, two of them, in my opinion, fall firmly into the low-risk category: Helen Gabrys and Ella Pentney. I suppose it could be argued that the Gabrys girl could possibly abscond, given her family links to Lithuania, but in the circumstances, I think she qualifies as low risk.'

'What about Red Pentney?' asked Greg. 'He's charged with at least one murder and an attempted murder, plus threatening behaviour and—'

'Yes.' Frank interrupted him. 'He's a more borderline case.'

'Borderline?' exclaimed Greg. 'I thought he'd be squarely over the line.'

'It could be argued,' said Frank in measured tones, 'that his more extreme actions arose from his deluded attempt to take over the Gabrys empire—'

'If he's delusional, and I think it's a strong probability,' interrupted Greg in his turn, 'to my mind that makes him *more* of a risk rather than less!'

'Okay.' On screen, Frank could be seen to shrug. 'Let me have a summary of why you think he constitutes a serious risk, and I'll take up the argument. I can't promise anything, but I'll do my best. See you again soon.' He waved goodbye and the screen went black.

Greg turned to look at Jim and Jill, sitting to either side in chairs the prescribed two metres apart. 'You heard the man,' he said. 'Pretty much what we expected.'

'As good as we're likely to get,' agreed Jim. 'By the way, I haven't said congratulations yet, acting Detective Sergeant Hayes.'

Jill smiled with open delight. 'Thank you,' she said. 'I just hope it's confirmed.'

'It will be,' said Greg with confidence. 'You passed your sergeant's exam ages ago, you smashed the interview and now it's just a matter of jumping and hoops. And I'm delighted, Jill, as I told you.

'Okay, let's not waste any more time on constipated courts. Back to work. I don't suppose those two leads on the Mirren children and their father have led us to anything yet?'

'Not as of a couple of hours ago,' replied Jill. 'We still haven't found the van from the abattoir that they, belatedly, admitted was missing. And there's been no signal picked up from either the phone or the iPad.'

'We're assuming either the father or the kids have the iPad?' checked Jim.

'All we know for sure is that it isn't in the house, so that's the logical assumption,' replied Jill. 'But we'll keep looking, and we're still checking CCTV for the van. But apart from a glimpse of it on the A143 near the industrial estate, nothing. We've just started to look out of county and the ports have been alerted.'

'Okay,' said Greg. 'I'll tell Margaret about the bail situation with our three cases. Let me know if anything comes up.'

As Jim and Jill left his office, he turned with a sigh to the despised paperwork, only to be interrupted by his phone.

'It's me,' said a very familiar voice.

'Hi,' he said. 'Did I forget to feed Tally again?' he asked half-jokingly.

'Not as far as I know,' replied Chris. 'But I admit, I didn't check before I left. I was out the door immediately after you this morning. I'm ringing because I think we may have something of yours.'

'Something of mine?' asked Greg.

'A van. A rather scruffy van, parked near the docks in Lowestoft.'

'Not?'

'I think so.' She read out a registration number as Greg shuffled through papers on his desk to find where he'd made a note of the missing abattoir van.

'That's the right number,' he said.

'I thought it was. The letters rang a bell. We've got the driver too,' she added casually.

'Not Mirren!' exclaimed Greg.

'No, I should have said, we've got the latest driver. It's a teenage joyrider. I gather the van was spotted being driven rather erratically on the A146 near the Barnby turning. When the squad car turned on its blue lights, it got even more erratic and made a run for it. They were so worried about it crashing they turned the lights off, hung back and followed at a distance until it did a couple of circuits of the car park here before being abandoned. The driver and one other got out and tried to make a run for it, but they were collared and brought into custody.'

'A van is an odd choice for a joyride,' commented Greg.

'That's what I thought, but it seems to have been a spur-of-the-moment thing. The attraction was twofold. First, it was unlocked, and the keys were in the ignition. I think that was a big part of it. Second, there was some meat in the back, which these two bright sparks thought they could sell. Good job we caught them,' she added, 'or we'd have had a mass outbreak of food poisoning to add to the Covid problems. It looks to me as though the meat was intended for pet food and it's a bit high, to put it no stronger.

'Incidentally, this is all being reported to your team through the usual channels, but I thought I'd give you a heads-up.'

Greg couldn't wait to ask the next question. 'Where did the joyriders find it?' he asked.

'In a pub car park not far from St Olave's Priory. Obviously, the pub is closed, which is why no one noticed the van.'

The door flew open as Jill and Jim jammed themselves in the doorway.

'I know,' said Greg, forestalling their comments. 'Chris just rang from Lowestoft. Jim, can you get down to the harbour with Ned and tactfully take over the van from our Suffolk colleagues? Jill, who do we have in this morning?'

'Bill and Steve,' replied Jill. 'Jenny's out with Turbo, checking around Ormesby for the two children. I'd suggest Steve to come with us. Bill's busy with the paperwork for the Pentney cases.'

'Okay. Meet me in the car park. We're going to St Olaves.'

In the car, Greg looked at Steve. 'Quickest way to St Olaves from here?' he asked.

'The long way round: A11, A47, A146,' replied Steve promptly. 'Especially with the roads quiet. The cross-country route is a nightmare.'

'Okay.' As they sped north on the A11, he said to Jill, 'Tell me again what Jenny and Turbo are doing in Ormesby?'

'It's a long shot,' admitted Jill, 'but we've tried everything else. Ned supplied us with some of the children's bedding from the house. Obviously, everything, to us at least, smells strongly of smoke. But Jenny thought it was just possible that Turbo might be able to pick up other scents from the inner bedclothes. You know, the sheets and so on, because they would both have been in closest contact to the children, and also had least contamination from the fire. She's giving it a go – in the streets we know the children walked.'

'After all this time, would there still be any scent that wasn't overlaid by others?' asked Greg.

'Normally no, but there isn't much movement on the streets at present. I said it was a long shot,' she added defensively.

There was silence after that, until they arrived at the closed pub on the banks of the River Waveney. Everywhere was deserted. As they looked around them, Jill took a phone call.

'That was Jim,' she said, putting the phone back in her pocket. 'The joyriders say they picked the van up from the far corner of the car park and that there was no one in sight.'

'How did they get here?' asked Greg. 'I forgot to ask Chris.'

'They were out for a bike ride, and I gather the two bikes are in the van. Jim says to tell you that SOCO should be joining us here shortly.'

'Let's take a look around, but shoe covers on first, and try not to tread on anything we shouldn't,' replied Greg.

They approached the corner of the car park cautiously and viewed, from a safe distance, some possible tyre tracks in a patch of mud.

'From here, that looks like van tyre marks over bike tracks,' said Steve.

'I agree,' said Greg. 'Can you get some tape up, Steve, to protect this area. We'll have a quick look at the pub.'

A stiff breeze was blowing off the river as Greg and Jill walked across the car park, through what, in more normal times, might be a beer garden, and onto the riverbank.

The pub itself was in darkness with a sign in one window which read "Keep Safe! We look forward to welcoming you back." Jill shook the doors to the main bar; they were firmly secured.

'If we need to get access to the pub itself or any of the sheds, we'll need someone with a set of keys,' she said.

'We'd need more evidence that Mirren went into any of the buildings first,' said Greg. 'I don't see anything at the moment.' He looked to where a bridge carried the A143 over the River Waveney, and then down at the water flowing rapidly towards Lowestoft and the sea. 'If he went in here,' he added, 'we'd be unlikely to find him, judging from the speed this water is moving.'

'Normally, there'd be a good few pleasure boats on this stretch, tied up on the moorings near the pub,' said Jill. 'But this year, nothing! This dire shortage of witnesses doesn't make our job any easier, does it, Boss?'

'No, it doesn't,' he agreed, turning away, then he stopped, staring downstream. 'Might be worth checking that out though,' he said, moving along the bank.

Jill's eyes followed his gaze, then she followed him towards what looked like a bundle of clothes precariously caught on a makeshift boom across a small inlet. As she watched, the current tugged at the bundle, which moved slightly but stayed put.

Greg got as close as he dared, conscious that plastic overshoes did not provide much grip on a slippery grassy bank. 'Jill, get a team here fast,' he snapped. 'I think it could be him.' His heart rose to his mouth as the current tugged again and the bundle looked like slipping free. 'Try Yarmouth police station,' he said. 'It's nearest. If we don't secure this asap it'll be on its way downriver, never to be seen again.'

***

As luck would have it, it was the now familiar team of Sergeant Briscoe and Constable Drake who joined them. Although less than half an hour had elapsed, it had gone very slowly for those watching on the bank. Several times the possible body had nearly left with the current. Both Steve and Greg had tried to reach it from the bank, but with clear memories of an unfortunate experience on the River Bure at Acle, Greg had concluded it should be left alone until more equipment and help were on hand. It was with relief he saw the two uniformed officers approaching, armed with an aluminium ladder, a bag and something on a pole.

'I found a boathook, sir,' announced Drake.

The sergeant added, 'DS Hayes here gave us a very graphic description of the problem. We thought, rather than waiting for an official boat, we'd better improvise.'

'So, I'm going to secure the item with the hook, in case it tries to bugger off,' said Drake. 'Oops, sorry, sir, I didn't mean...'

'It's okay,' said Greg. 'And the ladder?'

'I thought we could use that to bridge the inlet,' said Sergeant Briscoe.

As Greg watched, Briscoe balanced the foot of the ladder about a metre in from the edge of the bank, then half lowered, half dropped it until the other end rested on the opposite bank. Greg went to crawl onto it, but was stopped.

'Not yet, sir,' Briscoe said. 'I need to secure it first.' He produced two substantial stakes from the bag, and a mallet, with which he proceeded to hammer them into the ground between the top of the ladder and the first rung.

'Can't move now, sir,' he said with a grin. 'Drake, deploy the hook.'

Constable Drake swung the boathook over the water and with as much care as she could, twisted it into the clothing floating around whatever was caught on the boom.

'Got it, sir,' she said.

Looking up, Greg noticed that the clump of police officers had at last begun to attract attention. A couple of people were watching from the far bank and three more were approaching from the direction of the main road.

'Keep them at a distance, Jill,' he said. 'Steve, give me a hand, would you?' Exercising extreme caution, Greg began to crawl over the ladder. It lurched a couple of times as each end sank into the muddy banks, but showed no signs of collapsing under his weight, to his considerable relief. Eventually he reached a point where, lying on the ladder, he could reach the bundle of clothes floating below.

'It's him. At least, it's a body,' called Greg, as the bundle twisted in his grasp.

Up on the bank, Drake took up the strain with her hook and the body wallowed precariously, bobbing on the current.

'How do we get it out without doing too much damage?' asked Greg. 'Any suggestions, anyone?'

Steve had been scouting along the bank and spotted a small boat moored just the far side of the bridge.

'How about we commandeer that boat?' he suggested, pointing along the river. 'We could tow it to here using the mooring rope, and then recover the body into the boat.'

'Good suggestion,' said Greg. He was about to add an instruction, but Sergeant Briscoe was already heading along the bank to where Steve was pointing. Steve ran after him, and in a remarkably short space of time the two men had unmoored the small motorboat and towed her along the river.

Checking that Drake had her boathook securely entangled in the bundle of fabric, Greg let go of the body and retreated from his precarious perch on the ladder. Then with Jill on the forward mooring rope and Briscoe holding the one astern, Steve and Greg scrambled into the boat. Controlled by the two ropes, the current carried it the last few feet down the river and a final eddy brought it close to the mouth of the inlet. With some considerable difficulty and even more distaste, Greg and Steve between them lifted the body into the boat.

As Jill and Briscoe hauled the boat back into the bank, Greg did a quick check through pockets and held up a wallet in his gloved hand. It contained, among other things, a driving licence.

'It's him,' he said. 'We've found Kit Mirren.'

59

The nose knows

Over in Ormesby, Jenny was having a frustrating day with Turbo. Or, to look at it from the main protagonist's point of view, Turbo was having a frustrating day with his chauffeur. First, he'd been offered something that had some interesting smells overlaid by an overpowering scent of smoke. Then he'd been asked to find those smells in streets full of other smells, including a very intriguing aroma of in-heat bitch. Turbo had long since lost the wherewithal to do anything about an in-heat bitch, but he could dream, couldn't he?

He'd patiently patrolled street after street with Jenny. He thought for a moment he'd found something near a village duck pond, then again at the entrance to the village garage. Both had merited further sniffing, but he couldn't be sure, so he'd wagged his tail and moved on. Then, not far from the garage, he'd had a quick sniff in someone's front garden, and he was pretty sure he'd found what he was looking for. Not absolutely certain, but pretty sure. His signal to Jenny was, therefore, nuanced. It was a definite signal but lacking total certainty.

'Are you sure?' Jenny asked, looking at her dog.

No, I'm not sure, but I'm sure it's worth looking, so he wagged his tail again, slowly.

Jenny had sighed, looked at him hard, then gone to the front door of the small bungalow and knocked. After a short delay, a woman had come to the door and opened it, but not invited Jenny in.

'I'm sorry, I'm shielding,' she said. 'Can I help you?'

Jenny held up her warrant card and explained who she was. 'I just wanted to ask if you had seen either of these children in the last few days,' she said, holding up photos from the school.

The woman looked at the photos. 'No, sorry,' she said. 'In fact, I don't know why I'm looking because I haven't seen any children at all.'

'Okay, thank you,' said Jenny. 'Sorry to have disturbed you. Nice boat!' she added as she turned away.

60

Entombed

Karen had taken to scratching marks on the wall to indicate how many days she thought they had spent in the underground room. It was hard to be sure, with no daylight to check, but she assumed that each time the lights dimmed, it was night.

The first night the lights had gone off and Jake had started screaming and crying, Karen had hammered on the door, shouting, 'He's afraid of the dark. Let us out, he's afraid of the dark.'

The woman hadn't let them out, but the lights had come on dimly and that was enough to calm Jake.

They were fed regularly, and they had the toilet facilities in the annex behind the bookcase. Karen had wondered what would happen when the cassette needed emptying. Perhaps she and Jake would be able to rush up the stairs while the door was unlocked. But one morning she woke up after a very heavy sleep to find that it had been emptied during the night and a small TV had arrived.

The iPad was still their secret but hadn't been much use for communication. Down there, in the underground room, she hadn't been able to get a mobile signal on either the phone or the iPad. She had detected a faint wi-fi signal, but it was password-protected and she didn't have it.

Even so, each day she typed emails to everyone she knew: her friends, her teacher, even her father. But early each morning, or what she assumed to be morning, she would check, and all the messages would still be sitting in the outbox.

She had read her way through most of the books, even the old ones with cracked hardback covers. When the woman came back that afternoon with their tea – beans on toast, it was – she asked for some more books. *And some for Jake too*, she had said. The woman had looked startled but said she would see what she could do.

As she went back up the steps, Karen plucked up courage to ask, 'Who was Francis Chalmers?'

The woman stopped dead on the stairs. Karen wondered again, as she had wondered so many times before, if she and Jake tackled her together could they pull her off the steps and escape. But she returned to the same conclusion as before. Jake was too scared to join in any such attempt. Too scared of their father and, she thought, too scared of the outside world as well. Now they had the small TV, he seemed perfectly happy where he was, and she couldn't bring herself to leave without him. Not yet anyway.

'Frankie?' the woman said. 'How do you know about Frankie?' She looked almost scared.

'His name's in the books,' said Karen.

'Oh yes, of course. Frankie lived here once, but he was naughty.'

'Where is he now?' asked Karen.

'He went away, and now he's dead,' said the woman. 'That's what happens to naughty children.' She left and Karen heard the door lock behind her again.

Jake was watching the TV, of course, and Karen thought he hadn't heard a word that was said. She was right, but not for the reason she assumed. He was staring at the TV, with one finger in his mouth in a pose she thought he'd long since abandoned.

It was the last of the news, not his usual sort of programme, but it was just the tail end, the local bit. Now Karen was paying attention, she heard a voice say, '...as we said earlier. The body found in the River Waveney has been identified as that of Yarmouth man, Kit Mirren. Anyone who saw him in the last seven days is asked to contact Norfolk police on...'

She was so focussed on the TV that she hadn't heard the door open again. This time the woman just poked her head in.

'You're orphans now,' she said. 'You're lucky I took you in.' And the door closed with a finality that rang in Karen's head for hours.

THE END – FOR NOW